The Battle of Inchcolm Abbey

ALSO BY WILLIAM CLINKENBEARD

O is for Oval, Oswald and Osama
Ripples Across the Bay (Ed.) Forthwrite Writers
Writers at Bay (Ed.) Forthwrite Writers
All Published by iUniverse

The Contemporary Lesson
Full on the Eye: Perspectives on the World,
The Church, and the Faith (with Ian Gilmour)

Mind the Gap: Moving between Pulpit and Pew

All Published by the Bavelaw Press

The Battle of Inchcolm Abbey

WILLIAM CLINKENBEARD

iUniverse, Inc.
Bloomington

The Battle of Inchcolm Abbey

Copyright © 2012 by William Clinkenbeard.

All rights reserved. No part of this book may be used or reproduced by any means, graphic, electronic, or mechanical, including photocopying, recording, taping or by any information storage retrieval system without the written permission of the publisher except in the case of brief quotations embodied in critical articles and reviews.

iUniverse books may be ordered through booksellers or by contacting:

iUniverse
1663 Liberty Drive
Bloomington, IN 47403
www.iuniverse.com
1-800-Authors (1-800-288-4677)

Because of the dynamic nature of the Internet, any web addresses or links contained in this book may have changed since publication and may no longer be valid. The views expressed in this work are solely those of the author and do not necessarily reflect the views of the publisher, and the publisher hereby disclaims any responsibility for them.

Any people depicted in stock imagery provided by Thinkstock are models, and such images are being used for illustrative purposes only.
Certain stock imagery © Thinkstock.

ISBN: 978-1-4697-6079-7 (sc)
ISBN: 978-1-4697-6080-3 (ebk)

Printed in the United States of America

iUniverse rev. date: 02/03/2012

Contents

Acknowledgements ix
Chapter 1   Invitation 1
Chapter 2   Inchcolm 10
Chapter 3   Headwork 24
Chapter 4   The Wark 32
Chapter 5   The Abbeys 38
Chapter 6   The Poets 46
Chapter 7   Smoke 54
Chapter 8   Fire 59
Chapter 9   Gavin 63
Chapter 10   Belle Encounter 71
Chapter 11   Colm's Course 78
Chapter 12   Smile 85
Chapter 13   Offer 91
Chapter 14   Protest 96
Chapter 15   Joust 102
Chapter 16   Thread 106
Chapter 17   Morton 111
Chapter 18   Fracture 124
Chapter 19   U-Turn? 131
Chapter 20   Loss 136
Chapter 21   Watcher 140
Chapter 22   Walkabout 147
Chapter 23   Tales 157
Chapter 24   Fog 166
Chapter 25   Activities 170
Chapter 26   Walkabout II 175
Chapter 27   Table Games 186
Chapter 28   Requiem 192
Chapter 29   Cartulary 198

To Michael, Thomas and Katie, to Lewis and Anna, to Cooper, Alyx and young Jack: our grandchildren, who one day in the distant future may wonder how faith is possible.

Acknowledgements

I am much indebted to research information gathered from several websites: S.E. Murray's article *The Lands and 'Sisterlands' of Aberdour, c.1100-1650 in* www.irss.uofguelph.ca/artic was invaluable for an account of the history/legend surrounding Inchcolm and the Aberdour area. Also indispensable was the information provided by the Royal Commission on Ancient and Historic Monuments of Scotland, at www.rcahms.gov.uk/. The research into the monastery at St Jean-des-Vignes and the presentation of the results is a model of how historical and archaeological investigation ought to be done, found at www.Monarch.brown.edu. William F. Hendrie's book *The Firth of Forth* proved extremely helpful. Wikipedia provided useful information about Inchcolm. Frost's *Scottish Anatomy* provided a list of Scottish Saints. The *Spring 2011* issue of the magazine of Historic Scotland, kindly loaned to me by David Cooper, provided useful information about the secret war department map of the fortifications on Inchcolm. I am grateful to Carcanet Press for permission to quote a verse from Iain Crichton Smith's poem *Jean Brodie's Children*.

I am profoundly grateful to my wife Janette for her patience in bearing with me during the writing and for her enthusiastic reading and correcting of the manuscript. Several stories in the book have emerged from and been shaped by our conversations with Ian and Pat Brady over many years of friendship. Lee and Richard Young also read the manuscript and went several extra miles in checking things out. Their enthusiastic and intelligent support was invaluable. The members of the *Forthwrite Writers* group heard several chapters and responded positively. I'm grateful to all our adult children: to Robert for ideas about publishing, to Helen for setting up my website, and to John for designing the cover. Finally, I'm grateful to Margaret Paterson, whose question, *When is Bill going to write another novel?* proved to be the trigger.

This book was written mainly in our flat in Edinburgh which overlooks the Firth of Forth and Inchcolm in the distance and in Fountain Hills, Arizona. However, some writing was done in the home of David and Ann Lee in Bradford Pennsylvania before and after a fine week at the Chautauqua Institute in New York. I'm grateful to the Lees for their warm hospitality.

Most of the places in the book are real, especially Inchcolm with its wonderful abbey, and it deserves a visit. However, this is entirely a work of fiction. As far as I know, no Scottish agency, institution or government has any plans to treat Inchcolm as suggested in the book. The identity, actions and attitudes of all the characters, institutions and agencies are fictional. Any resemblance to the activities and attitudes of real people and institutions is entirely coincidental.

I returned, and saw under the sun, that the race is not to the swift, nor the battle to the strong, neither yet bread to the wise, nor yet riches to men of understanding, nor yet favour to men of skill; but time and chance happen to them all.

Ecclesiastes 9:11

CHAPTER ONE

Invitation

There was, towards the front of the house, a little *plump*, the unmistakable sound of something dropping on the floor. Since the mail had arrived half an hour earlier Davis Lane wasn't much bothered. It was probably one of the free Fife newspapers that always went unread in their house or a leaflet from someone offering to replace their old antiquated metal gutters. Whatever it was, it could wait. So when he did go through to the front he was surprised to see an envelope lying underneath the letterbox at the bottom of the door. The envelope had his name on it, handwritten, but no address and no stamp. Inside he found a ticket for a trip to Inchcolm on the *Maid of the Forth* on the Tuesday of the following week. Lane racked his brain. Had he accidentally ordered something online while surfing the web? Surely not, unless he was going bonkers. Could it be a surprise gift from Katriona? His birthday was coming up. A neat handwritten note on paper cut to be the exact size of the envelope answered several of the questions.

> *Please use this ticket to come to Inchcolm on the morning sailing next Tuesday. We have a proposal to put to you. Once you're there we'll find you.*

The note was unsigned. So it wasn't from Katriona and it wasn't the result of an accident on his part. The big question was still unanswered.

Inch in Scots means island. Inchcolm, along with Inchkeith, Inchmickery and several others, lies in the Forth Estuary, which in Scotland runs from west to east into the North Sea at Edinburgh. It had been named after St Columba, who was supposed to have visited there in the sixth century. Situated several miles down the estuary from Inverkeithing, it is an attraction thanks to the ruins of Inchcolm Abbey. Lane studied the ticket and read the note again. Then he read it for a third time, trying hard to squeeze out additional information from the spaces between the lines. He felt his heart beating faster, and the room beginning slowly to spin. He sat down and studied the note again, more carefully this time. He could think of no reason why anyone should invite him to the island. And who was the *we* in *we'll*? The note seemed to convey more threat and menace than kind invitation. It brought back painfully the last offer he had received. Little more than a year ago he had been invited to the premises of the Clan Caledonia Company in Edinburgh. Clan Caledonia ostensibly exported Scottish merchandise, mainly to the United States. In reality the company had proved to be a cover for the CIA in Scotland. Lane had accepted their offer to research a theological tome read by the president at the time. It was reported that each day the president read from and took seriously a devotional book entitled *My Utmost for His Highest*. The reasoning was that, as a theologian, Lane might be able to provide the agency with some foretaste of the president's thinking. This venture had cost him dearly in anxiety, not to mention sleep. The secret agencies of several other countries had also become interested in discovering his conclusions. Apparently everyone wanted to be able to predict the president's thinking. He had been tailed on the streets of Edinburgh. His house and study had been violated. He had lived in fear for weeks. Yes, it had enhanced his finances as an infrequently employed freelance theologian, but at great personal cost. That was only a little while ago, and now he's had *We'll find you* put through his letterbox. Perhaps what that really means is *We'll take care of you once and for all*. He put the ticket and note down and sighed, wondering what he should do next.

Later, after Katriona had arrived home, he made drinks for them and they sat in the lounge. It was already the middle of May and the days were growing longer. There were whitecaps sweeping across the water, and the sun was a red ball sinking slowly behind the Forth Bridges.

"So what did you do today?" Katriona asked, setting her gin and tonic down carefully on the coffee table.

Lane jiggled his glass, listening to the ice clink and watching the little waves in his malt, wondering if this was the right time. "Actually," he answered, "it was a curious kind of day."

"Curious", she said, "what do you mean by curious? What happened?"

"I got this letter," he said.

"Yes, I looked at the mail when I came in," Katriona said. "Looked pretty harmless to me."

"No," Lane said. "This was hand delivered through the letter box, just my name on the envelope, no address or stamp."

"So what was in it?" she asked.

"There was a ticket in it, a ticket to go to Inchcolm on the *Maid of the Forth*, plus a note, asking me to go next Tuesday. It just says that they have a proposal for me, some kind of job maybe."

"Could I perhaps see it?" Katriona asked.

Lane left the room and went to the study to retrieve the note and ticket. He handed it to his wife. She studied the ticket and read the note.

"Davis," she said, freezing him with a hard stare, "Ignore it, tear it up and throw it away. You are not going on a boat trip to meet some unidentified party. You've no idea what it could be about or what might happen. She paused for a moment. Unless of course . . ." She hesitated and the glimmer of a smile appeared. "Unless it's from your mysterious lover: a clandestine rendezvous on Inchcolm Island, how romantic."

"My secret lover," he answered, "is that likely?"

"Well, now that I think on it a bit, and looking at you, probably not," she said. "But seriously, I don't want you to get involved in some shadowy operation like you did the last time. You could have been hurt or even killed, messing about with the CIA and heaven knows who else. You're not a spy, Davis. You might like to think of yourself as a spy, but you're not. John Le Carre' is just for reading, not for playing at. You're a theologian. I'm satisfied with that. Please, promise me that you not have anything to do with this, whatever it is."

Lane took another drink, slowly turning the glass and wondered how to proceed. He looked up at his wife. "Look," he said, "I wish that I could just ignore it. The truth is that when I opened this thing and read it, it sent my heart racing. I relived that whole affair with *My Utmost*. But the larger truth is that I can't just turn down an opportunity to do some work. You're the one working fifty hours a week, you're the one bringing home most of the income, you're the one dead tired every night."

"Yes, OK," Katriona answered, reaching over to put her hand on his knee. "But I enjoy my job. You know that. I like what I do and I feel that it's useful. There's no reason for you to feel guilty. Please don't do this. Just forget about it."

"I can't just leave it," Lane answered. "I'll have to check it out. The chances are that it's somebody's idea of a joke. I'll be careful, and I won't get myself into trouble."

Katriona shook her head, got up from her chair and left the room.

Lane did not sleep well that night. In the dream he was fighting, defending himself against the intruder who had come into the house to steal the research from his last project. The man was threatening him and Katriona; their lives were at stake. At what he thought was a key moment, when the man was off his guard, Lane lashed out as hard as he could with a kick. So hard was it that he kicked himself right out of bed, landing on the floor with a thump.

Katriona sat up straight in bed. "Davis, what's the matter? What's going on?"

"Oh nothing," he replied, sitting on the floor, "I just fell out of bed, got too close to the edge." He climbed back into the bed, noting that his shoulder and back were sore.

The morning arrived all too soon, and Lane was up early, determined to get the information that might help him deal with his mystery invitation. He made breakfast for them and saw Katriona off to work. He elected to walk to Inverkeithing Station. The day was bright and warm, and the waters of the Forth were a calm blue in the distance. Taking the train would provide him with the chance to think. Katriona was right of course, as always: the sensible thing to do was to ignore the invitation. His last experience had been scary. He had been dealing with unknown forces, harassed by at least one of them. On several occasions he had felt that his life was physically threatened—hence the dream last night. On the other hand, it had also been exhilarating, and that was a rare feeling these days. Moreover, he had made money and brought some income into the house. That had made him feel useful. Still, the last time, Katriona had been working in Guatemala, so she had not been aware of his escapade. Now that she was back in Fife she might well be put into danger by any foolishness on his part. On the other hand, he was probably making far too much of this little mystery. He had blown it up way out of proportion. Most likely it was a joke, dreamed up by one or more of his old colleagues in the ministry. They were playing on his last experience.

The train pulled into Waverly and he walked up the ramp, grateful to leave the gloom of the station. His emergence into daylight surprised him as it always had done: the vertical sunlit architecture of another age rising up from the Mound, the green lawns of Princes Street Gardens studded by floral patterns red and white and yellow. It was hard to imagine a more spectacular city centre. If you turned to face the other direction of course, the beauty was quickly undone. Princes Street was still torn up, as it had been for years while the city tried to install a new tram. The work started and then stopped. They argued about what was in and what was not in the contract. They worried about running out of money. They changed the plans about where the tram was going to run and where it was not going to run. There was a different story about progress or the lack of progress every week. People responsible for managing the job came and went. No one in the whole world, not even God, knew what was happening with the trams of Edinburgh. Lane thought that it was incredible that a city such as this seemed incapable of managing a big project. But there it was, and he had to put it onto the back burner of the mind, like everyone else in Edinburgh.

He took the bus down Leith Walk and then walked to the premises of Clan Caledonia.

The building still looked a bit rundown, and the window of the shop featured pretty much the same tartan products as the last time he was here. It was the same blonde at the desk, still engaged with the monitor of her computer. She eventually looked up.

"Yes?" she said.

"Hello," Lane said. "Do you remember me?"

She studied him for a moment. "I'm sorry, I don't think I do. What can I do for you?"

Lane sighed. "My name is Davis Lane. I did some work with Robert McCord last year. I'd like to have a word with him, please."

"Oh yes, Mr. Lane, of course I remember you. Hold on a tick till I see if Mr. McCord is available." She rang the room next door and conveyed the fact that Lane was waiting. The door opened immediately and Robert McCord appeared in it, smiling and holding out his hand. Lane suddenly remembered how tall he was, but there was more grey in the hair and he looked older.

"Davis," he said, "Great to see you. What a surprise." He grasped Lane's hand and then his elbow and pulled him intro his office.

To his surprise Lane found that he was glad to see this man who had recruited him into so much trouble. He was the cheerful, ebullient, friendly sort of person that you could not help but like. They stood for several minutes exchanging small talk. McCord motioned to Lane to take a chair. Lane glanced out the window. The last time he had been there a crane was knocking down the building behind. Now a crane was erecting a new steel framework. Leith was constantly changing.

"I wasn't sure that you would ever want to see me again after the hot water I dumped you in to," McCord said, looking anxious.

"I wasn't exactly sure myself," Lane responded. "You realize that for a couple of weeks I was right on the edge. It was scary and then just when I needed you, you disappeared for a while."

"I know, and I'm sorry," McCord answered. "They called me back to Langley urgently. It wasn't just your project but another issue altogether. But you came through it nicely. You acquitted yourself very well. Mind you, Langley was not terribly happy when you wrote directly to the president and rather spilt the beans. But in Washington these days no one is ever very surprised by clandestine surveillance. In any event, you got the point across very forcefully that even the president is not God, that he can't equate what he wants to do with what God wants to do. I'm not sure that he ever really believed that, but what he was reading implied as much. So . . . well done, Davis Lane."

"I'm not so sure," Lane replied. "I was running scared at that point. I wanted to do the right thing, to warn you and the president, but I also just wanted out."

McCord nodded, but said nothing.

"Anyway," Lane continued, "I want to ask you something else."

"OK," McCord said, "but before you do that let me ask you something."

"Fine," Lane answered. "Fire away."

"It's just idle curiosity," McCord said. "Are you still being a freelance theologian, and if so, does it pay well these days? And if it doesn't pay well why are you doing it? I mean, why not get an honest job?"

Lane laughed. "Yes, I'm still a freelance theologian, and no, it doesn't pay well. Why am I still doing it?" He thought for a moment and became serious. "You know, being a theologian is a little bit like having a chronic illness. Once you've got it, you can't get over it. You have to go on through life trying to spell out the nature of God and the nature of man. It has to do with using your intelligence. That's it, I guess. I earn enough from time to time to make a difference to our income. Anyway, a minister is a kind of marked man. The society labels you as *religious* and won't permit you to do anything different even when you have the skills. So that's my story and I'm sticking to it."

"Right," McCord said, "I kind of understand you, and you have my sympathy." He shifted in his chair, as if to mark the change of subject. "Now, you were going to ask me something."

"Have you," Lane started and then hesitated, "have you given my name or somehow referred me to anybody else?"

"You better tell me why you're asking," McCord replied, "If you're able to do that, I mean. You appreciate that this is just between us."

"Yeah, of course," Lane answered, "I know that. It's just that something odd happened yesterday and I'd like to figure out what it's about."

"OK, go on," McCord said.

"A letter came through the door. All it had in it was a ticket on the *Maid of the Forth* to Inchcolm with a note asking me to take the morning sailing on Tuesday, and that someone would find me once I got there. Would you know anything about this, Robert?"

McCord studied his desk for a few moments, as if its surface supported a record of everything that had transpired in the last year. "I don't know anything about your mystery ticket to Inchcolm," he replied. "It seems a bit cloak and dagger even for me. But I suppose that I have mentioned your name a couple of times to other people, although that was quite a while ago."

"Well, what people, Robert, who are you talking about?" Lane asked.

"Well, let me try to explain," McCord answered, with a hint of weariness in his voice. "We run quite a good business here over and above the clandestine things we do. Clan Caledonia exports items worth thousands of pounds every year. So we naturally hook up with other Scottish business and institutions. We normally talk to the Scottish Tourist Board, to Edinburgh Tourism, to the Caledonian Society, and so on. We go to conferences organized by the Confederation of British Industry and so on. Now it could well be that at one of these meetings or in a conversation with someone we might well have mentioned your name, but it would have been a positive reference, Davis. You did a good job for us, you know."

"Yeah, well, thanks," Lane replied, pointing at McCord, "but when you say "we" what you really mean is "you", right?"

"OK, OK," McCord answered, holding up both hands in surrender, "I mean "me"."

"So it's possible, in fact it's very likely, that whoever wants me to take a mysterious trip might have been tipped off by you."

"I admit that it's possible," McCord said, "but I'm not prepared to say that it's likely. There are lots of other people in the world, Davis," McCord asserted. "Look, if you're worried about this thing do you want me to send one of our people with you on the boat?"

"Lane shook his head and sighed. "No, I don't even know if I'll go yet. Anyway, CIA protection is carrying things a bit too far. But listen, if I disappear next Tuesday promise me that you will get involved and do what you can for Katriona."

"I promise you," McCord answered, and then with a smile, "How about lunch sometime?"

Lane boarded the train for Fife and found a seat by the window. Other passengers drifted in with their free copy of the *Metro*. He made up his mind that during this journey he would come to a decision. Should he use the mystery ticket or not? He tried to lay out the pros and cons in his mind. By the time that Edinburgh Castle appeared in the window he had done the cons. He knew next to nothing about what was behind this. Perhaps there were still people who were sore over his last escapade. It would be easy for someone on the boat to quietly hoist him overboard. Or once on the island, assuming that he got there, it would be even easier for him to disappear. But even if his life was not at stake could he really be bothered to get involved in something else? By the time the train passed the Scottish Rugby grounds at Murrayfield he had laid out the pros. This thing was probably nothing at all to worry about. It might well be a practical joke. He was making far too much of it. If it were to be a genuine opportunity to work then he could earn some money. It would do wonders for his self-esteem to take home some money as a free-lance theologian. It could also prove to be a welcome challenge for him. It might even be exhilarating. The thought of it brought a smile. God knows he needed some kind of real challenge. In any event, he could turn it down if he wanted to, whatever it was. By the time the train was crossing the Forth Rail Bridge he had made his mind up. He was content to watch the sun shining on the water and a tanker being gently tugged into Hound Point.

Later that evening, when he had made a gin and tonic for Katriona and poured a *Lagavulin* for himself, she posed the question. He was ready for it.

"Well, what are you going to do?" Katriona asked.

"About . . . . , he answered?

"You know very well what I'm talking about," she said. "What are you going to do about your mystery invitation to Inchcolm?"

"Oh that," he said. "Well, I've spoken to Robert McCord. This certainly has nothing to do with the CIA. He says that he might have mentioned my name to one or two of the business people that he has contacts with. Most likely it's one of them. So I'm going. I think that it's safe enough."

She shook her head at him. "I can't believe this. If it's some kind of business proposition then why the secrecy? Why not just call you on the phone and arrange a meeting? And this *we'll find you* thing scares me."

"Yes, I know," he said. "But there's bound to be other people around. I can look after myself. Anyway, let's hear what they have to say. I can always just say no."

"Oh yes, of course," she said. "Do I know you or not? How many years have we been married?"

"A long time," he answered, coming over to kiss her. "Now, let's have another drink, OK?"

But once again that night he did not sleep well. At some point in the dark hours a faceless person was trying to throw him overboard and he was desperately clutching the side of the vessel to save himself. But this time he stayed in bed.

Chapter Two

Inchcolm

Just before mid-day on Tuesday, Lane pulled into a parking space on the south side of the Firth of Forth in South Queensferry. It was a blustery day, with darkish clouds scudding from the west towards the North Sea. Hawes Pier, home base for the *Maid of the Forth* lay just across the road from Hawes Inn, made famous by its appearance in Robert Louis Stevenson's *Kidnapped*. The flags flying in front of the inn snapped in the wind. Perhaps being kidnapped was not the best thing to think about at the moment. High overhead, the red steelwork of the Forth Rail Bridge began its lengthy crossing of the water. Lane sat in the car for several minutes, watching the waves breaking onto the rocks and listening to *The Afterlife* by Paul Simon.

> *After I died and the makeup had dried,*
> *I went back to my place.*
> *No moon that night,*
> *But a heavenly light shone on my face.*
> *You got to fill out a form first*
> *And then you wait in the line.*

Contemplating the afterlife wasn't such a good idea either just now. He was already anxious enough about this venture without underlining it with intimations of his demise.

The Maid of the Forth was berthed at the pier and a few passengers were ambling down towards her. Lane locked the car and walked slowly towards the pier. He passed by the ticket kiosk and the lifeboat shop and stopped beside the *Maid*. When you stood alongside, the vessel was much larger than she appeared from the road or from how she looked from the viewpoint behind his house. She must be about sixty feet long with a blue hull and a white cabin running almost the entire length. Two red funnels projected from above the bridge. Lane slouched, trying to look at ease while he watched potential passengers stopping at the ticket booth to buy their tickets. No one had been permitted to board yet, so there was ample chance to observe body language. Thus far he could spot no one who fitted the image of his island contact. But then, what exactly should he be looking for? He really had nothing to go on, and he had simply conjured up a godfather type of figure. So far, no one in the group on the pier looked like Marlon Brando or Al Pacino.

An announcement was made over the vessel's loudspeaker and people began to go on board. Two middle-aged couples went first, and it sounded like they were speaking French. Three younger girls in their twenties went next, wearing bright yellow and blue waterproofs and carrying rucksacks. Lane hung back, observing carefully as more passengers straggled down the pier and onto the gangplank. Two young couples with children went next. The first couple had a boy and a girl, and the other a boy, all under the age of five. The two couples were clearly together, the children noisy and excited about a big adventure. A stout lady in tweed wearing a trilby and carrying an umbrella came next, followed by a tall older man immaculately dressed in a white shirt and kilt. He was followed by a still older and rather fierce man with unruly white hair and beard. A younger couple, perhaps honeymooners, clambered aboard holding hands. A middle-aged man, neat in a sport jacket and business-like in his movements went next. He was followed by four younger people of Asian appearance, two boys and two girls. Still, Lane hung back and waited. No further passengers appeared and a final boarding intimation was given. Like it or not, the time had come. Lane went up the gang plank, handed over his ticket and boarded the *Maid of the Forth*. This was it, for better or for worse.

Lane heard the engine starting up and felt the deck vibrating. Smoke rose up from the stern and drifted across the deck. The lines were cast off and the vessel edged slowly away from the pier and out into the channel to begin its voyage under the massive span of the Forth Rail Bridge. White sheeting still covered large portions of the bridge, and underneath them crews were busy renewing the steelwork. Lane couldn't recall how long these sheets had been covering various portions of the bridge, five years anyway. The never-ending work of maintaining the bridge had begun a part of the language. As soon as you finished painting the Forth Bridge it was time to start all over again. Lane directed his attention back to his fellow passengers, trying to eliminate any of them from his mental list of suspects. Clearly it wasn't going to be the French people, nor was it going to be the waterproof girls. It was highly unlikely, though not impossible, to be one of the couples with children. It was even more unlikely to be the honeymooners. Asian tourists? Surely not. That left the lady in tweed, the kilted gentleman, the fierce white-haired man, and Mr. Sportjacket. Surely it had to be one of the men. The white-haired and bearded man had to be his prime suspect. Be that as it may, he felt relieved when he realized that the vessel was underway without any genuinely suspicious-looking characters having boarded. Maybe all his anxiety had been in vain. But the question remained: which of his fellow passengers was the one who would *find* him, and why?

The *Maid of the Forth* proceeded slowly farther out into the firth and then directly under the bridge, the recorded commentary pointing out how long it had taken to build the bridge, how many tons of steel had been used, and how many rivets had been put into place. It went on to point out how many men had died in the process: over seventy, as far as anyone knew. Lane remembered reading an old newspaper report on the construction, quoting the same statistics, but making light of the deaths. Wasn't it remarkable, the report said, that *only so few men* had perished in such an engineering feat? That wouldn't happen now, he thought. Perhaps now we were at least a little more sensitive to the value of human life. Lane had heard the details of the construction before of course, but the facts were still amazing. This really was one of the engineering wonders of the modern world. Turning his attention away from the bridge, North Queensferry could be seen on the north shore and farther along, Inverkeithing, where the Lane's house lay beyond the old quarry. On board, the three children were playing noisily, running in and out of the cabin and hiding under the benches. The French people had heads bent together, deep in conversation. The waterproof girls were studying a map and pointing to something on the shoreline of Fife. The honeymooners were preoccupied with each other. The kilted gentleman had his binoculars focussed on the bridge. The tweed lady and whitebeard were talking to each other, and Mr. Sportjacket was reading a paper. On the upper deck, the Asian people were taking photographs. No one was paying any attention to Lane. Maybe that was a good thing, but he began to wonder if this whole thing would turn out to be a wild goose chase.

The recorded commentary about the trip to Inchcolm Island came over the loudspeaker at regular intervals: *To starboard there is Hound Point, where huge tankers arrive to load millions of tons of oil piped down from wells in the North Sea. Farther over is Cramond, where the Roman Antonine Wall ran all the way across Scotland to terminate at a fort. Even farther over there is the skyline of Edinburgh, where you can spot the castle and St Giles Cathedral, Salisbury Crags and the tall flats at Granton and Newhaven. And right here in the estuary you might see a Forth Ports Pilot Boat, on its way to take a pilot out at high speed to navigate a cruise ship into the firth. On the port side there is the historic town of North Queensferry, where the old ferry landed. There is Dalgety Bay and St David's, where high-grade coal was once loaded. Farther along is Aberdour with its picturesque harbour, ancient castle, and historic St Fillans Church. Over there is Braefoot, where liquid gas is pumped into tankers. And soon,* according to the commentary, *we'll be arriving at famous Inchcolm with its beautiful abbey.* Lane noticed that most passengers paid attention each time the commentary started up again, but not Mr. Sportjacket. Now and then he would look up from his newspaper and scan his fellow passengers. Maybe, Lane thought, it wasn't the fierce white-haired man after all, but this man. Moreover, this man was younger and stronger. The line from the note asserted itself once again: *We'll find you, we have a proposition for you.*

As the vessel approached the island, the commentary provided more detail. *Inchcolm was one of four "inches" or islands in the Firth of Forth. The island had a fascinating history, due largely to the imposing ruins of the abbey. According to the story, in the twelfth century King Alexander I encountered a storm while crossing the Forth in the ferry of the day. In desperation the king prayed to St Columba for help. St Columba must have helped, for the ferry vessel made it to a small island, which was then called Aemonia. Fortunately, a monk who lived on the island was able to give Alexander food and shelter for the night in his cave. So, according to the legend, the king vowed to give the island to God and to establish an Augustinian priory there in the name of St Columba. A priory was indeed established in the twelfth century and eventually became an abbey. The abbey was extended over the years until it gained its final form in the fifteenth century. Today it remained the best preserved of Scotland's monastic structure, in spite of the extensive damage suffered during the Scottish Reformation, Later,* the commentary continued, *Shakespeare employed Inchcolm in Macbeth.* Lane had heard most of this story before, but there were some details that were either new or had been forgotten. He made a mental note to research several of these aspects of the story when he could find the time.

If you looked at it from above, the island was shaped a little like the head of a dragon, having a neck, small body, but good tail. The beast's mouth is open to the west, breathing a flame of black rock. The narrowest part of the island lies between the body and the tail, and it was on this stretch that the abbey was built, facing south and fronted by a bay with a nicely curved beach. The head and tail both enjoy high ground. As the Maid began to come round the high ground, the abbey revealed itself majestically from right to left, first the chapter house, then the square tower and finally the cloister. The sun was out now, throwing the abbey's fine stonework into bold relief against the green grass. All the passengers were now standing to watch as the *Maid* passed by and rounded the dragon's tail, apart from Mr. Sportjacket, who sat absorbed in his paper. Lane found himself becoming irritated with his this man, whether he was the mystery contact or not. The kilted man had moved closer to Lane, and was speaking to him, warning him about the island's gulls. Feeling their nests threatened, according to Mr. Kilt, the gulls attacked the passengers when disembarking. "Watch your head as you go up the path," the man was saying. Why had he singled Lane out for this advice? Lane thanked him and wondered . . . perhaps he was wrong about everybody.

An announcement over *The Maid of the Forth's* sound system requested that the passengers be seated as the vessel slowly negotiated its way into the narrow harbour. The parents were having a tough time getting their children to settle. Whitebeard, his hair blowing wildly in the wind, seemed eager to disembark. Eventually the boat was secure, the gangplank was wheeled out and the passengers began to leave. They were reminded that they had to be back in time for departure, otherwise they would be sleeping rough in the abbey. Lane again waited, watching the bodily movements of the others to see if he could get more clues. He tagged along at the end of the line as several gulls screamed and flashed by just over his head. Ducking down, Lane hurried up the path and steps as his fellow passengers were moving up the slope.

Lane reached the top of the slope and looked around. The abbey lay to his right, the toilets and gift shop to his left, tucked into the hill. It was one thing getting to the island safely: no one had tried to throw him overboard. But it was another thing to figure out what to do next. People had dispersed, and no one appeared to be waiting for him. He could see the backs of yellow waterproofs heading in the direction of the chapter house and several people going into the toilet, but that was it. It might be a small island, but clearly it was large enough for people to disappear. Where was he supposed to go? Lane wandered towards the cluster of monastic buildings feeling unsettled. This whole thing had been a wild goose chase. Katriona had been right. As usual, he should have listened to her. Indeed, perhaps the point had been to get him out of and away from his own house. The idea had not occurred to him before, but now that it had it was alarming. He wandered into the chapter house and stood for a moment. The waterproof girls were there but took no notice of him. He moved out and into the cloisters. No one else was around. He moved down to where he reckoned the cellars and kitchen had been, and stood looking at the ruins. From behind him he sensed movement and then a voice:

"Mr. Lane?"

He whirled to find . . . the tweed lady. Lane attempted to respond but found that he was suddenly speechless.

"I'm sorry," she said, "I didn't mean to startle you like that."

"It's all right," he managed to stammer, "I just wasn't expecting . . ."

"You weren't expecting a woman, right?" she said.

"You're right," he answered. "I'm bewildered by this whole affair."

"Yes, you must be," the tweed lady said. She was short and stout, wearing a trilby, out of which tumbled curly auburn hair. She was wearing sturdy shoes and carrying a compact red umbrella. She had a kindly face, glasses, intelligent eyes, and a bemused smile.

"Can you tell me what's going on, please?" Lane asked, more forcefully than he had expected.

"Of course," the tweed lady answered, "but why don't we move a little further away, down towards the beach, and I'll try to explain."

They skirted around the end of the ruined wall and walked on the grass a few yards towards the beach. The tweed lady stopped just before the sandy beach. Halfway up from the water's edge, the remains of seaweed formed a thick line all the way along. Dozens of gulls were strutting about as if they owned the place. Edinburgh Castle and Salisbury Crags were just visible across the water.

The tweed lady removed her hat and shook out her hair. "My name is Naomi Fowler," she said, holding out her hand. "I really am rather sorry about the secrecy stuff. We just thought that it was necessary on this occasion. You'll see why after I explain things to you."

"I was rather alarmed by all this," Lane said, "but just now you said *we*, and in the note you put through my door you also said *we*. But there is only one of you." When he said it the words sounded a bit pedantic, but they were intended to be.

"Yes," she said, "it must be confusing. It will be less so in a minute, but I must confess that even then . . ." She had an alto voice, which trailed off as she planted her feet farther apart, as if to ready herself for a robust explanation.

"The *we* is really a kind of confederation or consortium of Scottish agencies and institutions. I'm speaking for them at the moment. They are deeply concerned about a development plan which I'm going to sketch out to you just now. I'm sure that you won't have heard about this before. It's been kept under thick wraps for a very good reason. But it's inevitable that leaks will occur, and so I suspect that the story is going to hit the media very soon, perhaps in the next two weeks."

"What kinds of institutions?" Lane asked.

"Well, institutions such as Historic Scotland, the Royal Commission on Historic Monuments, the Scottish Tourist Board, Forth Ports, bird and wildlife associations, the National Trust, the East Coast Fishermen, even the Rambler's Association. The Scottish government is involved and Fife Council. You name it, and it's likely that it's in the group. You can see how diverse these groups are. That's one reason that a) I'm here by myself, and b) we are approaching you."

"I hear what you say," Lane answered, "but the pieces aren't falling into place yet."

"No, I realize that," Ms. Fowler said, "but they will if you'll be patient. All these agencies are concerned because a very well-known tycoon is hatching a plan for the island and the abbey. His name is Alexander Morton. He's American. Perhaps you've heard of him?"

Lane suppressed a snort. "Alexander Morton? Is there anyone who hasn't heard of him?"

"Only, perhaps, someone in the remotest jungle of New Guinea." Ms. Fowler giggled. "Anyway, to go on, Mr. Morton wants to create a luxury development here."

"Here, on this island?" Lane exclaimed. "You've got to be joking."

"No, Mr. Lane—may I call you Davis by the way? And call me Naomi. No, I'm not joking. Mr. Morton has presented a preliminary plan for developing the island, to be held and studied in the strictest confidence by the agencies I just mentioned. His plan involves the construction of an eighteen hole golf course, a five star hotel and a casino, right here. He claims that it's not intended to be the greatest golf course in the world but the holiest. Every hole will be named after a saint. And he says that the casino could be the most exclusive gambling establishment in the world."

"I can't believe what you're telling me, Naomi. He hasn't a hope in hell of a development like that on this island. I mean, it's under the care of Historic Scotland isn't it?"

"Yes, of course it is. Under ordinary circumstances there wouldn't be a hope in hell, but these are not ordinary times as you surely must know. I know that the idea sounds absurd, but the fact is that these are economically straightened times. Historic Scotland is struggling to maintain all the properties it is responsible for. There isn't enough money to do that. Unemployment is very high, especially in Fife. The Scottish Tourist Board is under enormous pressure to bring more tourists with money into the country. The Scottish government is being pushed harder every day to create jobs in the regions with high unemployment, and the Scot Nats would like to stay in power. Do you see where I'm heading?" She smiled at him, as if gently encouraging a child in gaining some new understanding that was at base quite simple.

"Well, yes," Lane answered. "I'm gradually getting the picture, but I still don't believe it. The island's too small for a golf course, and these ruins are historically very significant. You just can't do it. It's just absurd."

"That's what everyone says, Davis. But Alexander Morton has an answer for everything. He says that it will be an executive golf course. Now, I'm not a golfer so I don't quite know what that means, but he says it can be done. He promises to rebuild the monastery to its original configuration, which he says will bring in the tourists. He says that the hotel with its casino will be unique and attract even more people with money to spend. He has billions of dollars and he says he's willing to invest it right here." He tapped her foot on the grass as if to emphasize the assertion.

"Oh, I appreciate that he must have loads of money," Lane responded, "but there are limits to what you can do, even with money. I mean, it won't buy him more space to build fairways and greens. It won't create invisibility to hide the profile of a big hotel."

"Yes," Naomi answered, "but I'm told that he has thought about all these issues and has solutions for them."

"Oh come on, "Lane replied. "Somebody's been taking you all for a ride. This is not the first of April."

She grasped Lane's elbow. "Davis, I wish that it were April Fool's Day so that we could have a laugh and get on with things. But I kid you not: this is a serious proposal, and Morton may be rich enough and powerful enough to pull it off."

Lane shook his head. "I still don't believe it, but even if it were true I don't see what use I could be to you. Why would you need a free-lance theologian?"

"I'm coming to that," she said. She paused for a minute to let the two French couples, still locked in philosophical conversation, to walk on by. "Alexander Morton is an American. You are an American. This is the beauty of the thing: if you were to agree to work with us, whatever ethical position you might adopt, no one could accuse you of being a racist, of just being anti-American. See what I mean? I understand that you're also a golfer, so Morton couldn't accuse you of being an anti-golf-course person. You would have something in common with him. Do you get my point?"

Lane sighed. "More or less," he said, "but I still don't see what you would want me to do. All these institutions you've spoken of: they have enormous power. They surely can put a stop to this now."

Naomi shook her head and looked into the distance as if searching for patience. "But again, it's not that simple. You know that many people will oppose this to the hilt, but you would be surprised at the people who will probably be for this. Morton estimates that the construction part alone would create a thousand jobs. Then the hotel and golf course and casino would create another three or four hundred permanent jobs. There would need to be improvements to the infrastructure in Fife. Then there's the money that the tourists who come here would bring into the economy. Surely you can see that from a political point of view he has a very powerful argument. If the Scottish National members of parliament could say that the government had brought thousands of new jobs to Scotland and millions of pounds in fresh money in revenue . . . well, you can see."

"But what would you actually want me to do?" Lane asked.

"Well, we would want you to take a deep interest in the island and the abbey. We would want you to do research into the history of the order and the abbey itself. We would want you to be regarded as the theological expert on Inchcolm Abbey." Naomi answered.

"And if I were seen to be an expert on the island and the abbey," Lane said, "then what?"

"Then, in the midst of all the media interest that will be generated, in the midst of all the arguing and negotiations and hostility . . ." Naomi hesitated.

Lane jumped in, "In the midst of all that I would be ground down into this rock by the heel of your consortium or Mr. Morton's organisation. My remains would lie in this holy ground as part of a tee or green."

"No, we wouldn't let that happen," Naomi said, laughing. "We'd make sure that you would be seen as a fair and balanced interested party. People would respect your viewpoint without slinging brickbats at you. The point is that you could provide us with inside information and an independent voice and a kind of fulcrum to exert some leverage."

"Naomi, I'm not prepared to act as a spy," Lane interjected, suddenly remembering his last experience with the CIA.

"I know, I know that," Naomi protested, holding up both hands in self-defence. "We are not asking you to be a spy. We simply want you to be involved as an independent consultant."

"But look, would you not finally depend on me to take your line, Naomi? I think that when it came to the crunch you would expect me to come out against this project. But suppose that when I look into it and consider all the possibilities, suppose that I were to support this development?"

"In the light of everything you've just said, that seems unlikely does it not? But we've talked about that Davis," she said, touching his elbow again. "We have talked about that a great deal. Here's what we think. First, we don't think that you would be in favour of a golf course and casino here. It would destroy what is a significant historic monastery and a beautiful island. But if you did support it, if you really could live with it on your doorstep, then we would have to consider your viewpoint. We might have come out publicly against you, but we're willing to take that gamble. But that is really jumping the gun anyway. There's no guarantee that all the organisations under this umbrella will agree on a line to take. In fact, we're pretty certain they won't."

They walked a little farther along the line of the beach. The tide was going out. They would need to depart soon. Lane was beginning to warm a little to this woman. She was clearly intelligent and competent. He could see why they might choose her to represent their interests.

"Let me ask you several questions while all this soaks in," she said.

"Fair enough, fire away." Lane responded.

"I suspect that were you to be interested in this project and we put your name forward, some of our people wouldn't understand what a free-lance theologian is or does."

Lane laughed. "Tell me about it. I don't always understand what I do. No, the thing is this: We live in a secular age, especially in Europe. People have given up on Christianity or at least think they have. But you don't really give up doing theology. You're always making assumptions about the presence or the absence of God, about what he does or doesn't do. So most people haven't given up doing theology; they just do bad theology, childish or adolescent theology. I'm around to help people do a better kind of theological thinking. So I do a bit of teaching or a bit of preaching or some consulting, whatever I'm asked to do. But it's not a very profitable job."

"No," Naomi answered, "I can't imagine that it is. But were this project to come off it would be worth your while. What do you think so far?"

"To be perfectly honest with you," Lane answered, "the whole idea seems so far-fetched that I'm having difficulty taking it seriously. I just can't imagine anyone wanting to plant a golf course, hotel and casino on this little island. It's ludicrous. In the second place I can't imagine the authorities even considering it for an instant."

"Yes," she answered, "I'm with you all the way. I felt exactly the same when I first heard about it, and I'm not even a golfer. But believe me, we have to take it seriously. You'll be seeing headlines about this in all the newspapers before you know it. So . . . would you be interested in the project if the umbrella organisations do agree to ask you to serve as a consultant?"

Lane studied her and then looked across the Forth towards Edinburgh Castle. "OK, I suppose so," he said, sighing, "if they really want me."

Naomi reached for his hand and pumped it. She looked genuinely pleased. "Thank you so much," she said. She opened her handbag and searched for a moment. She brought out a card and handed it to Lane.

"Here's my card," she said. "This is my mobile number. You can always reach me here. If I don't answer, leave a message. Don't try to get in touch with me via any landline number. We will need to watch our security. But I'll call you as soon as I know what all the representative people in the group think. Now, on the other side of this card is a figure that we are proposing to spend for your help. I hope that it's sufficient, but if you feel it isn't enough, please say so."

Lane looked at the card and gave a low whistle. "You sure know how to tempt a guy," he said. "But how can you afford to pay me this amount for what I'm supposed to do? It seems a lot to me."

"I suppose it does to a free-lance theologian," Naomi answered, "but remember that when all these agencies chip in a little bit each it doesn't amount to a whole lot for them. Now, do you have a mobile number I can reach you on? I won't try your landline for the same reasons. It may not be secure."

"OK, Lane answered, "I'll give you my mobile number."

The Maid *of the Forth's* horn sounded the warning that the vessel would soon depart for South Queensferry. They began to make their way back to the harbour.

"I don't want to appear rude," Naomi said, "but I think it might be better if we split up here. You probably saw the younger man in the sport jacket on the boat. I'm not sure, but I think he's a reporter with the *Scotsman*. I'm just hoping that he didn't see us talking. That's why I brought you down here away from the others. We've suspected that there is an aroma of all this in the wind. They are snooping. I think that he comes out here to talk to one of the keepers of the property. He chats them up, hoping for information. So I'm afraid that it's back to the cloak and dagger again."

Lane managed a weak smile. "Whatever you say, boss." An afterthought suddenly struck him. "Listen, you haven't told me who you work for."

Naomi stopped and looked at him for a moment. "I know, and I'm sorry," she said, but can we hold off on that for a little? If the umbrella agrees to this project I'll tell you, promise."

Lane held back to let Naomi precede him back to the harbour. By the time he climbed on board most of the others were there. In another five minutes the *Maid* was making its way back towards South Queensferry. The passengers were strangely quiet on the return trip, but Lane reflected that this was the way with most trips he had been on. Going, people were excited and chatted to each other. Coming back, they were tired and mostly silent. He studied the wake made by the vessel and wondered if what kind of waves this Inchcolm event might make.

At home he was surprised to see Katriona's car in the driveway of their house. Surely she was home early. Once through the door the smell of . . . what was it . . . ? Lasagne embraced him lovingly. She greeted him at the door to the kitchen.

"Well, I am surprised," she said, smiling broadly. "You weren't kidnapped or thrown overboard."

"No, I'm still around," he said. "Still here to annoy you."

She came to him and planted a kiss on his lips. "I'm glad. I came home early just to make sure, and I thought you might appreciate *my* cooking tonight."

"Believe me, you've no idea," he said, sitting down on a kitchen stool.

"No," she said, "no sitting down yet. You have to open a bottle of Chianti first, assuming that's all right of course."

"Believe me," he repeated, getting up and going for the corkscrew, "you've no idea."

"Oh, by the way," Katriona said, arching an eyebrow, "did you have your rendezvous with your secret lover?"

"I did indeed," Lane replied, pulling the cork, "and she's very nice. But she's fairly large, wears tweed and a trilby and carries a dangerous umbrella."

Over dinner Lane related the story of his trip to Inchcolm.

"So, what are you going to do," she said?

"What do you think I should do?" he answered.

"I think that you've probably made up your mind already. Does it really matter what I say?"

"Why do you think I've made up my mind already?" he answered.

"Because I can tell by the look on your face," she said. "I can tell by the way you told me about it, and I can see that you've been charmed by the tweed lady. What's her name—Naomi? It's a challenge to you."

"You think so?" Lane asked.

"Of course it is," she answered. "I know you need a challenge or project of some kind. It's all right, go ahead. It doesn't sound like it's as dangerous as the last one anyway."

"No, I'm sure you're right," he said, toasting her with his glass. Deep down, however, in his heart of hearts, he wasn't really all that sure.

Chapter Three

Headwork

Lane awoke the next morning feeling positive. He made Katriona's breakfast and saw her off to Dunfermline. She was heading, rather reluctantly he thought, for a morning conference in the social work department. The world outside the window was dark with a steady rain hitting the glass and slowly making its way down. This would be an ideal day to be at the desk. He sat down and began to make a list of the issues that would need to be researched, assuming of course that this umbrella Naomi spoke for wanted him to do the job. It might not happen of course, but he had to assume that she had approved of him and it would go through. It was a little unsettling to think that you would be working for an unspecified collection of agencies, but they seemed to want it that way. She seemed unduly concerned about security, but she must have cause. In any event, it was good to have something to get your teeth into.

The list of issues that needed to be tackled was growing longer and longer in his mind. Inchcolm Abbey had been an Augustinian monastery, so he would need to remind himself not only about the nature of the medieval monastery but particularly about the Augustinian tradition. It had been a long time since he had studied monastic history in seminary. He remembered that it had been mainly the monastery libraries that had preserved classical learning throughout the dark ages when everything else was being sacked. Recovering the classics prepared the way for the renaissance. He recalled that the monks have given impetus to modern agriculture because of their disciplined approach to growing and harvesting. The monasteries had also been important for their technical achievements. Inventions such as the clock had arisen in order to enable the community to worship at the appropriate hours. In the next place, he would have to see if there were any archaeological reports on the Inchcolm Abbey itself. He would need to look into the geography of the island and study its relation to the mainland. And he would have to do some research on Alexander Morton himself. What kind of person might he be dealing with? He'd gone online already to plug the Morton organisation into Google, finding that there were Morton hotels all over the world. On this score, though, an idea had been slowly taking shape in his mind. He could find out a lot through the internet, but there might be a way to get more revealing information. He picked up the phone and called Robert McCord. He was put through immediately.

"Robert," he said, "it's Davis Lane again."

"Davis, good to hear from you. I take it that you survived your little trip intact. No problems?"

"No, it went fine," Lane answered. "But listen, the last time we spoke you offered to help me if required, right?"

"Yes, I do seem to remember that," McCord said, chucking over the line. "But it doesn't look like you need any protection."

"No, I don't need protection," Lane answered, "but I do need some information, and I suspect that you're the person who could supply it."

McCord hesitated for a moment, and then sounded serious. "What kind of information? If it involves anything that's stamped SECRET I can't help you."

"No," Lane said, "nothing along those lines. It's just information or even gossip that probably could be found in the public domain for the most part, so I figured that you might be able to add little titbits to the pot."

"You're not suggesting that I listen to or encourage gossip are you, Davis?" McCord asked.

"No of course not," Lane answered. "I wouldn't dream of it."

"Thank goodness," McCord said. "Acquisition is one of the tasks of the company, but it's facts we look for rather than gossip."

"I seem to remember," Lane said, "that J. Edgar did a pretty thorough job of collecting gossip."

"Well," McCord came back, "that was the F.B.I. What can you expect? Our company's different. Anyway, I do owe you one. Tell me what it is and I'll do my best."

"First of all," Lane said, "this needs to be confidential. I promised someone that I wouldn't break her confidence."

"Oh, a female is it?" McCord answered. "I hope you're not going to be caught in the embrace of a sulky, blonde Soviet agent."

"No, I wouldn't say that she was blonde, sulky or Soviet," Lane responded, laughing. "If I told you, you wouldn't believe me."

"OK, you have my word, total confidence it is," McCord said.

"All I want," Lane said, "is some background information on Alexander Morton, the American property tycoon."

"Morton, the zillionair property magnate with his worldwide chain of hotels?" McCord responded. "That's an odd request. What's he ... oh no, sorry, I can't ask you about that can I?" There was silence for a moment. "OK," McCord said, "I think we can do that. I'll see what I can dig up. Give me two or three days. I think I promised you lunch before. I could bring any nuggets I do unearth. That be all right?"

"Yes, "Lane answered, "But I'm buying."

"No you're not," McCord said. "This time I'm the supplier and I'm the buyer, and I'm also glad that this is a secure line. The drug enforcement agency would have a field day with this conversation. Look, I've taken a shine to a place just down the road from here, the *King's Wark*. Why don't we meet there three days from now, say about 12:30?"

"I've never heard of it," Lane said. "Where is it?"

"Just along the road from me, where the Water of Leith meets the Shore. It's right on the corner. One of the oldest pubs in the country. Good food, no pretensions."

"OK, sounds good to me," Lane answered. "See you then."

Lane hung up. So far, so good. There were some possibilities coming down the pipeline already.

It was still raining outside. Lane turned back to his list of issues. It seemed logical to start with St Augustine and the Augustinian tradition. He liked Augustine and rather relished the idea of renewing his relationship with the man who had been so important for western Christianity. Augustine may have been born in Africa in 354, but in some ways he seemed a thoroughly modern man. Much influenced by his Christian mother Monnica, he was sent to Carthage in North Africa to study rhetoric. There, at age seventeen he took a mistress. It blew Lane's mind to think of having a mistress at seventeen years of age, but Augustine held onto her for fourteen years, and they produced a son Adeodatus. Augustine started reading Cicero, and that seemed to awaken him to a search for the truth. He went to Rome and then to Milan, where he came under the influence of the great preaching of Ambrose. The difficulty was that Augustine began to feel keenly the difference between his high ideals and his conduct, between the desires of the flesh and the desires of the spirit, and so could pray, "Lord, grant me chastity and continence, but not yet." Seventeen centuries later people were still quoting, but seldom praying, that same prayer. How many people could say that their words would often be quoted seventeen centuries after they had been uttered?

Augustine then experienced a powerful conversion experience and went on to become the bishop of Hippo in North Africa. His theology had proved to be the most powerful influence on the western wing of the Catholic Church and then later in the Reformation. The rules he established for those monasteries under his control had endured, and Martin Luther, as a monk in the Augustinian tradition, had been familiar with them. The monks in every monastery would be reminded regularly of the purpose and basis of common life, the need for and proper conduct of prayer, of moderation and self-denial, how to safeguard chastity and correct a brother, of the care of community goods and treatment of the sick, of the importance of asking for pardon and forgiving offences, and of how governance and obedience was to be maintained. All of these things would have been stressed in the community at Inchcolm Abbey. Lane wrote down some of St Augustine's rules:

> *Call nothing your own, but let everything be yours in common.*
> *Be assiduous in prayer at the hours and times appointed*
> *There should be nothing about your clothing to attract attention. Besides, you should not seek to please by your apparel, but by a good life.*
> *No one shall perform any task for his own benefit but all your world shall be done for the common good, with greater zeal and more dispatch than if each one of you were to work for yourself alone.*
> *Whoever has injured another by open insult, or by abusive or even incriminating language, must remember to repair the injury as quickly as possible by an apology, and he who suffered the injury must also forgive, without further wrangling.*
> *And that you may see yourselves in these rules, as in a mirror, have them read to you once a week, so as to neglect no point through forgetfulness.*

Lane tried to reflect on these rules in the context of life in the twenty-first century. He doubted that they would be happily received by many men and women today. Indeed, in this acquisitive, fashion-conscious, self-seeking and celebrity-obsessed society culture, they would probably prove to be incomprehensible. It was a thoroughly secular society, and yet curiously influenced by several *isms* such as fundamentalism and scientism. Sometimes, Lane thought, it was uncanny how without invitation the lines of a song injected themselves into his thinking. This time it was Don McLean's song *American Pie*:

> *The church bells all were broken*
> *And the three men I admire the most,*
> *The Father, Son and Holy Ghost,*
> *They caught the last train for the coast*

He reckoned that for most people the Trinity had indeed fled, fed up with such a self-seeking culture. Or perhaps they had been pushed out by the very lifestyle that Alexander Morton was promoting. What would the monks, who strived at keeping Augustine's rules, have made of a hotel, casino and golf course on their island? Would Morton post these rules in every room of the hotel alongside the directions to be followed in case of fire? Or might he have them read at breakfast during a communal silence? It was too absurd to think about. Lane shook his head, closed the book and left the house to find Melvin's Mobile Barber Shop. A haircut might not only lighten the head but clear it as well.

He found Melvin's barbershop bus parked outside the metro-centre in Dalgety Bay. The mobile barber toured the area looking for customers in his barbershop bus. The sign attached to the side of the bus read simply:

> *Haircuts here*
> *No Parking, No Fuss*
> *Get on the Bus*

The rain was still coming down, so it was no surprise that there were no customers waiting when Lane boarded. Melvin was sitting in the barber's chair reading *The Daily Mail*. His old boxer was snoring in the corner. Melvin got up and held out his hand when Lane came through the door. The sweet aroma of hair gel greeted him as well.

"Mr. Lane, good to see you. It's been a while. Please, sit down," Melvin said, making a sweeping gesture towards the chair.

Lane sat down in the barber's chair. "I know, Melvin," he said. "Too many things have been happening lately. Are you well?"

"I'm fine, Mr. Lane," Melvin answered, "just feeling the world has gone crazy, that's all," shaking his head as he adjusted the cloth over Lane's shoulders.

"And why has the world gone crazy, Melvin?"

"I've just been reading in the paper about Rangers and Celtic," Melvin answered. "I can't believe this. The Celtic manager was attacked on the pitch. He's had bomb threats through the mail. I mean, can you believe that, Mr. Lane? In this day and age? These people are like . . . like dinosaurs."

"I hadn't heard about that, Melvin," Lane answered. "I can't answer your question. I don't know why they do these things. I guess that it's just sheer prejudice."

"But you know about religion, Mr. Lane, Melvin said. "If the good book says that we're supposed to love each other, then why do these people hate each other?" Melvin's boxer, perhaps enjoying a dream about chasing rabbits, was yipping softly in the corner.

"I think it's a kind of fantasy they have," Lane said. "It isn't based on anything real. They need some kind of purpose to live or reason to be. They need an enemy, someone to hate."

Melvin was working with the clippers and didn't respond except to shake his head. "I can't take my kids to the game," Mr. Lane. "No way are they going to hear all those bad words and see all that stuff. No way."

"Quite right," Melvin, Lane answered. "I wouldn't take anybody to a soccer match these days."

"Does this happen in America, Mr. Lane?" Melvin asked.

"No, not really," Lane answered. "You can go to almost any game, football, baseball, whatever, and there's no bad language, no violence. In fact the last time I went to a baseball game, they invited the kids to run around the bases after the game. It was good to see. They try to appeal to the family."

Melvin had pushed Lane's head forward and was working on his neck. "That's good. I don't know baseball though. It's like cricket right?"

"Well, sort of," Lane replied, "but it doesn't last so long, the scoring is much lower, and I can understand the commentary." He laughed to himself, but Melvin didn't pick up on his little joke.

"Do you want some off the top?" Mr. Lane, Melvin asked.

"Yes, please," Lane answered, wondering how much longer he could spare hair off the top.

Another customer came into the bus and sat down. Melvin finished off and removed the cover with a flourish. "Well, that's it for another while, Mr. Lane."

Lane stood up and wiped his forehead with the tissue. He searched his pocket for change and handed it to the barber. "Thanks again, Melvin. It's always a pleasure talking to you." He moved to the corner and petted the boxer, who gave no sign of recognition for the affection. He stepped off the bus at the same place he'd gotten on. Finally, the rain had stopped.

Lane pulled out of the metro-centre parking lot, and on the spur of the moment decided to head east. The next town along the Forth was Aberdour, which was the closest place to Inchcolm. The castle and the nearby church, St Fillans, both had an association with the abbey. Lane drove along the main street of Aberdour and tuned right to park on Hawkcraig road. He walked back to the castle and stepped through the gate in the high surrounding wall. Enough of the castle remained intact to provide an impression of what it must have been like when the abbey flourished. He studied the ruins and the gardens for a few moments to remind himself of its position and outlook in relation to the abbey. Clearly, Historic Scotland kept the ruins and garden in good repair. Stepping back outside the wall he headed down the narrow path towards St Fillans Church. The path ran along the castle wall and then turned right under a low buttressing arch, finally opening out at St Fillans' graveyard. They were repairing the castle wall, and the scaffolding cut out the light on the very narrow path. Fallen tombstone decorations, mainly those of skull and crossbones, had been laid along the side of the path. This might not be the place to be on a dark night. Stepping carefully, Lane walked to the south end of the graveyard and focussed on Inchcolm. It was a fine view from here. The church was open and no one was around. Near the door Lane found a booklet giving the history of the church. He left money for it and then turned back towards the car. No doubt he would need to come back here, but this was sufficient for the day. Back on the main highway he went west towards Inverkeithing and home. Then, suddenly, the skies were darkening again. It looked like more rain and it was time to get inside.

When Katriona came in, took off her raincoat and set down her briefcase, the dinner was ready. "Welcome home," Lane said, sliding a glass of wine in her direction.

"Oh," she said, "I didn't think you'd be home this early, but I'm glad. It's been a trying day."

"Yes, I'm home," Lane said, giving her a cuddle. "Why has it been a trying day?"

"Well, you know, protracted conference, unemployment, abused children, drug abuse incompetent parents and so forth. Were you expecting something else?"

"Sorry," Lane said, raising his own glass and nodding it towards her, "but you're home now and the dinner's ready, and you can relax."

"Good," Katriona said, slumping into her favourite chair. "How was your day?" she asked.

"Fine," he answered. "I've organized some help from Robert McCord, I've joined the Augustinian Order, I've been to Aberdour and back, and I've had a haircut."

"I noticed," she said.

Chapter Four

The Wark

It was the day for his lunchtime meeting with Robert McCord. Lane decided on this occasion to drive to Leith rather than take the train or bus. The PT Cruiser had not enjoyed a longer run for a few days, so a trip to Leith might do it good. He crossed the Forth Road Bridge hemmed in by large lorries. Business was said to be bad, the economy was said to be suffering, and yet the number of trucks on the road seemed to grow greater day by day. There had been signs warning that work was going on somewhere on the bridge, but he couldn't see any. He passed Cramond Brig and continued on Ferry Road. The traffic was bad. He'd read recently that Edinburgh had joined the top ten of the most congested cities in Europe. He could vouch for that. Moreover, the city must be number one for the bumpiest roads in Europe. They dug up the roads for cables and pipes and whatever, yet never seemed to full the holes properly. If only Edinburgh had a tram! Just a dose of irony for the day. He followed Ferry Road all the way to the end, and then took Coburg Street over the Water of Leith. No parking spaces leapt out at him. He crossed Bernard Street and turned right at the Malmaison Hotel. He found a space just past the old premises of the *Classic Car Club*. Maybe in a couple of years the club would be interested in buying his PT Cruiser.

Lane walked back along the road to the point where Bernard Street crossed the river. The sun kept appearing and disappearing behind the clouds, so it was chilly and he zipped up his jacket. In spite of that there were lots of people around, some of them sitting out at tables on the pavement having a drink or a meal. *The Kings Wark* stood on the corner, facing the Water of Leith. This water came all the way down from Balerno in the Pentland Hills and emptied here into the firth. Lane found a narrow door at the front and made his way in. The pub was old, dark wood and blackened stone with a right-angled bar and a fireplace. Robert McCord was sitting a table in the corner close to the fireplace. He rose, smiled and held out his hand.

"Hi Davis, good to see you so soon again. Have a chair."

"This is quite a place," Lane commented, scanning the room. "I've come through this intersection dozens of time and didn't appreciate that this was a pub."

"It's a great pub," McCord said, "apparently dates way back to the fifteenth century when James I had several buildings put up for merchants. *Wark* really means *Work,* so it was the Kings Work. I guess that over the years it's been used in lots of ways, even to store weapons at some point in history. But I think there's been a pub here for most of the time. I like it because the food is good and cheap and I can walk here from the office. I'm trying to get more exercise these days."

"I thought that I knew a lot about Leith," Davis said, "but you've stumbled over a piece of history I didn't know."

"I'm not sure that the Agency would like to think of me as stumbling. Anyway, what would you like to drink?" McCord asked.

The two men decided on the identity of their pints and studied the menu while they waited. Once the drinks were on the table and they had ordered, the business could begin.

"So," McCord began, "you've got some new project that involves Alexander Morton?"

"It's not definite yet, just being considered," Lane answered.

"And you're not able to tell me anything about it, right?"

"That's right," Lane said. "Sorry about that but I did promise. But knowing you and knowing what you do for a living, I just thought that you might be able to squeeze something out of the known unknown."

"Oh please," McCord said, "let's not bring Donald Rumsfelt into this. I may be able to add something to what you already know, but Alexander Morton is a powerful guy. There's no way of telling what the man might get up to. In any event, it doesn't sound like whatever it is should be life-threatening for you."

"No, probably not," Lane said, "but you never know, do you? Look what happened the last time."

"OK, Ok," McCord said, "but that's all water under the bridge now. Let me tell you what I know about Mr. Morton." The food arrived and McCord waited until the waitress had departed. A group of six younger people had come in and the pub was getting noisy.

"Well, you're probably already familiar with all the material that's online," McCord said. "Alexander Morton is a highly successful property tycoon who's made millions. He's got hotels in New York, Vegas, L.A., Central America and Asia promoted under the *AM* label, AM being Alexander Morton of course. They've got all the latest luxury fixtures, things like spas and gyms and negative edge pools. They all have exquisite rooms and high class restaurants and high prices as well. Some of his hotels have casinos. Morton seems to be pushy and arrogant and conceited, but most of his properties have been done with quite good taste, so I hear. I've never stayed in *AM New York* or *AM Vegas*, so I really wouldn't know. I mean, there's no denying that he is a very good businessman. He sees himself as a rival to a couple of other property developers. I'm told that if you drive down the Strip in Vegas the rivalry socks you in the eye immediately. Like the other guys he plays golf and enjoys gambling."

McCord dipped a chip into tomato sauce and thought for a moment. "He's unique in a way because unlike the other guys he is still married to his first wife. She's the homemaker type, not much into society. She spends a lot of her time looking after his houses in the rest of the world. He's got a son and a daughter who are both in the business, and he does seem to give them a lot of responsibility in managing the business. I hear that the daughter is attractive and the son is rude and unshaven, but that's just hearsay. How am I doing so far?"

"You're doing fine so far," Lane said, preoccupied with trying to get piece of haddock to stay on his fork, "but keep on going."

"Well, there's not a lot more to say," McCord said, "It's been rumoured that he has political ambitions. It could be true, but I don't know. It seems unlikely because he doesn't like publicity. He hates being in the limelight, especially when his image is flashed on the television screen. He enjoys making deals quietly and in private and then announcing a done deal only at the last moment. He's said to get pleasure from blowing away his competitors in this kind of operation. In any event, because of the money he can do just about anything he wants. He assumes that he can buy his way into anywhere and usually he succeeds. Morton is not adverse to bullying people. He's a formidable operator, not one to be crossed."

"OK," Lane said, "that's quite helpful. That pretty much corresponds to what I've learned already but adds to it from a more personal point of view."

McCord took another drink and set the glass down on the table a little too hard. He sat straighter and then leaned forward. "Now, there are a few other little things I've learned that aren't widely known. Do you want to hear them?"

Lane smiled. "Of course I do. You know that."

"I thought you would," McCord said, motioning for Lane to lean forward as well. "One of our guys," he said, "knows one of Morton's minders. He's got at least one minder with him at all times. He figures that he's a target. I suppose that someone might think of him as a kidnap mark, but that would be a difficult one to pull off. It's more to do with defending the boss against people who are angry with him for his techniques. Anyway, the minder told our guy that Morton is very superstitious. Seems strange, but he is. There's all kind of things he's afraid of: black cats crossing his path, meeting someone in a stairway, that sort of thing. He avoids the number thirteen like a plague. None of his hotels has a room or floor numbered thirteen or a multiple of thirteen. He's afraid of mirrors breaking, so all the mirrors in all his hotels are made of polycarbonate, which they say is two hundred times stronger than glass. He's a godsend to the manufacturers of polycarbonate. And he won't sit with his back to a door or window. Now I don't know about you, but I find this quite strange. You would think that a man that rich and that powerful would have conquered all this psychological stuff, but there you are. That's about all I've got for you."

Lane leaned back in his chair, let out his breath, and picked up his pint. "Robert, you're a very valuable guy. I forgive you for everything in the past. Thanks. I'm sure that all this will help."

"Gosh," McCord said, "here's someone who believes in forgiveness. Thanks Davis. Now, not to pry, but how will it help?"

Lane winked at his partner in secrets. "I've no idea," he said.

Lane walked back along the water towards his car. He stopped to look at the new sculpture in front of the Malmaison Hotel. It was a memorial to the merchant navy that had made such a contribution to the life of the nation in two wars. All over Edinburgh there were pieces of art designed to honour people who had made sacrifices in wartime. It was right, of course, and yet it underlined how much war had dominated the history of the nation. All over the country, in cities and in every little town, there were war memorials listing the names of the young men and women who had sacrificed their lives in wars. What impact, Lane wondered, does it have upon a country to lose so many young people from one generation? We talk glibly about remembering and learning, *so that this sort of thing can never happen again.* What rubbish, he thought. In this context *learning* was an empty word.

Lane found the Cruiser, turned around and headed home. He reached into the bin in the door, took the first CD that came to hand and put it in the player. *I Heard it on the Grapevine* by Marvin Gaye. If anyone were to question the source of his newfound knowledge of Alexander Morton he could say that he had heard it on the grapevine. But he needed to make sure that no one would ever ask.

The road home to Inverkeithing was fairly quiet, too early for the rush hour traffic. There were still signs forecasting work on the bridge and there was still no sign of it. Lane wondered if the proposed new road bridge would ever happen. If people were unable to get a tram to run through the city centre how could they possibly organize a span over this wide estuary? The idea of another endless and unsuccessful project filled him with gloom.

Lane put the car into the garage and started thinking about what they would have for dinner. Maybe he should have thought earlier and stopped at the supermarket. His mobile rang and he answered. "Hello, is that Davis? It's Naomi here."

"Oh, Hello Naomi. How are you?" Lane said.

"I'm fine," she said, "Is it convenient to talk just now?"

"Yes, sure," he said.

"It's about our little project," she said. "I'm happy to say that the umbrella of organizations has discussed the matter and have decided that they want you to take a part in this. Are you still willing to take this on?"

Lane hesitated for a moment and was conscious of searching his mind for a final answer.

"Davis, are you still there?"

"Yes, sorry, Naomi. I'm still here. Yes, I'm willing to do this job. I only have one request. Could you give me some kind of paperwork on this? I'm not sure exactly what I want, and I know it might be difficult for you. I just feel that I ought to have some proof that I'm consulting for others and not acting on my own behalf. Do you get my point?"

"Sort of," she said. "I don't think in the nature of things that I can give you a contract. But let me talk to some of the others. I'm sure that we can come up with something. Is that OK?"

"Yes, Lane said. "I'll look for something from you then."

"Good," she said. "And, I will see that you get a cheque in the post. Is that OK?"

"I wouldn't complain about that," Lane answered.

"Good," Naomi said, "When can you get started then?"

"Oh," he said, "I've started already."

Chapter Five
The Abbeys

Lane had said to Naomi that he had started work already. That was true, but he'd really only begun to scratch the surface. It was time now to dig far beneath the surface in order to unearth material of value. Indeed, he seemed to recall that he was supposed to become *the* theological expert on Inchcolm Abbey. Perhaps that was going a bit far. In any event, he had to get serious. He gathered together several books, earmarked several websites and poured himself a glass of *Macallan*. The dram was not part of his normal procedure, but he decided that it could be justified as a toast to a special occasion. It might get things off on the right foot.

He began by carefully reading and noting every piece of information that might prove helpful. If he were honest with himself this was the sort of exercise he really enjoyed. He looked forward to discovering information that sparked off genuine interest because it described a culture and a way of life so different from that he knew in the twenty-first century. The first barrier, however, was the lack of facts about Inchcolm Abbey. Yes, there was abundant archaeological information, but nothing about the actual life of the community at Inchcolm. He needed to look elsewhere for clues, and on the score he was lucky. Lane found a website that focussed on another Augustinian monastery: Saint-Jean-des-Vignes, near Soissons, northeast of Paris. It had existed from 1076 until 1567, during roughly the same period of time as Inchcolm Abbey. Exhaustive investigations had been carried out at Saint-Jean-des-Vignes and had been carefully set out on a dedicated website. Of particular significance was the fact that for this abbey both textual and archaeological information had been available. So between the two sources, detailed information could be gained about the architecture of the monastery, the identity and daily life of the inhabitants, and about their relationship with the surrounding community. True, Saint-Jean-des-Vignes was not Inchcolm Abbey, but Lane reckoned that since both monasteries were of the Augustinian tradition and existed at the same period of time, Inchcolm would, in general, share the same type of structure and organisation.

There were two kinds of textual evidence at Saint-Jean-des-Vignes: *obituaries* and *cartularies*. The obituaries provided the actual names of the officers and lay brothers of the monastery who had died and presumably been buried within the complex. The members of the community were not *monks* as such but *canons* or priests who had taken monastic vows, as well as lay brothers. The obituaries also contained the names of those from the town and region who had been associated with the community in some way and been buried within its walls. Clearly for some people who lived *outside* the walls, it had been very important to be buried *inside*. This, to Lane, seemed to be an important and recurring theme, and he made note. The word *cartulary* was a new one for him. Cartularies were lists of people who had given various kinds of gifts to the community or who had been involved in legal matters connected with the life of the monastery and its relation to the world outside.

The second kind of evidence was archaeological. The extensive archaeological excavation of Saint-Jean-des-Vignes provided an accurate map of all the buildings and structures of the monastery and the flow of personnel within it. A meticulous reconstruction could then be made of the daily life of the brothers, how they moved within the complex and what they did. Excavating the graves had provided crucial information about the location and gender of the remains, as well as about stature, age of death, nutrition and disease in the community.

In the Augustinian tradition the brothers of a monastery were not secluded from the world in order that they might be devoted entirely to prayer. They were *secular* in the sense that they were also to be involved with the outside world in service to God. Beyond the walls of the monastery they might take services of worship or exercise charity to the poor. At Saint-Jean-des-Vignes the parish church was on the perimeter of the monastic layout, so the members of the local community could come there for worship. This meant that there was certain amount of contact with the canons of the community. There was a strong emphasis on learning, and the reading of books was an important element in daily life. Nevertheless, contact with the outside world was still limited and strictly controlled. For example, one of Augustine's rules stipulated that when the brothers needed to go to the public baths or any other place, no fewer than two or three should go together.

The evidence from Saint-Jean-des-Vignes indicated that the in the earlier period of time the brothers had come from the local and regional nobility. Later on, more members came from the middle class. But there were also lay brothers serving as craftsmen who came from the lower classes. Lane was struck by the idea of *class* within the community. So even in a monastery the differences in social position continued to be of concern. In one of his rules, Augustine wrote: *But they who owned nothing should not look for those things in the monastery that they were unable to have in the world. And let them not hold their heads high, because they associate with people whom they did not dare to approach in the world, but let them rather lift up their hearts and not seek after what is vain and earthly. The rich, for their part, who seemed important in the world, must not look down upon their brothers who have come into this holy brotherhood from a condition of poverty.* It came as a surprise to think that someone who had *given up everything* to go into a monastery might well be better off than he had been before.

The officers of the community were called the *obedientiaries*, and the lay brothers were the *conversi*. The abbot was in charge of the entire monastery. The abbot was always to be respected and obeyed. Augustine had summed up his role: *Let him admonish the unruly, cheer the fainthearted, support the weak, and be patient toward all.* An extensive hierarchy existed under the rule of the abbot. Beneath him was the prior, under whom was the subprior, sacristan, pittancer and magister. There was a deacon, a record-keeper, a vestarer, a cellarer, a kitchener, a porter and so on. They did the jobs that their titles implied. Detailed textual evidence gave instruction about how these tasks were to be carried out and how worship was to be conducted throughout the course of the year. Lane was impressed at how tightly the organization was managed. So much for the monastery in France. How would this help in deciphering Inchcolm Abbey?

Lane reckoned that there must also have been written documents at Inchcolm Abbey, such as obituaries and cartularies. These were likely to have been destroyed during the Scottish Reformation. However, one important and unique piece had been found: The *Inchcolm Antiphoner*, a fragment of a manuscript service book with music that had been written about 1340. It had survived only because, regarded as waste material, it had been used in the binding of a book. Mainly Gregorian chant, the music may have originated as much as six hundred years earlier, with words adapted to honour St Columba. That helped to provide an idea about the kind of music sung at Inchcolm, but nothing else. Historians also knew that one Walter Bower had been the Abbot of Inchcolm Abbey in the fifteenth century. Bower had written a document entitled *Scotichronicon* that chronicled legends about medieval Scotland, but this provided little information about the actual abbey.

Fortunately, the archaeological evidence was much more plentiful. At Inchcolm Abbey the architectural ruins were there in the earth to be read, for this was, after all, the best-preserved monastic ruin in Scotland. The key reason for its remarkable preservation was its island setting. It wasn't easy, after all, for later generations to cross a deep channel of water to raid the buildings for stone. The Royal Commission on the Ancient and Historical Monuments of Scotland had carried out extensive archaeological investigations and had made numerous aerial photographs of the monastery. All this evidence permitted historians to show how the community had developed from its earliest form in the twelfth century to its latest in the sixteenth century.

The Inchcolm priory was founded in 1123 as just two small rectangular buildings, nave and choir. The community continued to construct additions to the monastery over the years. By the fifteenth century it had become an abbey, comprising a church with north and south transepts, nave and choir, a large cloister and cloister garden, a kitchen and cellar, a chapter house, and tower. Upper floors housed a dormitory, abbot's camera, warming house, guest hall and porter's lodge. Within the monastery, a number of burial sites had been excavated. In one case, the remains of a person buried standing up were found in an abbey wall. An impressive fresco had been found in a tomb recess. It portrayed a group of canons, perhaps processing to a funeral, yet the heads were missing. Someone had drawn a sketch suggesting how the original fresco might have looked. Another important feature was a stone screen at the bottom of the tower which divided the choir from the nave.

No doubt contact with the outside world was more limited at Inchcolm Abbey than at Saint-Jean-des-Vignes because of the island nature of the community. Going into the *world* meant going to the mainland, which implied a boat trip. On the other hand, the abbey had been given lands around the village of Aberdour to use for the purposes of agriculture. It had long been appreciated that the medieval monasteries were highly successful in their agricultural pursuits. But at Inchcolm it wasn't clear whether the brothers were involved with the actual raising of animals and crops or whether the land was rented out to others with payment being made in kind. In either case, however, it seems likely that some of the brothers made regular trips back and forth to the mainland.

An ancient ferry had apparently operated between the port of Leith and Fife. Lane measured the distance from Leith to Inchcolm on his map. It was six miles, making for quite a hazardous trip in stormy conditions. Travellers and pilgrims might well have stopped at Inchcolm on their way to Fife. Important visitors would have been welcomed and housed in the guest lodge. Women could visit only under strict conditions. Proceeding on to the mainland, travellers might well have worshiped in St Fillans Church in Aberdour, which Lane had visited the other day. It had been granted to the abbey by charter in about 1160, so St Fillans was in essence the parish church. Near to St Fillans was a curative well, said at various times to cure madness or blindness. Pilgrims were likely to have visited the well and then gone on their way to Dunfermline Abbey or to St Andrews. Supplies to the abbey would have had to be brought in often, and for that purpose and for ferrying people the abbey would have required a reasonable boat and a team of dedicated lay brother rowers. Lane tried to project himself back in time in order to visualise a medieval procession of traffic moving on the water to and from the abbey. The work involved in rowing was hard to imagine, given the ease of going over the Forth Road Bridge today.

Movement inside the abbey would have been strictly controlled. The canons could access rooms and spaces nearly everywhere. They would have used the night stairs for access to the sanctuary in order to worship during the night and morning. *Conversi* could access the nave, but not the rest of the sanctuary. They were excluded from the chapter house and cloisters. Most of their time would have been spent in the working areas such as kitchen, cellar and porter's areas. Given permission, women could have access to the gatehouse and parish church, the outer court and porter's lodge. If they were noble or religious they might obtain permission to visit the cloisters, the nave of the sanctuary, or the abbot's parlour and camera. In exceptional circumstances, high ranking women could be buried in the chapter house upon their death. Lay visitors to the abbey were restricted to the parish church, the forecourt, and the steward's lodge.

The daily routine of the community was complicated, but strictly ordered. There were numerous services of worship, such as Matins, Prime and Mass. The canons and novices were carefully instructed as to how to go two by two into the sanctuary, to put back their hoods and bow to the altar of Mary Magdalene, then proceed to the choir and bow in the direction of the main altar. Set prayers would be said, psalms would be read, the Lord's Prayer repeated, and one of the psalms sung in a high-pitched voice. Complete instructions were set out regarding keeping the religious calendar, the observance of feasts, on processions, personal washing, the use of relics, and singing. In many ways the chapter house, which at Inchcolm Abbey was octagonal, was central to the daily life. Here, meetings of the canons would be held, during which brothers would be disciplined, important decisions would be made, and novices instructed. Special events would be held here as well, such as the reception of novices and special liturgies.

Lane had long since finished his dram. It would be good to have another, but he resisted, opting instead to have a coffee to clear his head. The deeper you went into the depths of history and legend the more you cut yourself off temporarily from the world. Outside on the patio in the real world, the sun was shining and birds were singing. This was the downside of research. After his coffee, going back inside to the desk was difficult, and so he lingered a little.

Finally back at the desk and starting at where he had left off, he learned that, according to legend, some time around 1100 the island and some land in Fife had been given to the Norman-French Vipont family. When the male line in that family died out, Anicea, a daughter of John Vipont, inherited the land. Upon her marriage to Alan de Mortimer, the Mortimer family assumed control of the land. It was during Alan's lifetime that St Fillans Church had been built. Alan de Mortimer is thought to have given half of that land to the canons of Inchcolm Abbey in exchange for a burial place for him and his descendents in the abbey. There were echoes here of Saint-Jean-des-Vignes. However, Alan de Mortimer, according to legend, never made it to the abbey. The brothers came to the mainland to collect the body in a lead-lined coffin for burial in the abbey. According to the story, on the way back to the island, *they dumped the coffin containing poor Alan overboard between the mainland and the island.* Subsequently, that part of the Firth of Forth became known as *Mortimer's Deep,* as it is still known today. Stunned, Lane looked up from his reading and stared out the window. The questions *Why?* and *How Come?* came instantly to mind. What kind of holy men were these canons? Alan de Mortimer had been their benefactor, and yet they had dealt with him in an apparently disgraceful way. After all, St Augustine's very first injunction was to love God and the neighbour. Dumping Alan de Mortimer was an absolute denial of the principle. What had the man done to them?

But the mystery deepened as Lane read on. In about 1186, St Fillans Church became vacant. The abbot and canons of Inchcolm Abbey had been given the right to nominate a successor to fill the vacancy. However, William de Mortimer, Alan's son, insisted that his man, a certain *Robert*, the Clerk of David of Huntington, assume the role. This obviously upset the leadership of Inchcolm Abbey, for on the day when Robert was to be inducted to the charge, the abbot and a number of canons rowed ashore and barred the door to the church to prevent the induction. In response, William had his men physically beat up the canons. Lane tried to visualise the robed and hooded canons of Inchcolm Abbey standing with arms linked in front of the church door, being attacked by men armed with clubs. This surely was material suitable for a film. William's man Robert did then take up the position, but only for a brief period. After some time he resigned because of the continuing bad feeling between the two sides. Lane felt some sympathy for Robert: nothing like being caught in the middle of dispute between ecclesiastical power-seekers. Apparently William de Mortimer then finally acknowledged his misdeeds against the brothers of the abbey and signed over complete control of St Fillans to them. It looked to Lane like the canons of Inchcolm Abbey were a determined and troublesome bunch. This image did not square with the normal image of passive and peaceful monks. Lane was left with the suggestion that there was much bad blood between them and the de Mortimer family.

Lane was still at the desk when Katriona came in. She looked in on him and then carried several bags of groceries into the kitchen. Going back to the study, she placed her hands on his shoulders and gently massaged. "How's it going?" she asked.

"It's going," he answered, "but not easily. It's been a hard slog today, ploughing through several hundred years of history and legend."

"Sorry," she said, "but listen, I've got some good news for you."

"Really," Lane answered, turning around to look up at her. "What is it?"

"I went shopping on the way home and I'll make dinner tonight."

"Great," he said. "What are we having then?"

"Well," Katriona said, "I stopped at the fish shop and got some sea bass. And even better," she said, drawing out her words to create maximum suspense, "I got some fresh prawns and an avocado, just for you."

Lane got up from the chair and put his arms around her. "Fantastic. What would I do without you?"

"I can't imagine," Katriona answered. "I don't suppose, seeing that you're deeply involved in your work, that you'd want to open a bottle of Sauvignon Blanc to go with the seafood?"

"Are you kidding?" Lane answered, releasing her and heading for the fridge.

Chapter Six

The Poets

The next morning was calm, but darkish clouds were assembling as if for a tearful reunion. The water on the Forth resembled a jigsaw puzzle that had been stretched by the tide and current, resulting in complicated patches of water in varying shares of blue. Lane was working at his desk early when the telephone startled him. It was Naomi.

"Hello, is that Davis?" she said, her voice a bit querulous.

"It is," Lane answered. "Hello Naomi. How are you this morning?"

"I'm fine," she said, apparently reassured. "I was wondering if we could get together very briefly, so that you could tell me how you're getting on. I don't want to put pressure on you, but I think that things are moving faster than expected on this project. Do you have enough information yet to make a meeting worthwhile?"

"Yes, Naomi, I could do that," Lane answered. "You'll appreciate that it's mainly historical stuff I've been working on, details about the abbey and the island. I've learned quite a bit, but I haven't done that much on Mr. Morton yet." Guilt tugged a little gently at his sleeve. He had picked up some very interesting things from Robert McCord, but it wouldn't hurt to keep them up that sleeve for a while. "When and where would you like to meet?"

"Would tomorrow suit you?" Naomi said. "I know it's short notice, but I think it has to be very soon. The other thing is, Davis, it would help to meet in Edinburgh. Would that be all right?"

"Yes," Naomi, I think so," Lane answered, opening his diary with his left hand and trying to find the page for the next day. "Tomorrow would work for me and I can come to Edinburgh. When and where?"

"Let's make it for coffee. Then it won't take up too much of your time or be too obvious."

The Battle of Inchcolm Abbey

"Are we still needing to do cloak and dagger?" Lane asked.

"I'm afraid so," she answered. "This reporter is still dogging our heels. He's with the *Scotsman*. And his name is Swinton. We don't know how much he knows, but one of the team here has been assigned the task of buying and scanning the paper first thing every morning. The story's going to appear any day now."

"OK," Lane said. "That's the way it is then. I'll don my disguise. We'll meet for coffee then. Where?"

"Let's meet at the *Wellington*. Do you know it?"

"No," Lane answered. "Never heard of it. Where is it?"

"On George Street, on the corner of Hanover Street," Naomi said.

Lane was racking his mind, trying to picture the four corners. "Oh," he said, "on the northwest corner, down below? Didn't there used to be a newsagent or something there?"

"That's it," Naomi said. "They make a great long black there. I'll meet you downstairs. There are only a few tables so it's quite private, and I think we should be safe enough."

"Right, Lane said. "I'll be there. See you."

He sat for several minutes staring out the window after pressing the red button. Naomi was certainly extra cautious, and he wondered if she needed to be. He could have done without the secrecy thing, without this creeping into basement coffee shops. Sometime, maybe he could get a project that was just straightforward and completely above board.

Staring before the monitor once again, Lane continued to delve into the history of the island and the abbey. He learned that Inchcolm Island appeared in the works of Shakespeare, in *Macbeth* to be exact. At the battle of Kinghorn in about 1040 Macbeth went to battle with the Danes. According to Shakespeare, the Danish king paid to have his warriors buried on the island

> *That now Sweno, the Norwayes King,*
> *Craves composition:*
> *Nor would we deigne him buriall of his men,*
> *Till he disbursed, at Saint Colmes ynch,*
> *Ten thousand dollars, to our generall use.*

So, Lane thought, we have a king landing on the island in a storm, a king wanting to bury his dead warriors there, an abbey being constructed, and pilgrims coming and going: an awful lot of history was being crammed onto a small island. And now Mr. Morton was going to cram his golf course in as well.

But there was more to come. Lane learned that on the mainland at Aberdour there was a parcel of land called the "Sisterlands", set aside for a group of nuns of the order of St Francis. They operated a hospital called St Martha for the care of pilgrims coming through the area. The piece of land was about eight acres in size, and it had a close connection with St Fillans Church. The land had apparently been granted to the sisters by James, the 1st Earl of Morton. So at some indeterminate point, the land was said to be owned by the *Morton f*amily rather than the *de Mortimer* family. It wasn't clear if this amounted to an ownership change or a name change. Alexander Morton obviously thought of himself as belonging to that line. In any event, somewhere in the back of Lane's mind bells were ringing. According to the document in front of him, a tortuous family history was to follow. The Sisterlands was given back to the Morton Family, then divided up, and then finally wound up as the glebe of St Fillans Church. Most of this history, Lane reckoned, was not relevant. But what was interesting to him, buried as it was in the depths of this complex tale, was the fact that James the Earl of Morton was accused of complicity in the murder of Lord Darnley in the year 1580. So now Inchcolm even had a connection with Lord Darnley's wife, none other than Mary Queen of Scots. And in 1581 he was tried for treason and beheaded. The de Mortimers/Mortons certainly seemed to have suffered a lot of misfortune.

The following morning Lane took the train from Inverkeithing Station to Waverly in Edinburgh. He walked up the ramp in light rain. A dark cloud hovered over the castle and the Royal Mile. On the corner of Princess Street Gardens a piper played, surrounded by a smallish group of tourists. The piper's suitcase was open, but no one was flipping coins into it. He walked up the incline on South St David Street. Everyone had the head down, trying to escape the rain. St Andrew's Square, normally filled with people enjoying a coffee and a chat, was empty. Far to the north, towards home, the sky was even darker. He came to Hanover Street and found the Wellington coffee house, but it was too early, so he continued along George Street, thinking to buy a *Scotsman* and see if the story had appeared. But the bookshop was no longer there. Once this space had housed *James Thin, Bookseller*. Years ago James Thin, the old man, had sent theological books to his customers all over the world. Lane himself had ordered something back in the sixties, and it had been faithfully delivered across the spaces of the Atlantic Ocean and half of the American continent. All gone now. So many markers to the story of his past were now gone. The only thing impervious to change was change itself. He walked on. Gray's the hardware store was gone too. There was no place to buy a paper here, so he turned around and made his way back to Wellington. He was five minutes early but went in anyway, going down the steps into a dark basement. There was an empty table in the back corner and he took it. This ought to satisfy Naomi's need to security. At least the coffee smelled good.

She appeared five minutes later, right on time. She was still in tweed, clutching a book and carrying an umbrella, but this time it was dripping. At the bottom step she closed and opened it to shake the water off, then closed it again. Naomi peered into the room and smiled when she spotted him. He stood to greet her. She held out her hand and shook his vigorously.

"Davis, thank you so much for coming on such a foul day. I'm sorry to bring you into town on a day like this."

"Naomi, it's fine," he responded. "I have some other things to do anyway," he said, lying to ease her conscience.

"Now, what would you like?" she said, laying the book down and putting the umbrella carefully under the table.

"Well, a long black and perhaps a scone," he said. "I perused the bakery on the way in and it looks pretty good."

"Fine," she said. "That sounds OK to me as well."

Lane looked around the room while Naomi was ordering. Sportjacket wasn't there. There was no one there who looked remotely like a reporter. He guessed that they could relax. He turned her book slightly and studied the cover. She came back to the table and sat down.

"They'll bring the coffee in a minute," Naomi said, sitting and adjusting her chair closer to the table. "We should be able to speak freely here. It's not the sort of place they would look for a hot story."

"I guess not," Lane responded, smiling. The coffee and scones arrived, and they waited while it was being put onto the table. "I see that you're reading John Le Carre'."

"Oh yes," Naomi said, "I'm a big fan of his. I only brought it this morning in case you were late. So, please tell me about what you've found so far."

Lane sampled the coffee and put his cup down carefully. "OK, but I've covered quite a bit of ground. What kind of information would be the most help to you? You already know the basic facts about the island and the abbey."

"That's true, of course," she said, "but you get from the usual sources is superficial. The more you delve into the history of these ancient sites the more there is to learn. Anyway, I'm responsible to a number of properties, so I can only recall so many facts about each one."

Lane studied her and was silent.

"Yes, what is it? She said.

"You just said something very interesting," Lane answered.

"I did? Oh dear," Naomi said, blushing. "What was that?"

"You just said that you have a number of properties to be responsible for. I take it that that means you work for Historic Scotland."

"That was rather a bad slip wasn't it," she said, looking at Lane with the faintest of smiles. "I suppose it had to come out sometime anyway. Yes, I'm responsible for four properties, including Inchcolm. Now you know, but I can't imagine that it matters much if I can trust you to keep it under your hat."

"It's OK, Naomi," Lane answered, "I won't say a word to anyone."

"Now," she said, "can we get back to the main subject?"

"Well, "Lane began, "just as you said, there is a lot more history than meets the eye, and it gets more and more complex the deeper you get into it. I've found some things that aren't in the guidebooks. You know about all the work that's been done by the Royal Commission?"

"Yes," Naomi answered, "we've got all of that."

"It's great, very detailed," Lane said. "But it doesn't give you enough to piece together the lifestyle in the monastery or its relation with the outside world. I found a website that details an Augustinian Monastery in France that existed during the same period of time as Inchcolm. They have textual evidence as well. Now that allows us to make some very good guesses about the life in Inchcolm Abbey." Lane took a card from his pocket and wrote the address of the website on the back and handed it to her. "Take a look at this when you have a chance."

Naomi looked at the card and placed it into her bag. "Thanks, Davis. That's a good start."

"Oh, there's more," he said, watching her face for a reaction.

"OK, tell me," she said.

Lane racked his brain for a moment, attempting to filter out what he could tell her that would be useful to them at the moment without revealing what could be helpful to him later on.

"Well, you probably know that there are Norwegian or Danish warriors buried on the island."

"No, I didn't know that," Naomi answered.

"Apparently so," Davis said. "Shakespeare has some verses in *Macbeth* about Norway's king paying money to have his warriors buried on the island."

"I knew that Inchcolm appeared in *Macbeth*," Naomi said, "but I didn't know the substance of it. Is it true?"

"It seems to be likely," Lane said. "So I presume that some Scandinavians might object if Morton used the island to build a golf course. The idea of digging up graves to put in a tee or a green wouldn't go down well. Just imagine of that were to happen to UK soldiers on some foreign shore, even if they had been buried centuries before."

Naomi put her index finger up against her lips and shushed him. "Let's watch it," she said. "There may be listening ears in here. "But yes, that's a good point," she added scribbling on another card she had taken from her bag.

"And you'll know about the de Mortimer connection, I take it?" Lane asked.

"Well, I know that part of the channel in the Forth is called *Mortimer's Deep*. Is that what you mean?"

"Partly," Lane answered. "But it's called that because de Mortimer's body was supposed to be buried in the abbey. That would have been the normal arrangement for a benefactor to the monastery. Instead of that the canons from the abbey dumped his body overboard into the Forth. That's why it's called *Mortimer's Deep*."

"No, I didn't know that," she said, scribbling away again. "Most interesting. You really have accomplished a lot."

"Well, it's been hard work, but fascinating. I just hope that it will be of some help to the spokes of your umbrella, but I'll keep digging in for you."

Naomi stood up and held out her hand. "I'll have to run, Davis. Thank you so much. I'll be in touch soon to keep you up to date on what's happening." She picked up her book, retrieved her umbrella and turned to go, then turned back again. "Oh," she said, "I do need to remind you that we are quite sure this will hit the headlines soon. Please watch out for the media." And then she was up the steps and onto George Street.

Lane left *Wellington* and walked east along George Street. The rain was off, but a sharp wind was blowing from the North Sea. He turned right on South St David's Street towards the station. That allowed him to scan once again the poem by Iain Crichton Smith that Edinburgh Council had inscribed on the windows of the now empty insurance building on the corner:

> *Dear Edinburgh, how I remember you,*
> *your winter cakes and tea,*
> *Your bright red fire*
> *Your swirling cloaks*
> *And clouds.*

He thought he might add a bottom line: *And your empty tram lines.*

When Katriona arrived home that evening Lane had the dinner ready.

"Oh great," she said. "You've got everything ready. What are we having tonight?"

"We're having one of your favourites," he said, "grilled lamb chops with new potatoes and asparagus. And with it," he added, holding up a bottle, "some Shiraz from down under."

"Fantastic," she said, planting a kiss on his cheek.

Later, when they were finishing the wine in the lounge, Katriona posed a question: "So how did you get on with your girlfriend today?"

"Fine," Lane replied, "but she's not my girlfriend. She's a lady in tweed with a hat, an umbrella, and a book."

"But she must like you," Katriona said, smoothing out her skirt, "taking you to coffee and so forth."

"I've no idea," Lane said, "I think she just wants information from me."

"Oh, I'll bet it's more than that. I'm sure that she's charmed by you. Is she married?"

"Again, I've no idea," Lane said. "How would I know if she's married or not?"

"Well," Katriona answered, "sometimes when ladies are married they wear a ring." She held up her left hand and rotated it for Lane to see. "Like this, see. Does she have a ring on her left hand?"

"I don't know," Lane said, "I've never noticed."

Katriona smiled sweetly at him. "No, I suppose not. You're not really a noticer are you?"

Chapter Seven

Smoke

After breakfast the next morning Lane decided to walk into Inverkeithing: down one hill, up another and cross over the railway line. On the other side of Inverkeithing Bay a pall of black smoke hung over the breaker's yard and the air smelled acrid. Something had to be on fire, but was it rubber or metal? The yard featured such a high mountain of materials from broken-up ships that it could be anything. He guessed that the metal in the pile must be valuable. People were stealing the lead from church roofs and stripping out copper wiring in order to sell the metal. Nevertheless, the yard must surely be a far cry from what it had been years ago, when many of the most famous ships had been broken up there. The town around him was quiet, still too early for the hairdressers, cafes and charity shops to roll up their shutters. At the newsagent Lane picked up a *Scotsman*. He glanced at it on the way to the checkout and his heart sank.

MORTON VOWS TO CREATE HOLIEST GOLF COURSE

Lane folded the paper shut, suddenly felt exposed and guilty, as if this news was somehow his fault. He looked around the shop to see if anyone else had seen him reading the headline, expecting someone to point a finger and say 'Shame on you'. He handed the paper, headline facing down, to the girl at checkout and paid for it. He left the shop and headed home, studiously avoiding another glance at the poisonous object in his hands. Finally, he sat down to read at the kitchen table.

Alexander Morton, the American property magnate, announced plans yesterday to create the world's holiest golf course. Mr. Morton, known for his property developments across the world and flamboyant life-style, is asking for a ninety-nine year lease on Inchcolm Island in order to build a hotel with casino and an eighteen hole golf course. Inchcolm Abbey, a popular tourist attraction dating back to the twelfth century, is to be completely restored as a condition of the deal. The Morton organisation says that it is aware of the religious history of the island and that the project will be sensitively managed. Each of the eighteen holes will be named after one of the Scottish Saints. Mr. Morton indicated that he has a special fondness for Scotland and especially for Fife, which he believes was the home of his great-great-grandfather. He said that two of his adult children, James and Sophie, were going to lead in the development of the scheme and would travel to Scotland during the week. Historic Scotland, which is responsible for the island on behalf of the nation, declined to comment.

Having read it carefully several times again, Lane found it hard to catch his breath. It was one thing to think about Morton's project in abstract terms. It was another to see it spelled out in bold print in the newspaper. He'd been comfortable in the back room doing his research, but now he could be exposed in the firing line. What had he gotten himself into?

Lane found Naomi's card and number. She answered immediately.

"Hello, Naomi? It's Davis Lane here."

"Oh Davis, I know what you're going to say. I've seen it too."

"It's kind of shocking, seeing it on the front page. What happens next?" he asked.

"I know it is," she said. "Everyone here is like a cat on a hot tin roof. The Morton group are supposed to arrive in Edinburgh tomorrow. Not Alexander Morton himself of course. He'll leave the preliminary talking to his son and daughter. We'll have a better idea of what the next step is after tomorrow."

"But what do you expect me to do?" Lane asked.

"Davis, I don't think there is anything you can do at the moment. Just continue with your research. But you do need to be prepared for the onslaught of publicity. I should think that your name will be coming up when we have a little discussion with the Mortons."

"How will it come up, Naomi?" he asked. "I mean, what exactly is my role in this now?"

"You are the local expert on Inchcolm Island and Abbey," she answered.

"But look, Naomi," he said, "I've only just started. I'm not really an expert. You people, your umbrella organisation if nothing else, must have someone who really knows his stuff."

"Well," she answered, "we did indeed, but not anymore."

"Why not?" Lane asked.

"He died," Naomi said.

"What of?" Lane said.

"Of a heart attack," she answered.

"Oh great," Lane said, and hung up.

It was hard to settle to anything. Every time he walked past the coffee table with its copy of the *Scotsman* the story leapt out at him. Lane decided that he had to become occupied with something rather than dwell on what had already transpired that day. He turned to the geography and the wartime history of the island. The digital images taken by the *Royal Commission on Ancient Monuments* were illuminating. Their material included sketches of the monastery in the various stages of development over the centuries. These were based on the archaeological surveys that had been carried out. Aerial photography provided a number of images from above. The island was only about twenty-two acres in area, hardly large enough for an eighteen hole golf course. A fair amount of the surface area was already taken by the ruins of the monastery. If Morton built a hotel that would consume more land. Steep headlands dominated the island's eastern and western ends. Lane couldn't see how it would be possible to use the headland for the course. It was one thing to build an elevated tee, but an elevated tee with a sheer drop to the sea was surely something else. There were five small beaches, one of which was situated next to the harbour for incoming vessels. The harbour would need to be retained, probably even expanded. There were numerous rocky outcrops, especially towards the west of the island.

Inchcolm had been an important part of the defence network in both World War I and World War II. Danger had been posed to the Forth from warships, submarines and planes. The Forth Rail Bridge had been a target, as had Rosyth Naval Station and the aircraft station at Donibristle. German planes had used the Forth as a convenient route to follow to the west of Scotland with its heavy manufacturing complex in Glasgow. Defensive structures from World War II still remained at the east end of the island. A careful study of the map showed the remains of a number of gun emplacements and other fortifications. But a more recent article also indicated a tunnel, quite a long tunnel, running across the east end of the island and connecting to a large ammunition magazine and the gun emplacements. The existence of the tunnel had long been classified by the War Department and only recently de-classified. It wasn't mentioned in the literature for tourists, and Lane wondered if Morton knew about the tunnel? If he did, what did he intend to do with it and with all the obsolete fortifications? The structures certainly weren't beautiful, but military historians might well argue that they were a vital element of Scotland's wartime history.

Studying the images of the island, along with the Ordinance Survey map, Lane also began to realise just how close the island was to the Braefoot Terminal. Tankers berthed at Braefoot in order to load butane, propane and liquid petroleum gas on board. These were large ships, requiring the help of tugs from Leith. Between Inchcolm and Braefoot Terminal there wasn't all that much room to manoeuvre on Mortimer's Deep, somewhere above poor Alan Mortimer's watery grave. Moreover, Lane discovered that there had been a major incident at the terminal. In 1993 the tanker *Havkong*, subjected to a sudden violent squall from the west, slipped loose from her moorings. She had been loaded with six thousand tons of butane. The *Havkong* drifted a mile to the east before she was brought under control. Lane tried to visualise the Havkong or some other tanker drifting onto the rocks along Inchcolm Island. With a hotel and crowded casino on the island, such an incident could result in a major disaster. Lane couldn't see how Shell UK or the Forth Ports authority would welcome Morton's development and the increased Forth traffic it would create.

The diversion worked for a while, but the *Scotsman's* story continued to pop into his mind. No doubt, he thought, perhaps he was making too much of it. Naomi tended to be a worrier. Perhaps she was overstating the case in order to prepare him for the worst case scenario. The fact was that in relation to this story he was still an unknown, and hopefully it would stay that way for a while.

>When Katriona came in she greeted him with a curtsy.
>"What's that for?" he asked.
>"It's for you," she answered, "for my husband the celebrity."
>"What are you talking about," Lane asked.

"Well, you're in the papers," she said, "or almost in the papers at least."

"What do you mean?" Lane asked.

"Well," Katriona said, "one of the girls at work went out to get a paper and was reading it at lunch. She pointed to the story on the front page and said, "Isn't this what your husband is involved in?

Chapter Eight
Fire

Lane did not sleep well that night. In fact, he slept very little, not because of bad dreams, but because his mind kept working away at the story in the paper. He seemed to be at the centre of some drama, and the people around him were pointing and accusing. He got up at half-past-six and made the breakfast. Katriona left at eight. It was dry outside, but the sky was grey slate, against which wisps of smoke from the other side of the bay were still curling upwards. He washed the dishes and mentally planned a day's work in the garden. The domestic chores had been neglected of late. The lawn badly needed mowing, and the hedge need to be trimmed. Gardening was not really his *forte,* but some physical effort today was appealing.

The doorbell rang. He couldn't think who would be at the door before nine o'clock in the morning. The man standing on his door step looked vaguely familiar.

"Mr. Lane?" he asked.

"Yes," Lane said.

"I'm Steven Swinton," he said. "I'm a journalist with the *Scotsman*. I'd like to talk to you for a few moments if that's all right."

The penny dropped. It was Mr. Sportjacket, the man who had been on the boat on the trip to Inchcolm. It was the same jacket, worn with the same sort of assured intensity. "I'm sorry, Mr. Swinton," he said, "what is this all about? Why do you want to talk to me?"

The reporter's face was brushed by an air of innocence. "Oh well," he started, as if explaining something complex to a child, "we ran a story yesterday about Alexander Morton and his plans to build a golf course and hotel and casino on Inchcolm. We understand that you are a key figure in this enterprise."

"I saw the article in the paper," Lane answered, "but I'm not sure what that has to do with me."

"Swinton shifted his feet on the doorstep and rolled his eyes up past the roofline to heaven. "Come on please, Mr. Lane. We've been told that you're the expert on the island and the abbey. Morton's asking to take it over and, as we understand it, you'll be the one dealing with him. I'm just doing my job here. The boss says 'Go interview Davis Lane', and so I arrive here at Inverkeithing where I'd rather not be in order to interview you. Simple as that, OK?"

"Mr. Swinton," Lane said, "First of all, it would have been good to have some warning that you were coming. Secondly, I have done some research into the abbey, but I'm certainly not an expert on it. More importantly, I'm not the chief negotiator or whatever it is you are suggesting. I think that you've got your facts wrong."

"Well," Swinton answered, looking more conciliatory, "it could be that we've got some wrong info, but why not talk to me about the thing? I mean, the best way for you to put things right is to give me the right info, don't you think? So why not let me come in and we'll sit down and have a quiet little chat and put things right." Swinton's body language was speaking *door*.

Lane deliberated for a moment. There didn't seem to be a lot he could do. To deny the journalist an interview would undoubtedly pour fuel onto the fire. Moreover, it was conceivable that an interview might help to correct some misinformation. In any event, from what he had learned the project would never go ahead, so it surely could do no harm to put Swinton right on several issues.

"OK, fair enough," he said, and stepped back far enough for the man to come through the door.

Lane led the journalist through the hall and into the lounge. He invited him to sit and sat down himself.

Swinton surveyed the room. "Nice place you have here," he said. "Being a free-lance theologian obviously has its rewards."

Lane had to stifle an expletive and so was rendered speechless for a second. Recovered, he managed a smile and responded, "I'm glad you like it, Mr. Swinton. Free-lancing is rewarding, but perhaps not as you know it."

"No, maybe not," the man said. "Anyway, let's talk about Alexander Morton and Inchcolm Abbey. You're working for Historic Scotland, right?" Swinton asked.

"No, I'm not," Lane answered. "I'm acting as a consultant for a group of organisations. Historic Scotland is just one of them."

Swinton had his notepad and pen out. "OK," he said. "You're a consultant. So what does that mean? What do you actually do?"

Lane was taking his time, trying to decide what could be said honestly without giving much away. "I'm interested in religious communities like monasteries. You probably know already that this was an Augustinian monastery going back to the twelfth century. I'm doing some research to discover what the style of life of this particular community might have been like. I might be able to advise interested parties on that score."

Swinton lifted his pen and looked up. "So what do you think? Should Morton be allowed to build a casino and golf course or not?"

"That's not up to me to say," Lane answered. "My work is mainly descriptive. It's up to others to say if this is a feasible project and if it should go ahead."

"Correct me if I'm wrong, Mr. Lane," Swinton said, "but aren't you a moral man too? I mean, don't theologians carry a moral responsibility?"

Lane was taken aback. The man was no fool, however forward. "Yes, of course," he said, "I may well be asked to give an opinion on the morality of it all, but that's a long way off, and it is still up to others to make decisions."

"I see," Swinton said, writing again but clearly not impressed. He smiled and shifted in the chair, as if signalling a new start. "Look, give me something for my editor here. I'd like to come back to you for another chat when you've had more time. But what are your first impressions? Do you think this thing should go ahead or not?"

Lane thought for a few moments and tried to figure out what he could say that would be truthful but ambiguous. "First impressions, OK. My first impressions are that there would be a number of positives and a number of negatives. Restoring the monastery would be positive and that could be very educational for a secular society. It would also create a lot of jobs. On the other hand, unless the restoration was done sensitively it could ruin the ruins, if you see what I mean. Beyond that the island seems too small for an eighteen hole golf course, and I'm not wild about the idea of a casino. The obstacles are both practical and moral. So at the moment, I would have to lean on the negative side. Does that help you?"

"Yes, a little," Swinton said, writing again. "I can see that you are a two-handed man, but I'll do my best with it, thanks. Let me ask you one more question. Have you met Alexander Morton or any of his family yet? And have you done any research into how he has handled any of his other developments across the world?"

Lane shook his head. "No on both scores," he answered.

Swinton stood up and began to put his writing pad away. "Well I have to say to you, Mr. Lane, that I think you are being naïve about these plans. From what I've learned so far I think that Alexander Morton will push on until he gets this. He's a ruthless man and a very rich one. I hope that you're ready for the battle."

Lane led Swinton to the door where he mumbled a *thanks*, gave a wave of the hand and said goodbye. Lane watched him walk briskly down the path to his car. As he closed the door he became aware that his mood had changed. His eagerness for domestic duties had fled. He no longer felt like cutting the grass or trimming the hedge. In fact, he didn't feel like doing anything.

Chapter Nine

Gavin

It was raining the next morning when Lane got up. Dark clouds hung heavily over the Forth, and the wind drew wavy lines of rain across the water. Water steamed down the kitchen window, bringing the inhabitants' mood down with it. They ate breakfast, and Katriona left for work early, mumbling that it was going to be a long day. Lane watched the rain through the window and wondered what the plan for today was. His conversation with Steven Swinton, as unpleasant as it had been, had served to sharpen the dilemma of the island and its abbey. He guessed that at heart he felt the development was both wrong and impractical and so would never come to pass. But this was clearly at odds with what Swinton thought would actually happen, and that made the situation unsettling. It would help if he could talk to Naomi, but it was too early to phone. In any event, he was reluctant to be shushed into secrecy mode yet again. He decided to walk into town once again and buy a paper. If things were depressing he might as well deepen the gloom by battling with the rain. There was something to be said for making things as bad as possible in your imagination, so that you would be cheered up when they weren't so bad in real life.

It was quiet as he climbed the incline to Inverkeithing High Street. There were only a few moving umbrellas in the vicinity of the shops, black and red domes hiding their owners. He found a *Scotsman* in the newsagent, paid for it, kept his head down and left. It was too wet to scan the newspaper outside, so he headed home. A rusty tanker was being eased into place by two tugs at Hound Point.

Glad to be back inside a dry house, Lane made a coffee and opened the paper. The Morton story appeared on page three under the by-line of Steven Swinton. There wasn't much new information, but what there was focussed on Lane.

The Scotsman understands that Rev. Davis Lane, a "freelance theologian" is an expert on Inchcolm Abbey and will be asked to offer advice on Morton's plans for the development. Lane, a former Church of Scotland minister, has carried out research into monastic communities like the one on Inchcolm Island. In conversation with this reporter, Mr. Lane indicated that he believes there are serious practical and moral obstacles to the plans. James and Sophie Morton are expected to visit the island tomorrow.

Lane was relieved. There wasn't anything wholly inaccurate about the reporting. It put a more negative cast on his viewpoint than he might have wished, but it was more or less what he had said. Still, he had the uneasy feeling that there would be much, much more from Mr. Swinton. The phone rang and he was glad to hear Naomi's voice.

"Davis, are you all right?" she asked.

"Hi Naomi, yes I'm fine," he responded, "just feeling in the dark about what's going to happen next. I take it that you've seen the articles in the paper."

"Yes, there more or less what we expected. I understand and I share your feeling," she said. "There have been discussions with the Mortons. They're going to the island tomorrow. It would be good if you were there to meet them. I'm going with them and could introduce you. Would that be possible?"

"I suppose so," Lane answered. "I can't say that I'm looking forward to it, but if you want me to go I'll be there."

"Great," Naomi said. "We're going to take the *Inchcolm Express* from Newhaven Harbour, so if you go on the *Maid* you'll be there before us. After a while wandering we'll just sort of happen onto you."

"OK, Naomi, that's fine," Lane said. "What should I expect with these two?"

"Ah well," she said, I don't want to spoil the surprise. Use your imagination."

"But listen, Naomi, what do you expect me to do or say tomorrow? What line do you want me to take?" Lane asked.

"I think that you should just focus on some of the factual things you've learned about the abbey," she answered. "Perhaps it's too early to express any opinions for or against."

"OK," Lane answered, "that's the line I shall take. I'll see you tomorrow."

The Battle of Inchcolm Abbey

There was no doubt in his mind that he had sufficient information for his meeting with the younger Mortons the following day. He was confident that he could answer any general questions about the monastic set-up. It was all there in his head, but he would also take along his notes in case he was pressed. But there was something nagging at him. The difficulty with all of this information was that it was just that. It was interesting, at least to him, but also factual, a little dry and reeking with the aroma of ancient history. He didn't even have the name of anyone connected with Inchcolm Abbey except Walter Bower, who served as abbot in the fifteenth century. But little was known about Bower himself. He somehow needed a name or a person, someone that he could employ to make the life of a fifteenth century community spring to life in the twenty-first century. What about a fictional person? Trying to re-create the daily life of a fictional person would force him to ask those questions that would expose the inner dynamic of the monastery. So that could serve as the plan for the day, and he set to work. His research into St Jean-des-Vignes would prove useful.

The man of his creation would be *Gavin*, which he had selected as a good medieval name. Gavin would be one of the canons in the late fifteenth century. He would be twenty-four years of age, having entered the monastery as a teen-ager. Gavin could come from the local nobility, from the family seat at Couston Castle, several miles inland and just west of Aberdour. It was a pious family, and Gavin had a sister Marjory, a member of the Order of Grey Sisters of St Francis. Marjory and the others sisters ran the hospice of Martha, set up to minister to poor pilgrims visiting the curative well, depending on the small parcel of land called the *Sisterlands* that had been set aside to provide an income. Did Gavin and Marjory decide for themselves to enter the orders as they had, or was it their family's decision? It was hard to say, but certainly it wouldn't have done any harm for their parents' eternal prospects. Gavin and Marjory and their parents and most everyone else in that period of time believed unequivocally in the reality of heaven and hell. Their priests had hammered it home. The promise of heaven was real and a blessed prospect. The threat of hell was just as real, but absolutely terrifying. Lane had seen many paintings from the middle ages portraying the Last Judgement. Sinners were captured and tormented and led to hell by the devil's demons, images that would convince anyone that faith and commitment to the church was essential.

One way to ensure your faith and commitment and escape from hell was to join a monastery or convent. Through a life of obedience, chastity, prayer and good works one might be rewarded with a place in heaven. So Gavin's presence in the abbey and Marjory's good works at Martha's Hospice was not only beneficial for the young people themselves, but also good for their parents. Pleased as he was to be in the abbey, Gavin missed his parents and his siblings. He missed his friends and the life around the castle. Materially he was worse off at Inchcolm, and he might not be completely happy, but spiritually he was better off. Lane knew that twenty-first century people would find this medieval perspective very difficult to understand, so he hoped that in Gavin they might experience the tension between the two worlds.

Lane tried to re-create that day when Gavin first came to the abbey to ask about becoming a canon. He had been taken to the abbot seated on his seat in the Chapter House. Gavin had gone down on his knees to ask for bread and clothing and to be allowed to join the eternal society with the brothers. The abbot asked him if he was truly devoted to the faith and why he wished to join the order. The abbot told Gavin that keeping the vows was very difficult, that getting up in the middle of the night and early in the morning to worship was hard, that the daily work was demanding, and that constant obedience to the officers was required. He reminded Gavin of Augustine's rules and how they must be kept. He asked Gavin if he understood all of this and if he still wished to join the order. Gavin, trembling, said *yes*. The abbot then asked Gavin eleven questions. Were his parents legitimately married? Was he married or had promised to be married? Had he been excommunicated? Did he suffer from any incurable disease? Had he been accused of any crime? Did his parents suffer from leprosy, and so on? When Gavin had answered all these questions to the satisfaction of the abbot he was finally given permission to enter Inchcolm Abbey. The abbot then said to him, *These conditions having been fulfilled, I receive you to the year and time of probation. And if your conversation and life pleases us we will receive you to the vows, and if not, then not. And you will conformingly make a trial of our religion and conversation, and if it is displeasing to you, the clothes in which you have come will be given back to you, and you will be able to freely leave and go back to the world. In the name of the Father, the Son, and the Holy Ghost. Amen.* At that moment an overwhelming sense of relief and gratitude flooded through the boy as he stood in the centre of the Chapter House.

What came next? Gavin was then led through the abbey complex to the Vestarer. The Vestarer handed him his clothes: three shirts, drawers, a *rochet* or white surplice and a hooded cloak, two pairs of shoes, an undercoat, an overcoat and a fur lining. Gavin was reminded about modesty in getting up from bed, told how to make his bed, and shown how to fold his blanket neatly. He was shown the latrine on the very south perimeter of the abbey and was instructed in the ritual of purification required when using the *lavabo*. He was firmly told not to blow his nose on the hand towels in the *lavabo* and not to go barefoot. Gavin learned that he would eat two meals a day, except on fast days. Meals were served in the *Frater* or refectory, which at Inchcolm Abbey was located on the upper floor adjoining the kitchen on the south side of the cloisters. The foodstuffs would come from the cellar, presided over by the *cellarer*. Gavin would be a junior novice for a period of time, under instruction by the officers. As a junior, some restrictions were placed on him in terms of moving about the monastery, and he was not allowed outside the walls without being accompanied by a senior. Upon successfully completing his training he would become a canon.

Gavin would find that the liturgical year was divided into periods of time associated with Lent, Easter, Pentecost, Advent and Epiphany. Each period of time had its special feasts and services. But he would also have been aware of linear time, dating from the death and resurrection of Jesus. Every day would be marked by the observance of the canonical hours: *Matins, Prime, Terce, Mass, Sext, Vespers,* and *Compline. Matins* came at about two o'clock. Gavin and the others in the dormitory would be woken up by the *Sacristan* lighting a lamp and striking the bell. The brothers would proceed two by two to the latrine or *necessarium* to relieve themselves and to wash. They would then go down the night stairs two by two in an orderly manner and go into the church. Entering the church they were to throw back their hoods and bow to the statue of Mary Magdalene, go to the choir, bow to the altar and assume their assigned places. Some of the Psalms would be said and sung, and prayers were said, including the Lord's Prayer. *Prime* came at 6 AM, when a similar pattern would be followed. The *Cantor* was responsible for organising the liturgical services, including choosing the brothers who were charged with singing. Gavin, being a large lad, found that he was a baritone. After Prime the officers and canons would go to the Chapter. The meeting took place between seven and eight o'clock in the Chapter House, which at Inchcolm Abbey was octagonal. On one of the sides a higher, three-seated bench had been formed, fronted by two steps. Three gothic arches had been formed in the wall behind the seats. The Abbot, Prior and Sub-Prior would sit on the elevated seats, and the canons on the lower level seats around the remaining walls. A number of readings would be given relating to the liturgical calendar and the duties of various officers. During the meeting, plans for the day would be intimated. Discipline would be meted out for any of the brothers who had broken the rules. The brothers moved from the chapter house to the cloister, where they could sit by themselves or converse about things useful and proper. Other services would follow during the day.

Vespers and the evening meal took place at five o'clock, and a lesson would be read from St Augustine's rules while they ate in silence. The brothers were enjoined to be careful not to throw nutshells or eggshells in the refectory. No food could be eaten outside the refectory. At St Jean-des-Vignes *vino* was available for the brothers to drink. Lane thought it was probably not so likely at Inchcolm Abbey, Scotland never being known for its wine-making potential. A weak beer may have been served. After their meal the brothers moved again to the cloister for more reading and conversation. Lane suddenly wondered how the abbey got its water supply. It was unlikely that there was a supply of fresh water on the island. It was more likely that rain water was carefully captured and stored. In the latrine or *necessarium,* sea water was used to dispose of the waste material, and at Inchcolm evidence had been found that the latrine had been reconstructed, probably because of changing water levels. Gavin would soon learn that the cloister was at the heart of monastic life. All the routes of access to the various parts of the structure seemed to depend upon the cloister. The conversations that took place in the cloister must have profoundly shaped the life of the community. Did the brothers talk theology? Did they complain about the weather or the food or one another? Did Gavin talk about his early years at Couston Castle and indicate that he missed his parents and siblings? Lane could only guess at answers.

As a 'local' with knowledge of the area around Aberdour, Gavin was soon made responsible for obtaining the produce required for daily life. This meant that he, along with at least one other brother, would travel the abbey's *domaine* or area to collect what they could from the farms: grain, eggs, milk, fruit and vegetables. This would involve being taken to the mainland, perhaps to the small bay at Aberdour when the tide was in.

From thence he might climb the hill alongside the Dour and pass by St Fillans Church and the castle. Lane had walked this same path only days before. Then he would need to walk between the various farms and carry whatever produce he had collected. Gavin was a reasonably fit young man, and the exercise made him fitter still, unlike some of the brothers who had less rigorous work to do. Would be able to visit his sister his parents at Couston Castle or Marjory at the hospice as he went nearby? Perhaps, but only with prior permission. If his family had given gifts or made donations to the abbey their names would have been on the *cartulary*, and they would have expected burial within its walls.

Returning to the abbey Gavin and his partner waited on the shore for the boat, sometimes idly throwing stones into the water and speaking about their life before Inchcolm. When the boat arrived they loaded their supplies aboard, climbed in, and began the voyage back to the island. When it was calm, the trip was a pleasure. The sun was warm and bright on the water, smoke curled from houses in the village, seals lay warming themselves on the submerged rocks. But when the wind was up the waves made the trip a nightmare. There were times when Gavin wondered if they would make it. The rowers had to battle to ensure that the vessel headed in the right direction. On several occasions when the wind made travel too dangerous, the pair of them had to spend the night on shore, trying desperately to find some shelter from the cold. On reaching the abbey Gavin delivered the produce to the *cellarer*, who would store it in the bins within his cellar. If they were chilled from the crossing, Gavin and his partner asked permission to visit the warming house to get warm. After *Vespers* they enjoyed the evening meal, accompanied by another reading from St Augustine's Rules. Then later, after the service of *Compline*, Gavin would go to his bed in the dormitory, fall asleep, until the routine began all over again.

Lane read over his story about Gavin, printed it out, and put it into his pocket. It might be of use for his meeting with the Mortons on the island. It was only right that Gavin should discover what the Morton family intended to do to his island and abbey.

After they had finished their meal and were having coffee in the lounge that evening, Lane told Katriona about Gavin and asked for her opinion. She listened intently and then put down her mug.

"That's good. It's very realistic and I like it," she said. "He sounds like a nice lad."

"He is a nice lad," Lane said. "It doesn't bore you then?"

"No," she answered, "it doesn't bore me but I am sorry for him."

"Why are you sorry for him," Lane asked.

"Well, Katriona said, "it just seems like such a waste. He's young and strong and undoubtedly intelligent. He should be out in the world looking for a girl friend or something, not stuck in a monastery for the rest of his life. I mean, can you bear to watch him staying there until he's an old man and then dying without ever having really lived? Just think about how little of the world he will have seen."

"It's not up to me," Lane said. "He's made a choice and I guess he'll have to live with it."

"Katriona shook her head at him. "But it is up to you. You're the one pulling the strings aren't you?"

"Well, yes, I suppose so," Lane mused, as if he hadn't thought of that before.

Chapter Ten

Belle Encounter

The next Morning, Lane decided to make it easy on himself. Instead of driving to South Queensferry and take the *Maid,* he would go to North Queensferry and take the *Forthbelle*. It got to the island slightly later, but he would still be there before Naomi and the Mortons. He chided himself for not walking to the town, but parking would be easy and he wanted to be there in plenty of time. He remembered the time they had gone for a holiday in Corfu and had arranged to take the ferry to one of the smaller islands. As they were walking to the terminal, Lane saw the ferry pulling away. When they asked the man in the office why it had left early he simply shrugged and said that it was *full* and so had left. But the vision of Katriona running along the shore and shouting "Wait, wait, we're supposed to be on board" had stayed with him.

 He drove the switchback road to North Queensferry and found a place to park on the main street. The town was quiet. It was usually quiet. It was almost always usually quiet. Somewhere on the hill far above him stood the former prime minister's house, but that reign was no longer. A train trundled noisily over the rail bridge as he locked the car doors. There were lots of people standing on the town pier where the *Forthbelle* was tied up. He guessed that the tourist season had begun. Men, women and children carrying picnic baskets, flasks and cameras stood waiting patiently. The gangplank was rolled out, and they boarded. The *Belle* seemed a bit more down at the heels than the Maid, but it would provide a slightly different experience. It was a cloudy day, but dry and calm as the vessel pulled away from South Queensferry. He was feeling good, a bit elevated. Was it the cheerfulness of his fellow passengers or the idea of meeting the Mortons? He wasn't sure, but whatever it was he would go with it. Pulling out into the channel, Lane suddenly realized that he had accidentally made the right choice. A large liner was anchored just beyond the bridge. How had he missed that? He could have seen it from the house had he looked. It meant that the *Maid* would not be going from South Queensferry today. The pier would be closed in order to allow the liner's tenders to tie up for passengers to disembark. Had he gone for the *Maid* he would have missed going to the island at all.

The *Forthbelle* edged slowly around the liner *Serenity*, the captain giving his passengers a chance to look while he provided some commentary about the details of the ship. Notice the balconies, he said, everyone wanted a balcony of their own these days. Notice the tennis courts and the swimming pool on the top deck. Notice the driving range on the top deck. Lane wondered if he and Katriona would ever book a cruise on such a ship. With three thousand people on board he couldn't see it.

Nearing Inchcolm Island Lane spotted seals lounging on the platform of one of the channel markers. There were more on the rock outcroppings west of the island. He counted forty-six altogether. Some of them looked up and watched the vessel with their large eyes, clearly wondering who was invading their space. Lane was one of the first to disembark, no sense in wasting time today. He walked up the path past the toilets and the gift shop. Some of his fellow passengers were heading to the gift shop first, apparently oblivious to the beauty of the abbey. The lawn was thick with feathers. Here and there yellow dandelions poked up through the grass. A girl in overalls pushed a wheel barrow up the path, collecting rubbish. He studied the structure carefully, the square tower and steep octagonal roof of the chapter house, the green lawn sweeping down to the south beach. It really was quite beautiful and he had to admire those canons and lay brothers who had designed and built the thing. He was beginning to get a feel for the monastery, connecting the digital images he had been working with for days with the real structure.

Lane wanted to be out of the way when Naomi and the Mortons arrived. It would give him a few minutes to observe the representatives of the great man. He entered the southeast door to the cloisters and walked along the passageway. He stopped to look at the cloister garden and tried to imagine Gavin seated there attempting to engage in only useful and purposeful conversation. Lane left the cloisters at the west door and walked up the incline. A wide strip had been mown in the field to permit access to the west end of the island. But he didn't get very far. A large, fierce-looking gull stood in the centre of the strip, quite deliberately barring his way. Lane stopped. There had to be a nest in the grass beyond the bird. Would he keep going and trust that the gull would turn chicken or not? Should a man be afraid of a bird or not? He decided that in this particular case he was and turned around. After all, birds had descended from dinosaurs.

Lane saw the *Inchcolm Express* approaching and watched. Eventually Naomi appeared on the path with two people in tow. They hadn't spotted Lane, so he stood and studied the Mortons for a while. James brought up the rear, the shorter of the two, blue jeans with dark shirt and leather jacket. As Naomi pointed towards the abbey and spoke he continued to look in another direction, as if absorbed in a different world.

Sophie followed Naomi closely, listening to the commentary. Lane wasn't prepared for her to be so attractive. Long legs in tight jeans, blonde, blue top and a smart white jacket. She was smiling and looking where the lady in tweed was pointing. She seemed interested. As they neared the entrance to the chapter house Lane moseyed over towards them.

Naomi looked up and saw him. She interrupted her commentary and smiled. "Mr. Lane," she said nodding in his direction. He moved over beside them.

"James, Sophie, I'd like you to meet the person I've been telling you about. This is Davis Lane." Lane stretched out his hand. "James," Naomi said, "meet Davis Lane." They shook hands.

"Hi," James said, longish dark hair and sharp eyes. His face was wide and sported several days' growth.

"Sophie," Naomi continued, "please meet Davis Lane." Sophie held out her hand and Lane took it gladly. She was a stunner: rosy cheeks, blue eyes, warm smile. "Mr. Lane," she said, "I'm so glad to meet you. Naomi has told us so much about you."

"And I'm glad to meet the two of you," Lane answered, internally quite agreeable to what he was saying. "What do you think of the island?" Lane asked.

Sophie answered first. "Oh, now that I see it I think it's brilliant," she said. "Naomi has been trying to tell us about the history of the abbey, but I think we're still very ignorant."

Lane looked at James. "It's OK," he shrugged as he looked around. "We've got great plans for it."

"I think that we all ought to sit down somewhere and talk," Naomi said, looking intently at Lane. "Is that the best plan?"

"Sure, let's do that," Lane responded, heading in the direction of a bench overlooking the beach. "With any luck we can all squeeze in."

Sophie fell in alongside Lane and Naomi while James brought up the rear. When they had reached the bench, Sophie and Naomi joined Lane on the seat, but James continued to stand, looking out over the Forth towards Edinburgh.

"Davis has done a lot of research on the island," Naomi started off. "This is your chance to tell him about your plans and ask the expert for advice."

"Oh I'm hardly an expert," Lane said, "but I have I learned a lot in the last few weeks. It's a fascinating place. How much do you know about the abbey?"

James looked down at him. "We know that it has a lot of potential. If we put a golf course and hotel and casino on it it'll be outstanding," he answered.

Lane looked up and presented a quizzical smile, "But do you know anything about the long history of the abbey?"

"We've tried to read up a little," Sophie answered. "We know that it goes way back to the year 1123 and that it was started by the Augustinians. Is that right?"

"Spot on," Lane said "It operated for three hundred years until the Scottish Reformation."

James was using the toe of his shoe to gouge out little crosses in the soil. "I'm sure that all that history is interesting, but we're here to get this thing going. We're got a time frame here, so we can't spend a lot of time fooling around with the past."

"You do realize that you are going to face quite a bit of opposition from people who don't want a casino and golf course here?" Lane suggested. "It may turn out to be hard to keep to your time frame," Naomi and Sophie were quiet on the sidelines, as if watching the players in a tennis match.

"Of course I know that," James offered. "But there's been opposition to just about every project we've done in the world. Someone's always moaning. The Morton organization knows how to deal with all that."

Lane decided to reduce the heat. "What roles do you play in the organization?" he asked, looking directly at Sophie.

"I'm the interior design person," she said. "That's what I studied at university. Daddy expects me to come up with a motif for the hotel that will reflect the nature of the island. That goes for the golf clubhouse as well."

"OK," Lane said, turning to look at James, but he was looking towards Edinburgh in the distance.

Eventually, Sophie spoke for him. "James is responsible for feeding ideas about the positioning of the buildings to the architect and doing consulting with the course designer."

"Do you really think that the island is large enough for an eighteen hole golf course?" Lane asked. "It's only about twenty-two acres after all."

James decided to come back in from the cold. "Look, we wouldn't be here unless we knew it was feasible. This has all been worked out by the boss. He's already got his Dubai palm man ready to go."

"Sorry? You lost me there," Lane said.

"His Dubai palm man," James said. "You surely know that Dubai has been building artificial islands in the shape of palm trees and so on. Well, we've got Fadi Hussein. He was one of the experts who pioneered this."

"You're planning to build artificial islands around Inchcolm Island?" Lane asked, looking first at James and then at Naomi. She was nodding silently.

"Yes, of course," James answered, looking at Lane as if everyone else in the world had known this except him. "The islands will be used to build greens and tees. It's a completely new concept. You really ought to speak to speak to Callum McBain to find out how he's going to work the course."

"I'm sorry," Lane said, looking at Naomi, "you've lost me again. Who is Callum McBain?"

Sophie answered. "Callum McBain is the golf course designer. He's got a team working on this already, liasing with Fadi. James will be talking to him in the next few days."

"Well," Lane said, "I didn't realize that things were moving so fast. I guess that I've got a lot of ground to cover if I'm going to be any use to you all."

"It looks like that," James said," the glimmer of a smirk forming, "but I don't really know what you can do. We've got it planned out."

"Well, I guess then that you better tell me what else I don't know," Lane said, looking steadily at James.

Naomi answered. "The big thing is that Mr. Morton plans to restore the abbey completely. Isn't that right?" she added, looking at James.

"Yeah, that's a part of the deal," he said. "I suppose that's where you come in Mr. Lane. You can help us put it back together again. You happy with that?"

"I'm happy enough to offer what I can," Lane said, "but I don't think you can count your chickens before they're hatched."

"I've already stressed that to James and Sophie and to Mr. Morton," Naomi offered. "I'm not sure they appreciate the number of hurdles that would have to be jumped."

"Naomi," James said, putting his hand on her shoulder, "the Morton organization are experts at jumping hurdles. I don't think we've ever failed yet. The locals will soon see it our way."

"OK, fair enough," Lane said, "we'll see how things go. Let me tell you a little bit about what I've learned. Shall we walk around the monastery?"

They followed Lane into the cloister and the Chapter House and listened as he explained some of the features. They went outside again and then back into the ruins of the church. Lane tried to show them the details of the original structure and the movements of the canons as they gathered for worship.

Standing at his shoulder, Sophie said, "It's a lot to take in all at once."

"Yes, I appreciate that," Lane answered. "I think that you'll need to come back again and again in order to really get a feel for it."

"I suppose so," she said.

"Actually," Lane said, "I've done something to try to make it easier for you."

"I was hoping that you would say that," Naomi offered. "Please tell us."

"Well, I've created a fictional character, a canon, Gavin by name. I thought that if we could follow Gavin through a day in the monastery it would give you a better feel for it."

"Wonderful," Sophie said, clapping her hands. "Tell us about Gavin."

Lane removed Gavin's story from his pocket and scanned it, giving them a brief summary of a day in the life of Gavin, canon at Inchcolm Abbey.

"Fantastic," Sophie said, "would it be possible for us to borrow that so that we can read it back at the hotel?"

"Sure," Lane said, folding it up again.

"That's great, guys," James said, reaching out to take the paper from Lane's hand. "Now, I really need a coffee. I don't suppose there's a Starbucks on the island?"

When Katriona came home that afternoon, Lane told her the story of his meeting on the island. She listened patiently to his long story and then asked, "So what's she like then?"

"Who?" Lane replied.

"You know who I mean. Do you think I'm talking about Naomi? I know what she's like. What's Sophie like?"

"Well, she's quite personable and intelligent, much more likable than her brother," Lane answered.

"Yes, OK," Katriona responded, "but what does she look like? Is she attractive?"

"Yes, I suppose so," Lane said. "She is quite attractive."

"I thought so somehow," Katriona said. "What was she wearing?"

"What was she wearing?" Lane replied, "Am I supposed to remember that?"

"Well, I don't know, I just thought you might," Katriona said.

Lane racked his brain. "I think that she had jeans on and a white kind of top thing."

"Right," Katriona said, "so you are a noticer after all, just a selective one."

A little later, over dinner, Katriona asked, "Davis, would it tempt you back to this world if I offered you a second helping of curry and another glass of Shiraz?"

"I'm sorry I'm distracted," Lane answered. "Yes it would definitely help. I'm bothered by James. I wonder if his attitude reflects that of his father. I just can't get over what this guy wants to do with the island."

"I think I can see that," Katriona said, "but you're back on the mainland now. Do you want to hear about the unglam work of the West Fife Social Work Department for a while?"

Chapter Eleven
Colm's Course

Lane found the contact details for Callum McBain's golf design company online and phoned his office. He indicated who he was and was put through to McBain immediately.

"Mr. McBain," Lane said, "I'm Davis Lane and I'm involved with the proposed development on Inchcolm Island. It would help me if the two of us could get together and you could tell me about your plans for the course. Would that be possible?"

"I've heard about you, Davis," McBain answered, "and yes, it would seem a good idea to get together for a chat. You might be able to help move this deal forward for us. How about today. You doing anything today?"

Lane opened his diary and found the right page. "I could do today, yes. Where and when do you want to meet?"

"I'm at Aberdour Golf Club this morning," McBain said. "The pro's an old friend of mine. I want to pick his brain about annual weather conditions, construction people in the area and so on. Could you meet me there? We'll have a coffee and I'll tell you what we have in mind."

"I'll see you there," Lane said.

The road to Aberdour was surprisingly busy until he got to the fork for Kirkcaldy. Lane turned right on Shore Road and negotiated the narrow road heading down to the water. He turned right on Seaside Place and the golf club. He had played here a few times and liked the course. It was certainly scenic, overlooking the Forth as it did, but there were problems. The greens were very fast and the layout of the back nine was tortuous. Still, it would be nice to be playing today rather than working. Lane parked in the parking lot and walked up to the pro shop. The morning was windy but sunny. In the distance, the sun was picking out the outlines of the abbey. A green tanker was being manoeuvred into Braefoot by two tugs from Leith.

A tall, well-built man with sandy hair and ruddy complexion was standing near the first tee and looking out over the estuary. "You wouldn't be Callum McBain would you?" Lane asked.

"I would," he answered, holding out his hand, "and you must be Davis." They shook hands.

"I take it that you're studying Inchcolm from here," Lane said. "It's a great outlook isn't it?"

"Fantastic," McBain said. "I'm just trying to picture what the island will look like after we develop the course."

"I remember when you won the Scottish Open," Lane said.

"Do you really?" McBain answered. "It was a long time ago. These were the days. I don't even have time to play anymore, just build golf courses."

"That seems like a pity," Lane said. "So you're very busy?"

"Very," McBain answered. "Shall we sit down over here and chat about what's happening?"

They moved to the bench at the side of the first tee. Lane felt the bench shudder as McBain sat down. He was a big man, must have been able to hit the ball a long way in his prime.

"Before you tell me about your plan," Lane said, "tell me how it's possible at all. The island is only twenty-two acres with headlands at each end. I've studied it. I just don't see how you can fit an eighteen hole course on that island."

"You don't know Alexander Morton do you?" McBain said. "This is a very determined man. He knows what he wants and gets it. To be honest with you, when he came to us first I suggested that we could do a nine hole course, maximum." He reached into his shirt pocket, pulled out a pack of cigarettes, and held it out to Lane. "Smoke?" he asked.

"Thanks, no," Lane replied. "I don't."

McBain lit up and took a long drag. "Anyway, Morton said that it had to be an eighteen hole course. It could be an executive course, par three you know, but eighteen holes. It was going to be the holiest course in the world. He laughed when he said that. So I said that there wasn't enough space on the island for eighteen holes, and he came right back at me that he would make space. I asked him how he would do that and he said that we would make some islands. He would call in his Dubai engineer who knew how to make palm islands and we would just build some." McBain seemed to be breathless. Whether it was the cigarette or the story Lane couldn't tell.

"So he's got this engineer, Fadi Hussein is his name, who's going to make space for tees and greens. They're not really islands those, more like bridges. Here, let me show you." He pulled a piece of paper and a little scoring pencil from his pocket and drew a rough sketch of the outline of the island.

"You see here on the south bay," McBain said, "we fill in a narrow strip from the southeast corner of the bay and take it across to the southwest corner." He drew a curved strip the width of a fairway across the bay. "Then we put a bridge in the middle like this so that the water can go in and out with the tide. Then at this end on the mainland we put a tee, like so, and just before the bridge it widens out enough to put in a green, like so." The tee and green appeared on the sketch. "We don't need bunkers here because the water almost completely surrounds the green, and that is trouble enough, wouldn't you say?" McBain looked at Lane and grinned.

"Then," McBain continued, sketching again, "on the other side of the bridge we put in a tee and then another green on the mainland. Now, we need a bunker on the right-hand side of this green, but the beach offers sufficient trouble on the left. You see how this is working."

"Yes, I do see," Lane answered, "ingenious."

"Now," McBain went on, clearly relishing his lecture, "we can do this at two of the bays."

"OK, fair enough," Lane countered, "but that still doesn't give you the space for eighteen holes."

McBain took another long drag and through the cigarette away. "No, quite right," he said. "You've done your homework. But you know that there are outcroppings of rocks around the island. These will be built up to be genuine peninsular greens. The other holes will be on the mainland. They'll be done by cut and fill, and several will be blind holes. Now, bear in mind that all these holes will be short, hundred and fifty yards max, but they will be bloody difficult, I assure you of that. You do realise, don't you, that for all the links courses in Scotland, there aren't many that have greens actually in the sea? This course will be unique." He sat back and looked at Lane, clearly chuffed by his plan.

"But these outcroppings of rocks," Lane said, "there are seals on them. I was out there the other day and counted forty-six at three different places. What about them?"

"Yes, I know," McBain answered. "They are a problem, but Morton says that he knows how to deal with that. Leave it to him."

"I see," Lane said. "What about all the birds on the island? Aren't they are problem?"

"Yes, I know that," McBain said. "They're more of a problem than the seals in a way. But there are lots of other places they could go. I mean, Bass Rock is just down the road so to speak. Once they have golfers waving a club and shouting at them they'll probably pack it in and leave."

"I see," Lane said. "Tell me about the artificial island or peninsulas. How does this chap Fadi intend to make them?"

"Well, as I understand it," McBain replied, "they ship in thousands of rocks. I think they are more or less cubes. A crane lifts each one in place, guided by a diver. He ensures that they fit together as tightly as possible. Now, in the gulf they dredged up sand from the bottom and sprayed it over and into the rocks and crevices. The sand came up in great arcs from the water, 'rainbowing' I think they called it. That can't happen here because there isn't enough sand on the bottom. So the idea is to bring in tonnes of fine limestone grit, spray it on and then work it in. The grit helps the rock base to stay in place. Then they bring in topsoil and sow the grass seed and bingo, you have a fairway."

"Where do they get the rock?" Lane asked.

"Mr. Morton is going to ask Fife Council to reopen the old quarry, Millstonemeadow Quarry or something like that. He reckons there is enough stone there for the job."

"But that's on Gavin's old land," Lane said.

"Sorry?" McBain said.

"Oh sorry, just a slip of the tongue," Lane said. "Forget I said that."

"OK. Anyway," McBain went on, "Fadi seems to have checked it all out and says it's feasible. It'll cost a fortune of course, but Morton seems to have it. The good thing is that it will create jobs, lots of them. Not just for me and my team but for stonemasons, truckers, big machinery people, divers and guys with shovels."

"Yes, I can see that," Lane said. "At the moment we need jobs badly, all we can get."

McBain shifted in his seat and pulled out another cigarette. "You know that he's going to name each hole after a saint," he said, rolling his eyes back.

"I heard that, Lane said. "Are you happy about that?"

"Well," he said, grinning, "It's going to be all Scottish saints, and I'm a Scot, so that's fine with me."

"Care to give me an example?" Lane asked.

"Well, the signature hole, which is number five, will be called *St Columba.*"

"You no doubt realize," Lane said, "that Columba probably never set foot on Inchcolm?"

"I heard that," McBain said, shrugging. "Does it really matter? I mean the island and the abbey are called after him in spite of that, so I guess it doesn't hurt to name a hole after him."

"And what are the others?" Lane asked.

McBain thought for a minute. "Well, we've got *St Andrew, St Cuthbert, St Fillan, St. Mungo* . . . that's all I can remember at the moment. This is really Mr. Morton's thing. I'll leave it to him. He'll be happy to tell you all about it I'm sure."

"I hope he will," Lane said. "Look, I do have one other question for you. Do you have any reservations about building a course on this island? I mean, look at it just now in the sunshine. It's really a beautiful place. Doesn't that worry you a little?"

"I have thought about that," McBain answered. "I do like the ruins. They are beautiful, but golf courses are beautiful as well. They preserve green space which we need badly. If this course brings people here and they enjoy playing it, and if they visit the monastery, well, that's not a bad thing is it?"

"Maybe not," Lane answered.

"I'll tell you what," McBain said, rising up, "What do you say that you and I have a game when the course is done? I'll treat you."

"Fantastic," Lane said, meaning it. "I'll look forward to that."

"Now," McBain said, "It's really lunchtime. How about we go into the clubhouse, and I'll buy you lunch."

Lane followed McBain to the door of the clubhouse. McBain punched in the security code and the two men went up the steps and into the lounge. McBain led the way to the corner table.

"What would you like to drink?" he asked.

"A pint would be fine, "Lane answered. He stood surveying the Forth while McBain went to the bar. McBain returned with two pints and they sat down.

"I had forgotten just how fantastic the view is from up here," Lane commented.

"Aye, it's got to be one of the best views in the country," McBain said. "I come here and sit with a pint and try to visualise what the island will look like when we finish the course." He held up both hands, forming a rectangular screen like a film director. "If you can imagine pasting green fairways and tees and greens onto the brown patches you see now . . . ." He paused while Lane gazed at the island again. "I know that it's kind of romantic, but I like to think of it as an emerald in the midst of a blue sea. It'll be stunning."

Lane held up his glass. "I can see what you mean. Here's to your course. Cheers."

After dinner that evening, when they were having coffee in the lounge, Lane told Katriona about Callum McBain and the proposed course.

"And is Alexander Morton really going to name each hole after a saint?" she asked.

"That's what the man says," Lane answered.

"Is that not a bit peculiar?" she said. "I mean, can you imagine a golfer saying to his partner, 'Well, two bogies on St Cuthbert isn't too bad. Now, it's on to St. Mungo?"

"I agree that it sounds a bit strange," Lane answered, "but I think it's Morton's way of trying to show that he's maintaining sacred nature of the island."

"Well," Katriona said, "I think it's just plain silly. All I can think of is that when a golfer arrives on that tee and stands up to address the ball, he says:

> Here is the bird that never flew
> Here is the tree that never grew
> Here is the bell that never rang
> Here is the fish that never swam

Lane looked at her and said, "What on earth are you talking about?"

"Did you not know that?" she said. "It's a saying about St. Mungo, Glasgow's patron saint. The bird, the tree, the bell and the fish are all about miracles that Mungo performed. If you had grown up in Glasgow you would have known it. Every Glasgow schoolboy or girl could quote you those lines."

"No kidding?" he said.

"No kidding," she said.

Lane shook his head in wonderment.

The next morning, Katriona said to Lane, "You didn't sleep well again did you? You were thrashing about in the middle of the night. A nightmare again?"

"Not a nightmare exactly. I was playing golf on Inchcolm with McBain. On St. Mungo's green, which is out on the peninsula surrounded by water, I kept driving into the water, again and again. Splash after splash. It was so frustrating."

"Ah, she said, "That explains it. Here is the ball that never bounced."

Chapter Twelve
Smile

Lane decided to renew his research to the east end of the island, where most of the military fortifications were located. The idea didn't exactly enthuse him, as forts weren't high on his list of interests, but he wasn't satisfied with what he had found so far. If he were going to be an expert on the island then he had to know more than he did at the moment.

Lane was surprised to find that Fife had boasted more fortifications than any other region in Scotland, presumably because the Forth estuary provided more potential landing sites for a German invasion than anywhere else. Clearly it had been essential to protect the Forth Rail Bridge and the Royal Naval Dockyard at Rosyth. Fortifications had been built on the east end of Inchcolm for the First World War and then upgraded for World War Two. There were two very large gun emplacements at the top of the headland at about the one hundred foot level. At a protected lower level a large magazine housed the ammunition. He knew now that a secret brick tunnel ran from the men's quarters to the gun emplacements to allow the troops to get safely to their guns. At a lower level on the southeast side of the island light batteries had been installed to light up the sky or the sea. An anti-submarine net had been stretched into the Forth to protect the waters from German subs. But all these things he had noted already.

It was difficult to do much more. You could go further back in history of course. Inchcolm had been no stranger to war long before World War One. The English had attacked the abbey on several occasions, providing a reason why the canons had decided to erect fortifications around the abbey itself. Long before that had been the Battle of Kinghorn in the eleventh century, resulting in the Danish king paying Macbeth ten thousand dollars to bury his warriors on the island. It was ironic, thought Lane, that such a beautiful and peaceful island had known so much warfare. The idea that now Alexander Morton might induce a different kind of warfare nagged at him.

Beyond these general observations, however, it seemed impossible to go. He couldn't visualise what, if anything, Morton might do with the fortifications. And he didn't know to what extent such military relics were valued. He had managed to locate a group online that devoted itself to the study of wartime pillboxes, but they seemed interested mainly in sites south of the border. The remains of wartime fortifications in the country seemed to enjoy a peculiar status. Like the giant blocks of concrete tank barriers around the beaches, these things were just *there*. People didn't talk about them or even seem to notice them. Perhaps Morton intended to leave the east end of the island just as it was, or maybe he had other plans for the site if no one objected. Lane would have to leave it there.

He decided to turn back to other things, to things domestic. His last attempt, made in good faith, had been hindered by the intrusion of Steven Swinton. The garden hadn't been touched in days, the garage was untidy, and they needed shopping. Maybe if he did his domestic chores it would help to clear the mind and reinvigorate him. It was while he was emptying grass clippings into the brown bin that the idea came to him. He wasn't sure why he hadn't thought of it a while ago, just too preoccupied with Mr. Morton and the abbey. He checked his personal diary and the diary on their PC and then got busy.

Later, when they had settled in the lounge for a pre-dinner drink, Lane said to his wife, "It's Friday, you know."

"Yes, I do know that, Davis," Katriona said. "It always manages to come around after Wednesday and Thursday."

"What I mean," Lane said, "is that it's Friday, like the end of a working week. Do you see what I mean?"

"I do know that it's been a working week. I know how I feel, totally exhausted."

"Exactly," Lane said, "That's what I mean. Now, what to ordinary mortals do after they've worked all week?"

"Well," Katriona answered, "some ordinary mortals would take the weekend off, do something. But then, we're not ordinary mortals are we?"

"I'm pretty ordinary, but you're not. You're extraordinary."

"Davis, what on earth are you getting at?" Katriona asked. "You're milking something for all it's worth."

"Sorry," Davis said. "but you need a break, so I've organized a weekend off for us."

"Really?" Katriona said, sitting up and looking at him with arched eyebrows.

"Really," he said. "I checked my diary and there's nothing in it for the next two days. I looked at yours as far as I can and there's nothing in it either. So I've booked a room at Kinloch-Rannoch for Saturday night. Tomorrow morning we'll head up north, maybe stop at Pitlochry and look around, take a walk and so on. I might play golf at Taymouth Castle on Sunday if you feel like walking around with me. Does that sound OK to you?"

"It sounds fantastic," she said, and Lane thought that she looked better already. She rose from the chair, came over to him and sat on his lap. "It's brilliant. Thank you," she said, planting a kiss on his lips.

Lying in bed that night Lane listened to his selection of music from the ipod and tried to unthink his way into sleep. He was almost there when the tracks changed and called for his attention. He had to search his mind for a moment to recall that it was one of Strauss' *Four Last Songs*. There was something about it, an upward movement, a transcendence that lifted him above earthly cares. He knew that it didn't correspond with his theology. Unlike so much of scripture and the liturgy and the hymns that they sang, God was not *Up* but rather *Down*, in the deepest reaches of humanity. This music was taking him up, but at least it was far above and beyond Inchcolm Island and Alexander Morton, and it was good.

On Saturday morning they had coffee early and left in the Cruiser. Getting out onto the open road, onto the M90, did what it almost always did for Lane. It made him feel that he was getting away from things, leaving them behind. It made him feel good. They drove past Dunfermline and the social work department, they drove past the ugly opencast mine, they drove past Loch Leven shrouded in cloud. They followed the gentle downhill curve that revealed Perth in the distance. The drove past the wooded slopes of Dunkeld and along the flat bends of the Tay.

"I'm glad that you thought of this," Katriona said.

"I am too," Lane answered. "I'm beginning to feel free again."

"Good," Katriona said. "But promise me that you won't think about Inchcolm Abbey all the time while we're away."

Lane looked across at her and said, "I promise. And you promise me that you won't spend all your time thinking about the problems of West Fife."

"I promise," she said, looking straight ahead at the road in front.

In Pitlochry they visited the usual haunts, the woollen shop and the outdoor clothing store. They had lunch and walked across the dam, watching for salmon. The water was calm, permitting perfect reflections of the forest and sky around the loch. They walked on to the Festival Theatre and studied the billboard to see what was playing.

Back in the car, they headed north and found the turnoff west over the Garry. The road was familiar, turning and twisting alongside Loch Tummel. They pulled off at the Queen's View to have a look. Yes, there were buses and it was touristy, but it was also magnificent. The trees running down to the edge of the loch, the still water, the mountains in the distance sucked you into the country. How could you think about anything else?

At Kinloch Rannoch they checked into the hotel. The room was good, at the front and looking over Loch Rannoch. They unpacked and took a walk along the loch. There were no phone calls or texts. They had a swim in the hotel pool. They changed and went down to the bar for a drink. The bartender was tall and blonde and very courteous. She spoke with an accent. Lane thought it sounded like Polish and asked her where she was from.

"Latvia," she said.

"Latvia?" he said. "What's a nice girl from Latvia doing in a place like this?"

"Just working," she said. "I came to Scotland to find a job and wound up here. I like it because it is so beautiful."

"I'm surprised," Lane said. "It just seems like a long way to go for a job."

"Oh no," she said. "There are other people here, from Poland and Estonia."

"I see," Lane said, thinking that the world was changing faster than he appreciated.

The next morning seemed promising. Fog lined the hills and shores of the loch, but the sun was fighting to break through. They headed across the Tummel Bridge towards Kenmore. By the time that they pulled into the parking lot at Taymouth Castle it was free and genuinely warm. The course wasn't busy so there was no pressure on them. Katriona managed the trolley for him and he played not badly, considering that it had been a long time.

They went back into Kenmore and found a sunny outside table overlooking the Tay at the hotel, where they had smoked salmon sandwiches and sauvignon blanc. They couldn't believe how good it was. On their way back to Loch Rannoch they drove back via Fortingall and stopped to take another look at Europe's oldest living thing, the Fortingall Yew, nearby where Pontius Pilate was supposed to have been born. Lane reckoned that his idea had worked. They had managed to leave everything behind.

Until they got home. After carrying all the stuff back into the house, Lane switched on the BBC to see the six o'clock news. Bad Mistake. On the screen was an image of the Scottish Parliament building at the bottom of the Royal Mile. Standing across the entrance and barring the way stood a double row of people, arms linked. All of them were shouting something that sounded like, "Say No to Morton." Some were holding up placards. One sign featured a drawing of a puffin with a large tear rolling down its cheek. The sign said:

SOB
SAVE OUR BIRDS

Others were holding up placards featuring a drawing of the face of a seal. Their signs read:

SOS
SAVE OUR SEALS

The commentary explained that this demonstration was in opposition to Alexander Morton's plans to build a hotel, casino and golf course on Inchcolm. The camera then focussed on two men in the back row holding up a much larger sign featuring a mouth with its corners turned down. It read:

GIVE MORTON AN INCH AND HE'LL TAKE YOUR SMILE.

Davis Lane and Katriona turned away from the screen and at looked at each other in silence.

Chapter Thirteen
Offer

When his mobile rang early the next morning Lane knew that it was Naomi. The ring had a certain quality of urgency or desperation.

"Hello Davis," she said. "It's Naomi here. I suppose that you saw the news last night. How are you?"

"I saw it," he said. "I'm fine, but it shook me a little. I wasn't expecting to see very noisy demonstrations when I took this job."

"I know, I know," Naomi responded. "I'm sorry. I think that we should get together and talk about this. Are you free today?"

"Yes, of course," Lane said. "Where and when do you want to meet?"

"How about the same place as last time, about half-past ten. Would that be all right?" She sounded cautious, Lane thought, maybe worrying about someone listening in. Maybe she was now anxious about people hacking into mobile phones. He'd heard that certain newspapers were up to such tricks.

He couldn't help sighing, "Sounds fine, Naomi," he said. "I'll see you then."

Lane drove to the Park and Ride just outside Inverkeithing and boarded the bus for the city. It would forego any parking problems at either end. The traffic was light and the bus made good time. There was another passenger liner in at South Queensferry. There were buses lined up to take sightseers to the castle and the Royal Mile and wherever else they wanted to go. If they walked to the end of the Royal Mile would they find the demonstrators still there?

George Street was busy with pedestrians. Already he spotted several carrying bags advertising the liner he had just seen. Naomi was waiting for him down the steps and in the darkest corner of the coffee shop. She stood up, held out her hand and smiled. No tweed today, but a white blouse and blue skirt. Lane thought that she looked pale and anxious. He also noticed that she had no ring on her finger. This would be information he could take to Katriona, if she asked again. There was another John Le Carre' on the table. He offered to get the coffee and went back to the counter to order it.

When Lane returned and sat down Naomi was turning pages in her diary.

"You look a bit stressed," Lane offered. "I take it that it was the news last night. I couldn't believe it."

She smiled thinly. "Yes, that and just the whole thing. It's kind of taking over my life."

"But surely," Lane said, "you've got someone working with you, someone to share this with and help you organize."

"To be honest with you, no," she answered. "And that's one of the things that I want to talk to you about. I am the sole person who is supposed to be liasing on this project, issue, problem . . . whatever you want to call it, and I'm beginning to feel that I've been rather set up, if that is the current term. I'm taking all the flak on this. What's worse," she said, touching Lane's arm, "is that I feel I have now set you up. You're going to be the one who'll get most of the flak."

Lane thought for a moment. What she said underlined a thought that had been rolling around in his mind but hadn't before surfaced.

"I see," he said. "Are you saying that this has been a deliberate policy, to put us in the hot seat so that others can stay out of it?"

"Maybe," she said. "I don't know for sure. Maybe I'm just being paranoid. Anyway, I'm sorry that I got you into this. Obviously you are going to get publicity and then be confronted by people protesting against one thing or another. I didn't intend that. If you want to pull out now I would understand."

"You mean quit, give up now?" Lane asked.

"Yes," Naomi said. "That's exactly what I mean. I can see things becoming very acrimonious, and I don't see any reason why you should get bruised. It really isn't anything to do with you."

Lane looked at her as he drank some coffee. He set the cup down on the table. "Two points," he said. "First, if I pull out that would leave you on your own and I wouldn't want to do that. Secondly, it is to do with me anyway. I have an interest in what happens to Inchcolm Abbey and the island. We all have. I've come to have a real fondness for the place, and after all," he said, winking at her, "I've got to support my pal Gavin."

Naomi seemed visibly to relax. Her shoulders dropped, her hands moved to the table and a smile appeared. "Of course, Gavin," she said. "Thank you Davis. It really helps to know that you'll stay on the job. I do appreciate it." He wondered if that was moisture in her eye, but he wasn't sure.

"Tell me where we are in the thinking of your umbrella group," Lane said.

Naomi opened her diary again and took out a piece of paper. "Right," she said, studying the paper, "Historic Scotland is still unofficially open to the idea. We're under enormous pressure on several fronts. First, we've calculated that the revenue we might get from the Morton organisation could probably enable us to maintain at least six other important properties. This is quite a carefully done estimate and also a conservative one. Now, under the present policies, our funding for the next several years looks like being cut. So you can see how useful the injection of that much extra income would be. But also from the cultural perspective, the fact that Morton would restore the monastery is immensely appealing. Can you imagine how wonderful it would be to have a genuine medieval monastery for people to visit and learn from?"

"I can, actually," Lane said. "Everything I've learned so far opens up so many ideas and questions about a kind of murky age. It would be fantastic to see the place as it really was in the sixteenth century."

"Of course you can imagine it," she said. "I'm sorry. That was a stupid thing to say. If anyone would like to see it restored it would surely be you. Anyway, getting back to the point, the Scottish Tourist Board is very much for it. They think that would impact upon the number of people wanting the visit the country. Lothian and Fife councils are enthusiastic, as one might expect. Anything to bring jobs to the regions would be welcome. The Scottish government are not saying anything, again as one might expect. Behind their silence however, I think they would like to see it go ahead. But they're just realistic about the political fury it would invoke. On the negative front, Forth Ports look like being against it. It would complicate traffic on the Forth without that much economic benefit for them. We know that Shell UK would oppose it because of the risks to Braefoot. But the most vocal opposition will come from the bird and the wildlife people as you have already seen. I can't imagine that they would ever come round."

"OK," Lane said. "That pretty much agrees with my own assessment of the situation. So what is the next step? What do you want me to do?"

"Well," Naomi said, taking a deep breath and opening the diary again, "Alexander Morton himself arrives in three days time. I'm hoping that he will want to meet with you. I keep putting the idea into the heads of James and Sophie, although I'm not sure that it gets into James' head. He doesn't appear to be the listening type. Sophie's fine though. Are you willing to talk to Mr. Morton?"

"Of course," Lane said. "I'm looking forward to it with bated breath. Seriously, I am in a way. Having heard so much about him and met his son and daughter, I'm anxious to see what he's like. So what else can I do just now?"

"Brace yourself," she said.

"I will," he said. "Naomi, before we go, can I ask you something personal?"

"Yes, of course," she answered.

"Are you partnered to someone, or are you on your own?"

"Why do you ask?" she said.

"No particular reason," Lane answered. "I just wondered if you had someone to talk to when you got home."

"Right," she said. "The answer is no to both of the above."

During dinner that evening Katriona asked Lane what he'd been doing. He explained that he had gone into Edinburgh to confer with Naomi.

"Did you encounter any protestors on the way?" Katriona asked, but she wasn't smiling.

"No, of course not," Lane answered. "But she apologized for getting me into this," he said, "and she gave me the chance to back out."

"Did she really?" Katriona said.

"Yes, she did. I thought she looked stressed, and she admitted as much," Lane said. "She said that she didn't want me to get bruised by the controversy. I do feel kind of sorry for her. She's on her own."

"Now, let me think," Katriona said. "You thought about her offer very carefully. You recalled how stressed you got the last time you took up the CIA thing. Then you reflected on how anxious I am about this affair and how worried I am for you. And then you accepted her offer and said goodbye. Right?"

"No, not exactly," Lane answered. "You know that I can't back out now."

"Absolutely not," Katriona said. "Why am I not surprised?"

Chapter Fourteen
Protest

Lane was twiddling his thumbs. There had been nothing else about Inchcolm and demonstrations in the news. Hopefully, it might be quiet for a while. The next thing on the agenda was the much heralded arrival of Alexander Morton and a meeting with the man. He felt that he was more than ready for that. He had done his research into the abbey and the island, he had looked into the design of the golf course, and he had talked to James and Sophie Morton. He was receiving very little direction from above. He didn't know what else he could do until there was some further planned or unplanned development. He had to find something else to occupy his mind. All his research had been pretty straightforward, but it had also lifted up several important questions which remained unanswered. He might as well occupy himself with trying to find answers to these questions.

    He decided to tackle what he thought would be the easiest question first. It was about the reason for the headless fresco, now situated alongside the ruins of the church wall. He discovered that the fresco portrayed the funeral procession of John de Leycestre, the Bishop of Dunkeld. John had been the archdeacon of Lothian and was then elected to the bishopric on October 22, 1211. Lane already knew that the Romans had a fort at Cramond in 142, guarding the east end of the Antonine Wall. It followed logically that there must have been a church at Cramond in the thirteenth century. John must have travelled to Cramond from Dunkeld, probably to officiate at an important service of worship of some kind. While at Cramond he had died and had been transported to Inchcolm Abbey for the funeral service and burial. But why bury John at Inchcolm rather than take him back to Dunkeld? There were two possibilities. It would have been easier, since transporting a body all the way to Dunkeld would have taken several days. This also underlined the vast differences between the twenty-first and the thirteenth centuries. John's flock in and around Dunkeld wouldn't even have known about his death and burial for days after it had taken place, given the distance between Inchcolm and Dunkeld. No texting, no telephone calls, no radio, television or newspaper reports. The second possibility was that perhaps burial at Inchcolm was preferred because that holy place enjoyed a higher status. Lane thought that this second possibility was more likely. For these Christians, holy places were very important, especially if getting to heaven was high on your list of priorities. So burial on a holy island and within the abbey became a priority. John de Leycestre's funeral had clearly been a big event, featuring a clerical procession and a high service of worship. This was important enough to be portrayed in a fresco on the wall of the church. So the fresco was at Inchcolm because Inchcolm had been the place of John's funeral and burial, and that location was theologically important. Lane felt that he had answered that question to his satisfaction. But the other questions were more difficult.

The question that nagged at Lane more than any other was why the canons of Inchcolm Abbey had thrown the coffin of Alan de Mortimer overboard in the twelfth century. De Mortimer wanted his body to lay at rest at the abbey. He had given half of his lands to the abbey for its living, undoubtedly to ensure the fulfilment of that wish. The abbey was dependent upon this gift. It received rents from the land and produce from the farms. Try as he might, Lane found it impossible to exclude Gavin from his thinking. This, he thought, is precisely what Gavin would have done when he went out on his forays. He collected the produce or the rents. This is what keeps the abbey going. And yet, here are the canons, rowing back to the island with Alan de Mortimer in his lead-lined coffin. They come to the middle of the deep water between Aberdour and Inchcolm, rest their oars, very carefully stand up in the boat, lift up the coffin on the count of three and hoist it over the side. What on earth are they thinking? What is their rationale, to treat their benefactor in such a way? Theologically, how do they justify their act to God? Lane had thought often about this and couldn't work it out. They must have harboured some deep grievance against de Mortimer, but what that grievance was had been lost in the past. Lane could take the matter no further, so the question remained unanswered.

The one remaining question, Lane felt, could be dealt with more easily. There was at least some logic to it. The event in question took place in the late twelfth century, involving the succession of the vicar at St Fillans Church. Lane recalled how the canons from Inchcolm had gone ashore and barricaded the door to the church to prevent the induction of the new vicar. Why, he wondered, had the brothers taken so radical a step? There appeared to be two different ways to answer the question. The first one was to suggest that the canons of the abbey were really very troublesome people. It was a political power play. They simply wanted to retain the right to St Fillans for themselves. The dumping of Alan de Mortimer would support the theory of troublesome canons. Yet this theory seemed preposterous to Lane. These men had taken vows to live in harmony with others. They believed in the rules of St Augustine. They sang the psalms and said the Lord's Prayer every day. Like Gavin after them, they had taken the vows, had affirmed their commitment to the faith, and had committed themselves to Jesus Christ. Lane could not believe that they were no more than selfish rogues.

The other possibility was to suggest that the canons had some pressing moral concern about the vacancy and were prepared to back it up with moral action. His research into the abbey forced him to believe that this was the more likely answer. The facts were that St Fillans Church became vacant in 1186 through the death of the vicar, and that Inchcolm Abbey had the right of *presentation,* which meant the right to nominate someone to hold the post. However, William de Mortimer bypassed the officials of the abbey to nominate his own man, the clerk to David, the Earl of Huntington. This was an infringement of the abbey's rights. But the issue was much more than the infringement of a legal nicety. Lane found that David, the Earl of Huntington was also and at the same time the Earl of Northumberland, the Earl of Lennox, the Earl of Carlisle, the Earl of Doncaster, the Earl of Garioch, and the Earl of Cambridge. At least some of these honours must have resulted from the fact that David had been a great commander under Richard the Lion Heart during the First Crusade. But, Lane thought, if David's clerk is to function as the vicar of St Fillans, he will never be there. He must surely have bureaucratic functions to fulfil in Northumberland, Doncaster and all the other earldoms. So St Fillans would become like many of the other Catholic churches of the medieval period; they would have absentee priests or vicars. The man might be there once or twice in a year, if they were lucky. Moreover, he would be entitled to collect the tithes and rents of the people. It was a wonderful position: there is nothing like collecting a reward for doing nothing.

If this was the correct interpretation of the incident then, Lane went on to wonder, how had it come about? The canons must have discussed this proposed induction in the Chapter House, probably over a number of days. They must have agreed that it was wrong and that something ought to be done about it. Individually, the canons must have talked about it to one another in the cloister at length. If they were enjoined to engage only in useful and purposeful conversation, then this moral issue surely qualified. It wasn't simply an issue that affected the abbey, but an issue that affected the ordinary people of the parish. It was the people who worshipped in the church. Did they not deserve a priest in residence rather than an absentee one? Lane tried to visualise the canons talking quietly about this with one another, tried to hear their arguments, to see their gestures, their furrowed brows, the shaking of heads. They must have resolved to take action. So, did a number of the brothers slip out quietly on the morning of that day, unbeknownst to the abbot and prior? Did they row to shore and barricade the door to St Fillans and wait for Robert and his men to turn up? Lane thought that this was unlikely. There was no way they could have done this secretly, without the knowledge and permission of the abbot and prior. The punishment meted out by the abbot would have proved disastrous, both for this earthly life and for the life to come. *So the act of defiance at St Fillans must have been approved by all the brothers or at least by the officers.* This surely was a major decision by the abbey, *a corporate act.* Lane went on to visualise a dozen or more of the canons linked arm in arm, lined up against the door to St Fillans. And when that vision came it brought with it moral insight. Was this not the same kind of protest that he had seen at Hawes Pier in South Queensferry? The canons of Inchcolm Abbey were only asking for the keeping of a promise, for fairness in the appointment of a new leader in the parish church. Were the people who were concerned about the birds and seals, the people who wanted to wanted to preserve the ruins as they were, were these people not making the same sort of moral protest? Were they not only asking for what was right, for fairness?

Lane went on to visualise Robert and his men leaving the castle for the induction, turning the corner and marching under the flying buttress to St Fillans. When they went round the corner of the church they must have been surprised to see a human chain of canons barricading the door against them. The ordinary people who had come to join in the service must have stood back from the church, framed against the sky over the Forth, wondering what would happen next. Robert spoke to his men, giving them firm instructions. He must have said to them, 'We can't have these people, these lowly canons thwarting the will of David, the Earl of Huntington. Move them away from the door. Do whatever you have to.' The canons would not have responded to violence with violence. Coming before all the rules they knew so well was the rule that they must love God and their neighbour. And so they must have tried desperately to hold together, lying down and refusing to move. Then they were punched and beaten and kicked until they have been moved away and the door to the church was clear.

How the canons were able to make their way back to the boat and row back to the abbey with their injuries Lane couldn't imagine. Upon their arrival, they were helped by the brothers to file in to see the *Infirmarer*, who did what he could. They would have suffered broken ribs and bruises over their bodies, as well as broken heads. Upon hearing their story, the abbot was deeply shocked and angry and vowed to withdraw all support from Robert and from William de Mortimer.

The story must have spread quickly through the parish. It was expanded and distorted no doubt, but the core facts of what happened on that day were lodged in the minds of the people. When the parents of young canons like Gavin heard they also were shocked. They may well have been unhappy with the actions of their sons, no matter how well intentioned. After all, it was important that they remained on good terms with the clerk to David, the Earl of Huntington. He was a powerful man, who could take away favours as easily as he could give them. Perhaps these same parents, concerned about their sons, and after several days of trying, were finally given permission to visit them in the porter's lodge. Sympathy was given, but also an explanation of their parental displeasure. The young canons said that they understood, but they had done what they thought was right in God's eyes. The abbot had given them permission. Was this kind of holy and moral activity not what their parent's had intended when they had been encouraged to enter the abbey? More and more to Lane, Inchcolm seemed like a battleground.

After dinner that evening Lane told Katriona the story of the protest and beating at St Fillans Church.

"I don't understand," she said, "how Robert's men could have been so brutal to the canons from the abbey. Did they not fear the wrath of God for beating these people up?"

"Well, yes, I suppose they did," Lane answered, "but probably not as much as they were afraid of the wrath of David, the Clerk of Huntington and of the king behind him. The wrath of the king could be immediate, remember, while the wrath of God was a bit more distant."

"Was there not something in the Church of Scotland similar to this kind of protest?" Katriona asked.

"Exactly," Lane answered. "Middle of the nineteenth century the evangelical wing of the church walked out, ministers and congregations because they wanted to choose their own ministers rather than having them chosen by the lairds or landowners."

"So," Katriona said, "there's not a lot that's new then is there?"

"I guess not," Lane answered. "It's always been about power and money in the church."

"I just feel very sorry for that boy," Katriona said.

"What boy?" Lane answered.

"Gavin," of course," Katriona said.

"No," Lane said, "Gavin was much later. Anyway, we've got to stop talking about Gavin. You're doing the same thing that I've been doing. He's fictional. He's not real. Get over it, please."

"I know, I know," she said. "I'm sorry, but I can just see him lying there with bruises and a broken rib."

Chapter Fifteen

Joust

Lane had assumed the next day would be uneventful, a day away from the obligations of Inchcolm, a day that could be whittled away with some domestic duties and some simple pleasures. He was wrong. He drove into Inverkeithing, went to the fish shop, bought a few groceries and the paper. When he sat down to read the paper at home, it was there on the bottom half of the front page.

Gulls in Skirmish with Monks over Morton Plans

As Scotland awaits the visit of Alexander Morton to explain his plans for Inchcolm Abbey, a gull scrapped briefly with a monk yesterday in South Queensferry. As this paper has previously reported, Mr. Morton seeks permission to restore Inchcolm Abbey and build the world's holiest golf course, as well as a hotel and casino on Inchcolm. A large body of demonstrators has once again barred the way to Hawes pier, preventing passengers from boarding the Maid of the Forth. Protestors against the scheme were wearing gulls' heads and screeching loudly in order to demonstrate their opposition to the Morton organisation's plans. A number of the gulls were also carrying placards which read **Save our Birds**. *The gulls were joined in their opposition to the plans by demonstrators wearing seal heads featuring large brown eyes and whiskers. Many of the seals carried signs reading* **Save our Seals**.

The gulls and seals did not, however, have it all their own way. Among the demonstrators was a group dressed as monks, who were protesting in support of the restoration of the abbey. The monks were silent, but carried signs saying **Restore Our Abbey**. *Some onlookers to the demonstration were clearly alarmed by the monks in the mistaken impression that they were "Hoodies".*

During the demonstration a brief skirmish ensued between a gull and a monk. Apparently, the gull accidentally struck a monk in the head while jostling for position and waving its sign. The monk retaliated by punching the gull on its beak. Several other monks separated the two demonstrators. It is understood that no one was seriously injured.

Representatives from the several groups were interviewed after the demonstration. Morris Falconer, speaking for the Save our Birds protestors said that the bird life on Inchcolm would be decimated. 'Some of our bird species, especially puffins, are already under threat by human development,' he commented. 'This development will make it worse. Besides that, the birds themselves will resist any effort to develop the island. Anyone expecting to interfere with this bird habitat should expect to be dive-bombed by gulls and terns and who knows what else.' Mr. Falconer went on to say, 'Over and above or rather beneath the birds, we like the ruins as they are. When we walk among the ruins we feel transported back to an earlier and better time. We do not wish the ruins to be ruined. We believe in ruins.'

The Save our Seals group was represented by Miss Betty Duthie. After removing her seal head, she commented, 'The seals have been coming to this island and lazing on the outlying rocks for years, probably for centuries for all we know. We will not stand idly by and see them expelled from Inchcolm. We are totally opposed to this proposed development, and we will be relentless in pursuing those who support it.'

No one was able to speak for the monks. However, the monk who appeared to be in charge showed produced a printed statement in response to questioning. It indicated that the monks were unable to speak as they had taken a vow of silence, but that they wished the abbey to be restored. To quote from the statement: 'Inchcolm was an absolutely beautiful abbey. To see these walls rise again, to see the beauty of the church and the chapter house would be marvellous. Just think of how educational it would be for people to see how an abbey actually functioned. Think how many tourists it would bring to the island. Restored, this abbey would be an ideal place to worship in the midst of the noise and violence of the world.' Should the restoration not proceed, according to this piece, the monks might organize a hunger strike or a sit-in in the cloister.

On one issue the various groups all seemed to agree. It has been rumoured for several days that the remains of one identified monk has been discovered by Davis Lane, the expert on the abbey. The remains of a fifteenth-century canon named 'Gavin' is thought to have been found and disinterred. Many details about Gavin's life have been unearthed by Mr. Lane. All the groups demonstrating yesterday expressed the view that it was morally wrong to disturb his remains.

Lane discovered that he was holding his breath and that his heart was racing. He read the story again and then again for the third time. How on earth had Gavin made it into this story? He decided to throw caution to the wind and ring Naomi.

"Naomi," he said, "I take it that you've read the paper this morning."

"Yes Davis," she said, "I saw it first thing this morning. I couldn't believe it. I was going to ring you but I was afraid, to be honest. The thing about the gulls and seals and monks was bad enough, but I thought you would blow your top when you saw Gavin's name there."

"Tell me how Gavin got there, please," Lane said. "I haven't talked about him to anyone except you, the Mortons, and my wife. How do all these other people know about Gavin?"

"I've been thinking about that," she said. "Do you remember when we were on Inchcolm with James and Sophie and you let them see your little sketch about Gavin? Did James not keep that?"

Lane searched his brain. "Yes, you're right," he said. "James took it out of my hand. I didn't really think anything about it because it's on my PC. Do you think that he might have told someone about Gavin?"

"That's what I'm wondering," Naomi replied. "Let me look into it, will you?"

"Yes, please," Lane answered. "I'm beginning to wish that I had never created Gavin, but I'll be angry with James if he's told some reporter about this."

"Leave it with me," Naomi said, "but don't get too upset about it. I mean, we may have a circus with birds and seals milling about and monks watching on, but you don't need to act as the ringmaster."

Lane hung up the phone, not much comforted by Naomi's assurances. He was surprised that people were already going to such lengths to demonstrate, but more than anything he was angry with himself for allowing James to keep his paper on Gavin. He had intended for Gavin to simplify his understanding of the abbey, but now the fictitious canon was complicating it. He would need to wait to see if Naomi could clarify things. Now, the major concern was how to break the news of the demonstration to Katriona. It was too much to hope that perhaps she wouldn't see the newspaper or watch the television news. He would need to make a plan.

Katriona came in early that afternoon, but fortunately he was ready.

"Hey, welcome home," he said, giving her a hug. "How was your day?"

Katriona took off her jacket and hung it onto the hook in the hall. "Pretty much as usual," she said. "Drug abuse, anti-social behaviour, truancy, plus a meeting that went on beyond its shelf life."

"Sorry," Lane said, "but listen, I've got two bits of good news."

"Really, she said, brightening up. "Tell me."

"First," he said, "we're having your favourite tonight, sea bass."

"Great," she said. "That's nice. You went all the way to the fish shop?"

"Just for you," he said.

"Thank you," Katriona said. "What's number two?"

"Well," Lane answered, shaking his head dismissively, it's this story in the paper about Inchcolm. Apparently they were all out demonstrating at South Queensferry yesterday, lions, bears and monks. It's very funny. You'll need to read it sometime."

"Well," Katriona said, "I might as well read it now. We're not in any great rush for dinner are we?"

"Well, no," Lane answered, "but some things are nearly ready. I wouldn't want to hold dinner much longer. You could wait and read it tomorrow."

"No," she said, "it shouldn't take long. Where is the paper?"

Lane busied himself at the worktop, glancing at her now and then out of the corner of his eye. Unfortunately, she wasn't laughing.

"Davis," she said, putting down the paper, "this is awful. It's not funny at all. It was one thing when they were demonstrating against Morton. But now they're going to be demonstrating against you. You're going to be right in the middle of all this . . . this conflict. I don't want that. They've been at South Queensferry. The next thing you know they'll be here in Inverkeithing. Do you want that? Beyond that, I don't understand this about Gavin."

Chapter Sixteen

Thread

It had been yet another largely sleepless night. Lane had tossed and turned in bed trying to get the images of menacing gulls and whiskered seals out of his head. He kept having conversations with hooded monks, explaining to them that they were canons rather than monks and that they weren't bound by a vow of silence. 'Speak up for restoration,' he kept saying to them. He finally gave up, got up and made the breakfast, trying to formulate a plan of action. Katriona was silent over her cereal and coffee, clearly not in the best of moods. He jumped when the phone rang just after nine.

"Mr. Lane," the voice said, "it's Steven Swinton here. I'd like to interview to you again about this latest turn in the Morton project. Have you seen my article about the demos? Would it be possible to have a word today?"

"No," Lane said.

"I'm sorry," Swinton responded. "Do you mean 'No, it's not possible today,' or 'No it isn't possible at all'?"

"I mean, 'No, I want to question you first.'" Lane said. "I'm really annoyed by this Gavin material in your article. When can you get here?"

"Oh I see," Swinton said, a defensive note sounding. "I suppose I could be there early afternoon if that's OK."

"I think you should make it late morning," Lane said.

"I'll do my best," Swinton said and hung up.

Lane stared out the window. The sun was trying hard to break through a cloud bank in the east, but overhead there were ragged patches of blue sky. A plane followed the Forth as it descended on its way towards Edinburgh Airport. It was difficult to come up with a plan of what he ought to do next. His mind kept focussing on the images of the protestors and the story about Gavin. The whole thing was getting out of hand and he couldn't figure out how to get it under control again. The doorbell rang just after eleven and Lane opened the door to the reporter, leading him through to the lounge. It was difficult to be courteous. Swinton had a blue anorak with white strips down the sleeves, no tie on a white shirt. Lane didn't offer to take his jacket.

"First of all, Lane said, "I want to know where you got the story about Gavin."

Swinton shook his head. "I'm sorry," he said, "but you must know that I can't reveal my sources."

"Look," Lane said, "you know very well that the information in that story came from me. It's fiction, pure fiction. I only made up Gavin in order to get some kind of handle on the history of the abbey. It was just a way of personalizing things, just as you might . . ." Lane was struggling to find an analogy. " . . . just as you might personalize the toolbar on your laptop. He was just a means of access to a community and a way of life. He simply helped me to ask certain questions about the monastery. Gavin doesn't exist. He isn't real. He never did exist."

"Well, the way it was written, Gavin looked pretty real to me," Swinton said.

Lane couldn't believe it. "So you actually saw my paper, the thing I wrote," Lane asked? "You saw my sketch on Gavin and just used it for your own purposes?"

Swinton looked at Lane and smiled a little guiltily. "Yes, I did see it," he said. "I confess, but it was so well written that it had me convinced."

"O come on," Lane said. "Don't try to flatter me. You knew that it was fiction and figured that it would spice up your story a little. You just used it without any further confirmation."

Swinton was silent.

"Now, what I really want to know," Lane said, "is how you got your hands on that paper. Who let you see it?"

"Well, I have to be honest with you," Swinton said. "James Morton told me about it, and when I said that I'd like to read it, he gave it to me."

"James Morton gave it to you?" Lane said.

"That's it," Swinton said, "but I don't see what the fuss is about. It's a good story."

"It's fiction," Lane responded. "Surely you can see the difference between truth and fiction."

"Mr. Lane," Swinton answered, "I think that you're a bit behind the times. The line between truth and fiction has become about as reliable as a line in the sand when the tide's coming in. The two things are always merging these days." He sat up straighter and leaned forward. "Look, I'm only a lowly reporter. I've done that for a long time now. I've thought about chucking in this job and really trying to write some good stuff, a novel, you know. And every time I make some notes about what I think might make a good story, reality shoulders its way in. You've no idea. Some true story comes along that's so similar that it blows my story line away. The truth these days really is stranger than fiction."

Lane listened, not unsympathetically, as Swinton went on.

"I mean," he said, "take this thing about the gulls screeching and the seals moaning and then the monk nearly decapitating a gull. If I wrote that as fiction you would say that it was too fantastical, wouldn't you? In fact, take this whole project by Alexander Morton and look at it in the light of day: build a golf course and hotel and casino in a beautiful place next to a ruined monastery? Do you not think that strains credulity past the breaking point? Yet, there it is, on Morton's drawing board. And because this man has money and ambition he may well bring it about. You see what I mean about truth and fiction merging?"

Lane felt a wave of sympathy for the man, not a big wave, not a surfing wave, but a little one nevertheless. "Yes, I do know what you mean, but you did go overboard about Gavin."

"Yes, I suppose so," Swinton acknowledged, "but it seemed close to the real thing and it was a good story."

"OK," Lane said, "but I'd like you to put things right again. Let's put Gavin back into the box. Make some kind of retraction in the paper."

"I'll do what I can," Swinton said. "The trouble is that the editor really liked that story. He may not be very happy to make a retraction."

"I'm not concerned about your editor," Lane said. "I just want people to have the facts about this project. We need the issues clearly laid out in order to come to a decision. That's my job and I want to do it well. There is another thing, Mr. Swinton." Lane looked steadily at the man.

"Yes, what's that?" Swinton asked.

"The person I relate to in this job is continuously worried about security. I keep having to look over my shoulder and I'm tired of it. I want your assurance now that neither my landline nor my mobile will be tapped or hacked or whatever else your people sometimes get up to. Can you give me that assurance?"

"Mr. Lane," Swinton answered, "I don't even know your mobile number, but I think I can say that I'm pretty sure that your phone isn't tapped."

"Is that the best you can do?" Lane asked.

"Look," Swinton said, "us guys in the field, the ones who do the legwork, we don't always know what goes on behind our backs. Like I was saying before, even in the operations of the newsroom truth can be stranger than fiction."

Lane was on the phone to Naomi as soon as Swinton left. "Have you found out anything about how Gavin got into the picture?" he asked.

"Alas, not much," she said. "I have talked to Sophie and she said she didn't know anything about it. I asked to speak to James, but he seems to be unavailable at the moment. I think he's enjoying some of Edinburgh's hotspots just now. Sorry."

"No, it's all right," Lane said. "I know how it happened. I just talked to Steven Swinton, the reporter. He confessed that James had simply given him by little blurb about Gavin."

"Really," Naomi said? "He handed your paper over just like that?"

"Apparently so," Lane responded. "I can't figure out why he would do that because it surely wouldn't improve his case for the project. I'm inclined to think that it is just James wanting to be important. Anyway, Swinton promised me that he would try to make it clear that Gavin is fiction, but I'm not absolutely convinced."

"I see," Naomi said. "At least now we know how it happened. Maybe Gavin will now die a natural death so we won't have to worry about it."

"Maybe," Lane answered, "but somehow I'm not as confident as you. Anyway, what else is happening?"

"We're in suspended animation," Naomi said. "Everyone is just waiting for the great man to arrive. For all the preparation and suspense it might as well be the president of the United States coming in to town."

"It's that bad?" Lane asked.

"It's that bad," Naomi answered. "You should see my boss, pacing up and down, flitting about here and there, consulting with important people. He's like a cat on a hot tin roof. I think that we have reached Plan F, where F stands for Farce."

Lane couldn't help laughing and it brought some relief. "I'm sorry," he said. "What do you want me to do now?"

"Try to avoid gulls and seals," she answered. Stay away from monks. Watch the space around the Caledonian Hotel. Wait a little longer and then brace yourself again."

They had a more serious talk that night, Lane and Katriona. He told her about his conversations with Swinton and Naomi.

"Davis," she said, "please tell me how this is going to end up. I feel that you, we, are getting drawn into something that's intruding into our life together. I see enough shouting in the homes I visit in Fife. Now I see all these people shouting on behalf of birds or seals or monks or whatever. Next thing you know they'll be here shouting at you. I don't want that."

"I know," Lane said, "and I feel that way too. But they're really aiming at Alexander Morton. When he gets here he'll draw all the fire. I can't really see this going on for very much longer, and then we can get back to normal."

"I hope you're right," Katriona said, but she was shaking her head.

Chapter Seventeen

Morton

The next day turned out to be the big day. When Lane switched on the news at noon he saw Alexander Morton's private jet landing at Edinburgh airport. There was a line of protestors outside the airport door, the bird people and seal people mostly, holding up their signs, **ABORT MORT,** and **GIVE HIM AN INCH AND HE'LL TAKE YOUR SMILE.** The commentary was largely drowned out by the noise of the protestors. Lane watched as Alexander Morton came through the airport door led by several policemen and accompanied by James, Sophie and another man. Morton stopped for a moment, looked around, smiled, and waved to onlookers. The police gently but firmly made a way through the protestors to allow the entourage to cross the bus lane and proceed to a black Bentley in the pickup lane. Preceded by two cops on motorcycles they quickly pulled away. Minutes later the coverage moved over to the Caledonia Hotel, where Morton and the others were seen arriving at the front door on Rutland Street. He was greeted by the manager at the front door and whisked into the hotel. The report went on to summarize Morton's plans for Inchcolm and reported that he would be meeting with representative groups over the next several days. Lane switched off and felt his pulse quicken.

Later in the afternoon when the phone rang, he knew it was Naomi.

"Hello Naomi," he said.

"No," the voice said. "It's not Naomi. It's Sophie here, Sophie Morton."

"Oh, sorry," Lane answered. "I thought it was Naomi. I don't know why. I saw you on the news a little while ago. Anyway, how are you?"

"That's OK, Mr. Lane," Sophie said. "I suppose you know that Daddy's here now. He arrived this morning. We've given him an update of your research into the abbey and he wants to meet you. Could you do that?"

"Yes, Sophie, of course," Lane said. "I'll be happy to meet him and give him any information that's relevant."

"Great," Sophie said. "What about tomorrow afternoon at the Caledonian Hotel. Do you know it?"

"That's fine, Sophie," Lane answered. "I know it, and I'll be there. Will you be around?"

"Oh yes," she answered. "James and I will both be here. Now that the boss is here we won't get any free time at all."

"I'm sorry to hear that," Lane said. "By the way, Sophie, I do need to speak to James about something important when I come."

"OK, I'll tell him," she said, "See you tomorrow."

Up early the next morning, Lane tried to prepare himself for the meeting. He printed some of the more important notes he'd made and also printed out his narrative on Gavin. It shouldn't be necessary, but it probably wouldn't hurt. He shouldn't be nervous about this meeting, but he was: that sinking feeling in the pit of the stomach that he sometimes used to get when he was performing at some important service or occasion. He had decided to take the train in. There would be scant parking at the west end, and even if he found a space it would be expensive. He would get off the train at Haymarket and walk the rest of the way.

The train arrived and left on time and it wasn't crowded. He picked up the free paper and read the front page to divert his mind for a while. The day was actually very pleasant, a blue sky and a cool breeze from the east. The Forth sparkled as he crossed the rail bridge. Haymarket Station was fronted by a maze of yellow and red barricades separating off the tram work from the station. You had to think ahead and plan your route in just in order to get across the roads. Lane walked along towards Shandwick Place, dodging pedestrians and looking into the occasional shop window. He was still a little early. The Caledonian Hotel was an imposing red sandstone building standing sedately at the west end of Princes Street, at the corner of Rutland Street. The noise hit him as he rounded the corner into Rutland Street. A chain of protestors blocked the entrance to the hotel. People in gull's heads were screeching and waving signs. The seals were there, groaning beside the gulls. Several yards along from the birds and animals were a half-dozen monks, holding up signs asking for the abbey to be restored. Lane noticed that there were also a number of people holding up signs reading, **Say Yes to Mort**, and **Inchcolm Means Jobs**. Several policemen stood between the two groups in order to keep them separated. Standing in front of the demonstrators, the doorman in his nineteenth-century blue suit and top hat seemed agitated and red in the face. Dealing with a demonstration was not in his job description at the Caley. A policeman stood watching at either side of the entrance. Lane tried to think what to do. It wouldn't be easy to get through the line without calling attention to himself. He watched for a few moments and decided that there might be a better way. He walked down Rutland Street and scanned the entrance to Henry J. Bean's pub. Bean's was really a part of the hotel, but had its own separate entrance. There were several people standing near the entrance, but they weren't demonstrating and no one was blocking the way. This surely had to be a better way in. Lane put on his *I know exactly where I'm going* look and strode through the door. One of the men standing near the entrance studied him but offered no resistance. Lane wandered through the pub and out into the hotel to the reception desk. When he told the desk clerk that he had an appointment to see Alexander Morton, she rang the room and informed him that he could go up. "It's the top floor." she said. "When you leave the lift, turn right. It's the King Suite at the end of the corridor." As he ascended in the lift, Lane thought of a wedding in the hotel that continued to live in his memory. It had begun well, featuring the music of a string quartet. But once the bride and groom were in place, the event had been spoiled by a pushy photographer who kept getting in his way. The photographer moved first to his right and then to his left, then under him and then behind him. The wedding became merely a photo opportunity, not a coming together of two people.

Lane knocked on the door and it was opened by Sophie. She was dressed down that day, blue jeans and a black and white striped top. The man he had seen accompanying the Mortons at the airport was standing beside her. Slightly shorter than Lane, but very broad with a prop forward's neck; surely this couldn't be Alexander Morton.

"Hi Davis, come in, please," she said, grabbing his hand. "It's great to see you." She gestured towards the man beside her, "This is Lanson Brand, Daddy's PA." Brand looked Lane up and down, then shook his hand without smiling. The man had a vice for a hand and a small tattoo on the wrist. He released Lane and returned to a chair in the corner. This guy, Lane thought, must be the minder. Sophie led him into the suite, where one large window looked out onto Edinburgh Castle. Two steps led up to another part of the suite, featuring a smaller window which looked down onto St Cuthbert's Parish Church. James sat at a desk on the upper level studying a monitor.

"James," Sophie said, "it's Mr. Lane."

James turned briefly and looked at him. "Hi," he said and turned back to the monitor.

Sophie motioned to the couch and invited Lane to sit. She sat down in the chair opposite.

"How are you?" she said.

"I'm fine," Lane responded. "How are you? Have you been able to get some time to see the sights?"

"Yes, I've been all over the place," Sophie said. "Edinburgh's wonderful, so different from Manhattan."

A door opened, and a man came into the room whom Lane took to be Alexander Morton. He was not quite what Lane had visualised. Morton was shorter than expected, but trim and athletic, reminding Lane of a physical education teacher he'd once had in high school. Short dark hair flecked with grey, receding slightly in the middle of his head, but doing fine on the sides. He wore an expensive blue suit and light blue shirt, open at the neck. He moved quickly towards Lane and gave the impression of being in charge of everything in the room. He arrived at Lane and held out his hand, firm grip.

"So this is Davis Lane," he said. "Alexander Morton. My friends call me Mort. I'm glad to meet you finally. I've been hearing a lot about you lately."

"Glad to meet you," Lane said. "I've been hearing a fair bit about you too."

"Oh, I'm sure you have," Morton said, the flash of a smile, "and most of it will be negative I bet."

"Well, no, not all of it," Lane said, trying to be gracious.

"Sophie's got quite a thing about you," Morton said. "She's been telling me about your research into the abbey. I keep hearing about 'Mr. Lane' this and 'Mr. Lane' that."

"Oh well, that's good," Lane said, embarrassed. He wanted to ask if James had been heaping praise on him as well but managed to restrain himself.

"And you're a golfer I believe?" Morton asked.

"Well," Lane answered, "I do play, but not very well."

"Tell me about it," Morton said. "Well, that's enough small talk. Let's get down to business." He took Lane's elbow and manoeuvred him to a seat at the table. Lane was surprised to see Morton move round and take the chair in the very corner, so that he was looking back into the room instead of outside. After all, the window provided one of the most spectacular views in the city. Then he recalled one of McCord's pieces of information. *Morton never sits with his back towards the door or a window.*

"So, do you know all that we're intending to do on Inchcolm?" Morton asked.

"I've talked to Sophie and James," Lane answered. "I've heard about your plans in general terms from news reports, and I also talked to Callum McBain about the course design."

"Good, good," Morton said. "And what do you think?" Lane was struck by the intensity of his gaze.

Lane wasn't sure how he ought to answer if he were to maintain and underline his neutrality. "Very interesting," he said, "but also very challenging. It's not going to be easy."

"No, of course," Morton said, "but these things never are easy. My philosophy has always been that obstacles are there to be overcome. Now, let me show you exactly what we have in mind."

Morton stood up and looked over to James. "James," he said, "stop being a recluse and bring the laptop over here for Davis to see."

James rose from the desk, rather reluctantly Lane thought, and moved to the table carrying his laptop.

"James has been working with the architect and with his geek friend in order to produce some images of the restored abbey and the new golf course," Morton said. "Let's look at the plans for the abbey first."

James pressed several keys on the keyboard and brought up an external image of the ruined abbey. The camera circled slowly, revealing the partially standing walls and the foundations. James pressed another key and the computer began slowly to build up walls, add beams, restore windows and the roof. Lane found himself saying 'Wow' under his breath. It was one thing to study the foundations and mentally imagine walls and roofs, doors and windows. It was quite another to see the abbey as it must have been, a genuinely beautiful structure on this island. James pressed yet another key and the camera began to move around the restored abbey on a 360 degree tour. Lane was entranced. It was all there, the cloister and cloister garden, the high walls of the church, the octagonal sides of the chapter house. Lane was moved. The whole thing was stunning.

"Well, what do you think?" Morton asked.

"I'm amazed," Lane answered. "It really is absolutely beautiful. You've done a great job."

"Oh," Morton said, "it's James here. He's the expert on the computer. I'm an ignoramus with the thing, but he's mastered it."

Lane looked at James, who glanced up at him, showing a small smile.

"Right, James," Morton said, "Take us inside." James pressed several more keys and the camera went inside the chapter house and then the church. The nave and transepts began to appear, then the gothic arches supporting the roof.

"We're not done yet with the interiors," James said. 'It's harder to structure the inside of the complex because we don't have as much to go on, but this gives you an idea."

"Well," Morton said, "this is what I want the abbey to look like after we get done with it. We'll go on working on the interiors until we're satisfied. It's important that we do it as accurately as possible. But you can see just how big a job this is, so we need to bring in stonemasons, carpenters and various kinds of craftsmen. Now, let's have a look at the hotel."

James pressed several more keys and a rectangular building appeared.

"This is the hotel and casino," Morton said. "Sophie's been working on this."

Lane couldn't recognize the location of the building on the monitor. "Where is this exactly?" he asked.

"You know where the gift shop and toilets are now?" Sophie came in. "They're going to be demolished since they're pretty unattractive anyway. Then the hotel will be built in their place and extended right into the hill behind. As you can see the building has quite a low profile so that it doesn't spoil the site. Some of the rooms at the very back will be dark, but we accept this as the price we have to pay to maintain the profile. We've got the architect working on this issue."

"The casino will be in the hotel interior," Morton said, "apart from the high-roller's poker room. There will be the standard poker room within the casino, but I'm planning another poker room that will be the most exclusive room in the world. It'll be in the chapter house. Obviously the game won't be going on during the day, so it won't intrude upon the sanctity of the place. But it will come into its own after ten at night. The carpet and the table will be specially made and brought in, as well as special lighting. Never mind the Concord in Vienna or the Aviation Club in Paris or even the Bellagio in Vegas, this will be the place for the high rollers to play. Maximum of eight players and a thousand pounds entry."

Lane looked at Morton and raised an eyebrow. "I hate to say it," he said, "but you could encounter problems there."

"Why's that?" Morton asked. "What's the problem?"

"The problem is one of the chapter house rules," Lane answered.

"How's that?" Morton asked.

"I'm sure," Lane answered, "that one of the abbey chapter house rules would say that games using dice or chess in the abbey should be avoided, any game in which something might be lost. I think you would have to agree that while poker doesn't involve dice, money will definitely be lost."

Morton was studying him, quiet for a moment. "Are you sure about this?" he asked.

"Yes, Lane said, "I'm sure about it."

"It doesn't matter does it?" James said. "We're not in the sixteenth century now."

"No, it does matter," Morton said. "I don't want to defame the abbey. I'll have to think about this. The poker room is very important to the whole plan. Thanks for pointing that out Davis. I don't want to create any more issues then there are already."

Silence fell over the group for perhaps half a minute. James and Sophie looked at their father who was obviously deep in thought. He finally looked up at Lane. "OK, we'll deal with that. Now let's move on now to the golf course. McBain has told you all about it has he?"

"He gave me a pretty good rundown," Lane answered. "I didn't see how you could get an eighteen hole course on such a small island, but he showed me how you intend to do it. I hadn't thought of artificial peninsulas or islands."

"No, of course not," Morton said, "but people need to think out of the box, and they don't tend to do that. I had to learn that a long time ago. Anyway, this is going to be a great course. It may be a short course, but it will be difficult, believe me. There will be more challenging holes on this course than any other in the world."

"It's being written up as the holiest course in the world," Lane suggested.

"Well, yes," Morton said, "but I don't remember using those words myself. We're naming the holes after Scottish saints, but that doesn't make the course holy. It's my little tribute to Scotland. I just like to think of it as being different from any other course I've ever seen."

"I follow you," Lane said.

"Now," Morton said, "We've done the specifics, but I want to provide a kind of overview of things for you. What does this development mean for Scotland? That's the question that people have to ask. First of all, it means jobs. In the initial period, the construction and restoration project, I figure that it could mean seven to eight hundred jobs, both on the island and onshore. Remember that we need to transport lots of materials to the island. I'm looking at establishing a base at Burntisland, where there is a vacant building and a deep harbour. There will be jobs there. We'll need to widen and deepen the harbour at Inchcolm, so there will be jobs there. The building of the course will take lots of work, and much of that will be the laborious type, so that will benefit people without particular skills. Now, these are jobs that will last perhaps two to three years. We'll need to improve the ferry service from South Queensferry and add another service from Fife, maybe from Inverkeithing or Aberdour, so that's more jobs. Then when the abbey is done and the hotel built and the course done, there will be jobs for hotel clerks and chambermaids and casino workers and green keepers and so on. I figure that there could be over two hundred permanent jobs involved. You can see what that means for Fife and Lothian in this economic climate."

Morton was winding up rapidly to his subject. Lane watched as he grew more animated. Sophie and James were silent, rapt in their attention. "But now listen," he went on, "just think about what this means for Scotland. Most every plane that flies into Edinburgh airport flies over Inchcolm. People are going to look out their window, see this island and say, 'I want to go there.' You realize that every ocean-going liner that goes up to anchor at the bridges goes past Inchcolm, so every passenger on that ship is going to look at the island and say, 'I want to go there.' And every serious poker player in the world is going to say, 'I want to play at Inchcolm.' Now, I think you can see that this is going to bring in millions and millions of pounds for the Scottish economy. And this is not a short-term thing. You're going to have a restored abbey and a great golf course to attract people for years to come. Do you see what I'm getting at?"

Lane had to nod his agreement. "Yes, I do see," he said. James and Sophie were nodding as if they were hearing this for the first time. The man did have vision and charisma. Still, Morton had not really acknowledged the now quite obvious problems. Lane felt they had to be mentioned.

"Mr. Morton," Lane said, "When I arrived at the hotel there were demonstrators at the entrance. I believe that they were protesting against your development plans on behalf of the bird and seal populations on the island. What are you going to do about that?"

"Davis," Morton answered, "please call me *Mort*. Birds and seals. Yes, we'll have to deal with these issues. I do understand that people are concerned, but on all my projects I've managed to solve these problems. As far as the seals are concerned, we're going to build and fix soft platforms for them."

"Soft platforms?" Lane queried.

"Soft platforms," Morton responded. "As you know, at the moment the seals lie on the buoy platforms, which are hard. It can't be all that comfortable for them. Better than rocks I suppose, but still pretty hard. We're going to construct floating metal platforms covered with thick waterproof material and fix them to the sea bed. It's not difficult because it's very shallow in that area. This is the same reason we can build artificial islands fairly easily. The seals will be lying on cushions, so I think that they'll find their relaxed style of life much enhanced. The seal people are afraid that this development will drive the seals away. Well, just the opposite: seals from all over the place will want to come to Inchcolm because it's so comfortable."

Lane had to stop himself from grinning. What an idea! But, he supposed, it was feasible.

"Now, as for the birds," Morton went on, "it is more difficult. I'm consulting several experts about the possibility of colony definition."

"Colony definition?" Lane asked.

"Colony definition," Morton repeated. "The experts say that there might be a way of improving or marking the territories of the several species in order to persuade them to stay within certain bounds. Obviously we don't want seagulls lifting golf balls from the greens and placing them in nests. That would confuse both the golfers and the birds. This sounds a little dubious to me, so I'm taking it with a grain of salt until I hear more from the experts. If it doesn't work then I would hope that the birds will move on. There are plenty of other places for them along the Forth."

Morton leaned back against the wall. "Now, Davis," he said, "you're probably wondering why I'm so keen on this. I would have to be, wouldn't I, with these people outside demonstrating against me?"

"Yes, I do wonder," Lane answered, "because these people are really very serious and very determined and they have important moral concerns. I can't see them giving up easily."

"Yes," Morton answered, "I know that. I respect their views, but let me tell you why this is so important to me."

"OK, go ahead," Lane said.

"My great-great grandfather came from Scotland," Morton said. "In fact, he came from Fife, somewhere around Leven I think. He told stories that came down to me, and these stories indicated that the Morton name was connected with the de Mortimers. You know about that family, I think?"

"Oh yes," Lane answered, "I know a lot about them."

"Well," Morton went on, "I always felt that because of that I'm really a Scot, and that I owe something to Scotland, especially to Fife. So when I saw Inchcolm I knew this was it. I had to develop this island." Morton leaned forward and smiled. "That's it, that's the greatest part of the story."

"Right," Lane said. "I see. Thanks for telling me that. But what do you mean when you say that it's only *part* of the story?"

"I'm just coming to that," Morton said. "To be completely honest with you, ego is involved as well. There are a couple of other guys who develop property on this same sort of scale. If you've done your research well you'll know who I'm talking about. The three of us sometimes go head to head in a property game, trying to outdo each other. We've done that in Vegas and also in Cancun. It's a game with us, just like poker. One of my competitors focuses on art, so he's got great art in his hotels. The other one loves golf, so he goes for golf courses. I like golf as well, but I also love history, so I like to incorporate as much history into my places as possible. I went for the Mayan culture at Cancun. Anyway, that's what appeals to me about Inchcolm. To bring back a part of the medieval culture really enthuses me. So now you've got the whole story. Anyway I think it's time for a break."

Morton offered coffee sent up to the suite and the four of them talked for a while about the agencies and institutions Morton would need to deal with. Having already agreed to meet Morton on the island soon, Lane decided finally that it was time to make an exit. He stood up but then hesitated. "Oh, James, I almost forgot. You remember that little thing I wrote about Gavin, a bit of fiction?"

"Yeah, sure," James answered. "*Gavin.* I like it: *Gavin the Canon* I call it. What about it?"

"I think that I gave you the piece assuming that you would read it and keep it under your hat. But somehow it seems to have been picked up by the media. Some people think that Gavin is a real person and that's confusing things."

"Sorry, what is this about?" Morton asked.

"Oh, Davis wrote a thing about a monk," James said. "I just liked the sound of it, you know. And then I thought: canon, like *cannon*, like Mon's Meg Cannon up in the castle, the one we saw the other day. And then it progressed to *Gavin the loose Canon*. I thought it was a kind of neat idea so I passed it on to a reporter. I didn't really think it mattered."

"Who exactly is Gavin?" Morton asked.

"Gavin is a fictional canon at the abbey," Lane replied. "I just created him in order to ask the right questions about daily life there. I made a narrative about him and he kind of took on a life of his own. But when James gave the paper on Gavin to a reporter, some people thought that he was real."

"I see, or at least I think I do," Morton said. "I'll need to study this. Do you still have a copy?"

"Well, yes I do," Lane said, "but I don't want this issue to get any larger."

"No, I understand," Morton said. "If you give me the paper on Gavin I can read it and sort things out. OK?"

Lane reached into his pocket and pulled the paper out reluctantly. "I'll give it to you, but please read it and then discard it. Gavin is fictional. He is not real."

"That's fine," Morton said. "I get it. Don't worry about it."

"OK, I'll leave it with you," Lane said, "but I really don't want any more confusion about Gavin. Anyway, I think it's time that I was on my way. Thanks for showing me your plans and for being so straightforward about things."

Lane shook hands with Morton and James and turned to leave.

"I'll walk you to the elevator," Sophie said. As they moved to the door Lanson Brand stood up and nodded to Lane.

"What's with the name of your dad's minder?" Lane asked Sophie as they waited for the lift.

"Lanson?" Sophie answered. "Oh it's a good story. Lanson was a professional wrestler, quite a good one I think. He made a good living at it but then needed to find something else when he got too old. Once when Daddy was in Vegas they met, and Daddy offered him a job. He's a bit overbearing at times but fiercely loyal. Anyway, the story goes that when he was born some friends of his parents came by to congratulate them and brought a bottle of champagne. Lanson's father had never opened champagne before, so when he tried to take the cork out, it blew, and the cork hit his forehead and left a mark. His parents thought this must be some kind of sign and named their baby Lanson."

Lane had to laugh. "Oh well," he said, "I guess it could have been worse."

"How is that?" Sophie asked.

"Well," Lane answered, "I suppose the champagne could have been Bollinger or Dom Perignon." Sophie was laughing as Lane stepped into the lift.

Lane strode through the lobby reflecting on the meeting. He had to admit that in spite of his earlier preconceptions he was impressed with Alexander Morton. The man did appear to have and to exercise values as well as entrepreneurship. He reflected on his conversation as he walked through the hotel lobby and past reception. But as soon as the front door of the hotel opened for him, Lane realized his mistake. The line of protestors was still there, looking facing him, and in the centre of the line was a man Lane recognized from television news. What was his name again, "Falconer" or something like that? He was staring right at Lane.

That evening, when Katriona came home, Lane made her a gin and tonic. He poured himself a dram. "It's possible," he said, "that I might even have a second one of these tonight."

"Now, let's see," Katriona said. "Why would you want to do that?"

"Well, I met with the great man today," Lane said.

"Oh, of course," Katriona said. "I'm sorry. I forgot all about that. Give me the whole dramatic narrative. What was he like?"

"Well, I have to say that I was impressed," Lane answered. "He's a nice looking guy, quite intense and very much in charge. He has vision and imagination and drive. He's perceptive and larger than life. The images he's produced of the restored abbey are marvellous."

"So you liked him?" Katriona asked.

"Yes, in a way. We got on all right," Lane answered. "I will tell you one thing though."

"What's that?" she asked.

"If Alexander Morton had been in charge of the tram project in Edinburgh the trams would be running by now."

Chapter Eighteen
Fracture

Lane couldn't believe that it could have been organized so quickly. When he and Katriona were in the middle of their meal that same evening they heard noises from the front of the house. They went to the front window and peered out. The sky was darkening, and in the west a jagged line of red capped the hills. In the foreground he was astonished to see a line of protestors stretched across the *cul de sac* behind his driveway. Lane could see a dozen people waving signs and shouting. The bird people were there with their **Save our Seabirds** signs. The seal people were there with their **Save our Seals** signs. Lane opened the door and moved out to the front porch. They were used to an almost total quiet in the evenings, apart from the occasional car turning in the *cul de sac*. Now, on the front porch in this quiet neighbourhood, the shouting was quite startling. Lane wasn't surprised to see the neighbours on either side standing on their porches as well. Jennifer, his neighbour to the right, called to him.

"Davis, what on earth is going on?"

"I'm not sure, Jennifer," he called back, "but I'll find out." This didn't seem like the time to provide a lengthy explanation.

When Lane got down to the group he recognized Morris Falconer, the man who had been at the Caledonian and had spotted Lane coming out of the hotel. He walked straight to him.

"I know you," Lane said to Falconer, a tall bald man with a long face.

"And I know you," Falconer responded. "You were at the Caledonian Hotel this morning doing your dirty business."

"Why are you people demonstrating outside of my house?" Lane asked.

"Because you're aiding and abetting Alexander Morton in destroying Inchcolm," Falconer said.

"But I'm not supporting Morton," Lane said. "I was only asked to do research into the abbey in order to give advice. I'm a theologian, not a developer."

"I don't think so," Falconer said, pointing angrily to Lane. "I think you're in his pocket. I saw you sneaking into the hotel to cosy up to him this morning."

"Could you perhaps ask your people to stop shouting so that we could have a reasonable conversation?" Lane asked.

"Aye, I'll ask them to be quiet," Falconer said, "but only for a minute or two. The shouting will only stop once this project is stopped." He turned towards the demonstrators and held his index finger to his lips.

"Thank you," Lane said. "Now maybe we can have a sensible conversation. Look, I'm neither for nor against this thing at the moment. I'm simply there to advise both sides on the nature and history of the abbey. You're barking up the wrong tree if you think that protesting outside my house will do any good."

"You may know something about the abbey, Lane," Falconer said, "but do you know anything about the seabirds on the island? Have you given any thought to them? Did you know that Inchcolm hosts more species of seabird than almost any other island in the Forth? Did you know that at least a dozen species make their nests there and live there and that some of them are endangered? I'll bet that you didn't know that, Lane, and I'll bet that you don't give a damn because you're being handsomely rewarded by Alexander Morton."

"I did actually know some of those things, Mr. Falconer," Lane said, "and I do value the bird life and the other wildlife, but I did also hope that you and I could talk sensibly about the issue rather than shout at each other."

"What is there to talk about, Lane?" Falconer said, holding out upturned hands in a gesture of hopelessness. "It's really only about seabirds. Morton's development will destroy their habitat and we're not going to allow it. Tell him to go off and build his golf course and casino somewhere else."

"But surely, Mr. Falconer," Lane said, "it's not only about birds. What about the abbey? Wouldn't you like to see it restored? What about the other heritage sites that could be maintained if Historic Scotland gets income from Inchcolm? Would you not like to see some other important sites benefit? What about people, their jobs and living conditions? Do you not care about these things as well?"

"Look," Falconer came back, "we care about the seabirds on this island. We are their voice. They can't discuss things or argue their case in the corridors or power. We are the voice of the birds and we say no. OK?"

At that Morris Falconer turned his back on Lane and with his hands cupped around his mouth shouted to the demonstrators to begin again. "Let's go, everybody," he said. And the shouting began again. This time it was a well-rehearsed unison chant: *Morton-No, Morton-No. Morton-No, No, No.* Lane turned and made his way up the driveway and back into the house.

Katriona had been watching at the door and moved aside for him to come in.

"Davis, what was that all about?" she said.

"Well," he responded, "that was Mr. Morris Falconer. According to their signs, they represent the *Forth Seabird Society*. He seems to be speaking for them and apparently for the seal people as well. I was trying to reason with him but it was pretty difficult. He accused me of being in the pocket of Alexander Morton."

"And did you set him straight?" she asked.

"I tried to," Lane said, "but he wasn't much into listening to me. I was trying to say to him that there were a number of moral issues involved, but he only wants to see one: the seabirds. I didn't really enjoy that confrontation."

"Davis," Katriona said, "we don't want confrontations like that. This isn't really your battle to fight, and I don't want you to have to deal with people like that. Is this going to go on and on forever? Are we going to have demonstrators outside every day and night now until this thing comes to an end?"

"I don't really know, Katriona," Lane answered. "I hope not, but I don't know. They seem very determined. However, I think that we should shut the door to block out the noise and then go and finish our meal."

"Fine," Katriona said, looking not at all convinced. "But you'll need to phone the neighbours and explain to them what's happening because they won't have a clue."

"Yes, of course," Lane said. "You're right, although I wouldn't be surprised if they had figured it out by now."

The Lanes finished their meal mostly in silence, each of them reflecting on what had just happened. At eight o'clock Lane went to the front door and looked out. There were no demonstrators, no signs, no shouting. There was, in fact, not a soul to be seen. He heaved a sigh of relief and locked the front door. That was it for the day. Maybe that was it, period. The demonstrators had made their point and they didn't require to do any more. It was quiet. Maybe the Lanes could relax.

The relief held only until ten o'clock precisely. Lane turned on the news and at the same time heard a crash followed by the sound of tinkling glass towards the front of the house. They both ran through to the front hallway. There was nothing amiss there. They moved quickly to the study. In the study there was glass everywhere, on the desk, on the floor and on the top of all the books on the lower shelves of the bookcase. In the middle of the carpet was a stone the size of his fist. Wrapped around the stone was a piece of folded paper, held firmly to the stone with a red rubber band. Lane took out his handkerchief and picked up the stone gingerly. He removed the rubber band and carefully unfolded the note. It read:

LEAVE INCHCOLM ALONE OR YOUR A DEAD MAN

They stood for a moment thinking about the note and looking at the broken glass littering the room. Silence reigned for a full minute.

"Well," Lane said finally, "obviously we'll need to phone the police."

"Yes, *now* please," Katriona said.

Lane found the number for the Inverkeithing Police Station and rang. He was told that someone would be there as soon as possible. In the meantime Katriona began gingerly to brush the broken glass into a dust pan. "We'll need to be careful in here," she said. "It'll take ages before all this is away. We can't come in here without shoes." Eventually she went for the vacuum to run over the carpet.

After about forty-five minutes a policeman and policewoman arrived at the house and rang the bell. Lane went to the front door and asked them in. They introduced themselves as PC Kevin Michie and WPC Joan MacAndrew.

Lane explained that there had been a demonstration outside the house earlier in the evening and who was involved. He told them about his confrontation with Morris Falconer. He showed them the stone and the note.

"Have you handled this?" Michie asked.

"No," Lane said, "at least not with my bare hands. I used a handkerchief to avoid putting my prints on it."

"That was good thinking," Michie said. "We'll get it dusted for prints tomorrow. Someone should come in the morning and do that. I doubt if it will yield anything very useful, but we'll give it a shot."

"Fine," Lane said. "Would there be any prints on the paper?"

"Possibly," Michie said, "but it's doubtful. Whoever did this would probably be careful, wear gloves when they were working it up."

"What do you make of the note?" WPC MacAndrew asked.

"It's difficult to know," Lane responded. "It's a little scary, but I find it hard to take it too seriously."

"But do you think that this was launched through your window by someone who had been here demonstrating?" she asked.

"I don't think so," Lane said.

"Why not?" she asked.

"For two reasons," Lane said. "First of all, the stone was thrown quite a while after they had left. I suppose that one of them could have hung around or come back, but somehow that doesn't seem likely. In the second place, it's the wording on the note."

"You mean the *your* rather than the *you are.*"

"Yes," Lane said, "or even the contraction *you're.*"

"Why is that important?" MacAndrew asked. "Well," Lane said, "the demonstrators were reasonably intelligent people, or at least Morris Falconer seemed to be. He was really the only one I spoke to. He was articulate and he wouldn't have made that kind of grammatical mistake. And I guess I assumed that the other people in the group would be reasonably intelligent as well. I mean, I have respect for the people who want to protect wildlife and so forth. I can't think that they would make that kind of mistake."

"Unless," PC Michie said, "they deliberately wanted you to think that it was someone less intelligent."

"Yes, that's possible," Lane admitted.

"Surely," WPC MacAndrew said, "you must recognize that the stone throwing has to be connected to the demonstration in some way. It can't be a separate or random incident. It's possible be that someone has attached himself to the demonstrators and then taken the chance to exercise his own little piece of vandalism, but the two things surely must be connected."

"Yes," Lane said, "I guess you're right. So what comes next?"

"Someone will come tomorrow to do an inspection of the premises and look for prints." Michie said. "But it looks like the demonstrators may well come back again, and if that happens you probably need police protection."

"You're not serious?" Lane asked.

"Yes, I'm afraid so," Michie said. "We can send several constables up here to protect you and the property."

"Do you really think it's necessary?" Lane asked.

"Read the note again," the constable said. "Do you not think it's necessary?"

Lane sighed and looked at Katriona. "Yes, I suppose so."

"There's one other thing we need to do here," WPC MacAndrew said. "We need to get that window boarded up."

"Yes, I had forgotten about that," Lane said. "But surely we'll have to wait until tomorrow for that."

"No, tonight," Michie said. "We know someone who will do that tonight. Then you two can get to bed. Would you like us to give them a call?"

"Even at this time of the night?" Lane asked.

"Yes, Michie said, "even now. That's their speciality. They do it all the time."

"OK," Lane said. "Give them a call."

At 2:00 AM the joiner arrived with a heavy plywood panel which he quickly fitted over the study window. "That should do it in the meantime," he said.

"Thanks very much for coming in the middle of the night," Lane said.

"That's all right," the joiner said. "I do it all the time, especially in this town. I'll send you a bill."

"Katriona," Lane said as they were getting into bed, "I'm sorry about all this. I didn't think it would turn this ugly."

"I'm a little scared," she said simply, pulling the sheet over her eyes.

"Yes, I know," Lane said. "So am I, but I can't take it too seriously. Surely no one is going to commit murder just because they're unhappy about a golf course on a little island in the Forth."

"No, I agree," Katriona said, bringing the sheet far enough down to speak, "but just because it seems ludicrous to you and me doesn't mean it's not a death threat. Someone out there has threatened your life, Davis."

Chapter Nineteen
U-Turn?

Detective Inspector Malcolm Hewitt arrived at the Lane house late the following morning. He introduced himself and followed Lane through to the study. The plywood boarding blocked out all light to the room. Lane switched on the light and gestured towards the desk. "Here we are," he said.

"You must have had quite a mess in here," Hewitt offered.

"The glass was everywhere," Lane said. "In fact, please be careful because there's got to be some shards left that we haven't found."

Hewitt stepped towards the desk and studied the stone and note. "Is this the offending object?" he asked.

"This is it," Lane responded.

"Have you touched this?" Hewitt asked.

"No," Lane said. "I picked it up and read the note using by my handkerchief."

"OK, good," Hewitt said. He took a pair of plastic gloves from his pocket, put them on, picked up the note, unfolded it and read it. "Ordinary paper, ordinary rubber band and ordinary stone." He placed the items in a plastic bag. "I'll take these and have a look, but I doubt that we will get much mileage from them. I better tell you that it's unlikely we'll ever find out who lobbed this through your window. Sorry about that."

"No, I really thought that's what you would say," Lane said. "but what about the death threat? What do I do about that?"

"You have to take it seriously," Hewitt answered. "Remind me of what happened here last night and what the issue is"

"There was a protest demonstration last night," Lane said. "Several different groups are unhappy about Alexander Morton's plans for Inchcolm. We had people acting as gulls and seals here. It was directed at me because I'm acting as a consultant, even though I'm not really for it or against it at this point."

"Right," Hewitt said. "It's unlikely that anyone would want to take your life over this kind of issue, but you never know. Some of the animal rights people are very serious and very committed."

"Do you really think we ought to have police protection?" Lane asked.

"Yes, I do, at least for the next few days," Hewitt said. "I'll organize that, but I'd like you to phone the station if the demonstrators assemble here before we come to check on you. OK?"

"OK," Lane said.

After D.I. Hewitt had left Lane phoned Naomi. "Naomi, I need to talk to you about my situation here, and it needs to be now, over the phone. I don't want to mess around with a clandestine meeting."

"I understand," Naomi said. "Go ahead then."

"We had a band of demonstrators outside the house last night, shouting, waving their signs and so on. I had a little confrontation with Morris Falconer of the Forth Seabird Society, and then after they left a stone was thrown through the window."

"Oh Davis, I'm sorry," she said.

"Moreover," Lane went on, "there was a note attached to the stone."

"Oh dear," Naomi said.

"Want to know what it said, Naomi?" Lane asked.

"Yes, I guess so," Naomi answered.

"Well, it said 'Leave Inchcolm alone or you're a dead man.'"

"Oh dear," Naomi said.

"Naomi," Lane responded, "it's a little bit more worrying than an 'Oh dear'. We really got quite a fright. We had the police up here last night, then a joiner to board up the window, and a detective here this morning. Things seem to be getting out of hand. I haven't had much direction from you or from your umbrella organization for a while, so I'd really like to know what's happening."

"Yes, of course, Davis," she said. "I do understand and I'm sorry. Let me try to bring you up to date."

There was a pause on the line, and some background chat. It sounded to Lane as if the woman was consulting with someone or trying to collect herself.

"Well, let me ask you something first," Naomi began "You saw Alexander Morton and the family the other day, right?"

"Yes, Sophie phoned me and invited me up to the Caledonian. We had quite a reasonable conversation."

"And what do you make of Alexander Morton?" Naomi asked.

"I was fairly impressed," Lane answered. "The restoration of the abbey as it's modelled on his computer is great. He's a very positive, go-ahead sort of man. By the same token there are things in his plan that will be hard to sell."

"Yes," Naomi said, "that pretty much agrees with my assessment."

"Naomi . . . ?" Lane paused.

"Yes?" she said.

"I want some direction here. I seem only to be hearing echoes of what I'm saying."

"Well, Naomi," answered, "the Mortons are talking to all the organizations involved, lumped together in twos are threes according to their various interests. People are being very canny about what they think. Everyone wants someone else to put their toe in to test the temperature. I think that Historic Scotland and the government are leaning to the positive side, but they're afraid of the political backlash. You've gotten a hint of that already through the demonstration outside your house. Fife Council is positive and so is Lothian. Forth Ports and Shell UK are not positive. I'm sorry to be so vague, Davis, but that's just the way it is."

"The bottom line of that approach, Naomi," Lane went on, "is that I'm left in the lurch. I'm the only visible figure in all this. I'm the only one who's there to absorb the flak."

"Yes, I can see that," Naomi said. "I am sorry about that. I'm sure that it wasn't intended to be this way though."

"When you have a death threat hanging over your head," Lane said, "that isn't a lot of comfort."

"No," Naomi said. "Look, you don't need to go any further with this if you don't want to. You can withdraw now if you wish."

"I'll think about it, Naomi," Lane said. "I'll think very seriously about it. The only thing is that I don't think that would make much difference. The people who have targeted me would never believe that I'm out of it. This chap Falconer, for example; he's tough and determined. You could put a notice in the newspaper to the effect that Davis Lane has no connection with Inchcolm and he would never believe it."

"No, you may be right," Naomi said.

"Yes, I am right," Lane answered. "However, I am going to think about pulling out very seriously, and I'll let you know." Lane hung up before she had the chance to respond.

Lane sat down in an easy chair to try to think things through. Things had turned too personal. He had been threatened and Katriona was alarmed. The logical thing was to withdraw, get out of it altogether. But could he? What he had said to Naomi was true. No one would now accept that he was out of it. The demonstrations and the harassment would continue anyway. It was impossible to see a way through.

Lane needed something to take his mind off it for a while. He went online to find something to cook for their dinner, a new recipe of some kind, something he would have to organise and think about for a while. He found a possibility and it was working to a degree, occupying his mind and meagre culinary skills. But his heart sank when he heard noises from the front just after five o'clock. When he opened the front door they were there, more demonstrators than yesterday, cheer-led by Morris Falconer. But there was a division this time, a gap in the line, for the monks were there as well. He felt the anger rising in his chest as he launched himself down the steps towards Morris Falconer.

"Mr. Falconer," Lane said, "why are you back here again?"

"Well Mr. Lane," Falconer said, smiling, "nothing has changed has it? We'll be coming back as often as it takes until we block Alexander Morton's plans."

"Was it you who threw the rock through our window?" Lane asked.

"I saw the boarding up over your window. I wondered what had happened there. I don't know anything about that," Falconer said. "This is a peaceful demonstration."

Lane shook his head and moved past the gap to one of the hooded monks. "Why are you here?" he asked.

The monk shook his head and pointed to his mouth, zipping up his lips.

"Are you saying," Lane asked, "that you can't speak because you're taken a vow of silence? Is that what you're saying?"

The monk nodded.

"Well," Lane went on, "you're very badly informed because Inchcolm Abbey was an Augustinian monastery and the brothers were permitted to have profitable and serious conversations. They didn't take vows of silence. Maybe you ought to check that out. Anyway, you appreciate that I might just be on your side on this issue? It's stupid of you to be here."

Lane was aware of someone touching his arm and turned quickly, ready to swing at whoever was there. But it was PC Michie.

"Please, Mr. Lane," Michie said, "it would be better if you went inside."

Lane found himself being gently urged up the path and through the door by WPC MacAndrew as Michie turned back towards the demonstrators. They were still shouting.

Later, Katriona was fuming as she walked in through the door.

"You realize that I had to honk the horn several times in order to get into my own driveway?" she said.

"Yes," Lane said, "I heard you. It's ridiculous."

"I also had a little skirmish at work today," Katriona said.

"No, really?" Lane asked.

"Yes. One of the other social workers, Sandra. I don't know her very well. Anyway, we were all having lunch in the staff room. She turned to me and said, 'Katriona, why is your husband helping this man Alexander Morton?' I was so angry with her."

"That settles it," Lane said.

"Yes," Katriona said, "it does settle it. This is getting out of hand. We need to come to grips with this."

"I know," Lane answered. "I've thought about it all day long. I called Naomi and talked to her. She said that I can pull out if I want, and that's what I've decided to do."

"Pull out?" Katriona asked. "You mean give up?"

"Yes," Lane said. "I'm not willing to have you put through all this stuff."

"No way," Katriona said. "We're not giving in to these people. You're only trying to do a legitimate and important job here. You can't let single-issue people run things. No, we're in this to the bitter end. The lady's not for turning."

"Katriona," Lane said, shaking his head, "you're a wonder."

"I know," she said.

Chapter Twenty

Loss

It was necessary to get away. The demonstration the previous night had lasted until eight o'clock. The Lanes had ignored it, but he'd had too much shouting, conflict and threat. He decided to drive around Fife looking for Melvin's Mobile Barbershop. It wasn't really time to get another haircut, but it was a good excuse to escape for a while. Beyond that, he had another motive. A bank of thin white cloud hung over Fife with an occasional patch of blue sky stitched in, but the day was dry and warm. A train was running alongside Lane on the Fife Circle. He passed it when it stopped at Dalgety Bay and headed on towards Aberdour. The long building housing the shopfitting works in the industrial estate had an *Available* sign on it. Companies and individuals were struggling to stay afloat in these times. Lane drove along the coastal route and then down the narrow main street of Aberdour. It didn't take long to reach Burntisland, where he found the barber's bus parked in the parking lot. There was a customer in the chair, so Lane picked up a copy of the local paper. Lane turned towards the corner, but Melvin's boxer wasn't there. The front page of the paper featured a story about the Morton plans. He started to read it when Melvin released his customer, nodded at Lane and waved him into the chair.

"Hi, Mr. Lane, how are you?"

"I'm fine Melvin. How about you?" he answered.

"I'm OK" Melvin said, fastening the paper collar and black cloth around his neck.

"Where's your dog today?" Lane asked, but as soon as he said it something in the circumambience told him he shouldn't have. There was a long pause, signalling that there was something amiss in the bus. Melvin put his hands holding scissors and comb down gently on Lane's shoulders. They had the weight of grief.

"Oh Mr. Lane," he said, "My dog is gone. His hind legs gave out, you know, just gave out. He couldn't even get out of the door to go outside. I had to carry him to have a pee. It was pitiful to see. I called the vet and he came. He looked at the dog and said what I knew he would say. I had to put him down, Mr. Lane. The vet gave him a shot and I held him. I just held him until the end. He slipped away quietly."

Lane glanced at Melvin in the mirror and then quickly looked down to give the man space for his grief. "Melvin," he said, "I'm so sorry to hear that. I knew that something was wrong when I came in. Your dog has been here every time I've come in for the last I don't know how many years."

"Yes," Melvin said, "he was a good dog. He was fourteen. I got him as a pup from the *Dog and Cat Home*. A good dog."

"Yes, he was a fine dog, Melvin," Lane said.

Melvin raised his comb and scissors. "What would you like today, Mr. Lane?"

"Just the usual, Melvin," Lane said.

Lane decided that a change of subject would be beneficial. "What are your customers talking about these days?" he asked.

"My customers?" Melvin said. "My customers are not talking much because they don't come is as much as they used to. They're trying to save money. They wait as long as they can. When they do come in they have long hair and they talk about the economy and bankers and football. That's about it."

"Yes," Lane said, "I think you told me before that they're not coming in so often. Do they ever talk about Alexander Morton and his plans to build a hotel and golf course on Inchcolm?"

"Oh sure," Melvin said, "a lot of them."

"And what do they say about it, Melvin?" Lane asked. "Are they for it or against it?"

"Some people laugh about it, Mr. Lane," Melvin said. "They think it's a really crazy idea and they make fun of the man. They think that he's greedy and just out to make more money. They say that he will spoil the island. But other people, most people maybe, say that they want it to go ahead because he will make some jobs. They think that if it goes ahead it will help Burntisland because he will need to base his construction there. That would be good for the whole area. Fife's not good now. It's a depressing place. We need jobs."

"And what about you, Melvin?" Lane asked. "What do you think?"

"Me?" Melvin said, "What do I think?" Melvin held his scissors and comb in midair while he thought. "I think . . . what is it that the Americans say . . . ? I think it's a no-brainer. Is that the right word, Mr. Lane? A no-brainer?"

"Yes, Melvin," Lane said, "that will do nicely."

"I mean that if you can build something on the island that brings jobs and houses and a better life to people, then why not?" Melvin said. "The abbey, the ruins, are beautiful. I've been there, really beautiful and good for a picnic, but you can't live in them or eat them. You know what I mean, Mr. Lane?"

"Yes, Melvin, I do know what you mean," Lane said. The men were silent for a while Melvin worked. He finished up the haircut and held up the mirror behind Lane's head.

"That's fine, Melvin," Lane said, "thanks for the haircut once again. Good job."

Melvin removed the cover and handed Lane a tissue to wipe his face. Lane got down from the chair, reached into his pocket and passed money to the barber with his right hand while placing his left hand on the man's shoulder. "Melvin, I'm sorry about your dog, but I think that he would want you to get another dog," he said.

"I don't know, Mr. Lane," the barber said, shaking his head and turning to put the money into the till.

Lane took another look towards the empty back of the bus, exited and headed for his car. The way out of town took him past the empty structure which Alexander Morton probably wanted for a base and then back onto the road for home. A mile down the road he knew he wasn't quite ready. Home at the moment had become a different place for him, a place disturbed and violated by others. Just a little more away-time would help. He found a CD at random from the pocket in the car door and pushed it in. He pressed *play* and made a right turn at Moss Cottages. *Let it Be* by John Lennon came on. This back road went up to Cockairnie and then to Couston Castle. The song nearly had the texture and words of a hymn:

When I find myself in times of trouble,
Mother Mary comes to me,
Speaking words of wisdom
Let it be

    He didn't agree with the theological assumptions of the song, but it had the right sentiment. Bad theology, good song. Mary hadn't really understood what her son was up to. He was an embarrassment to the family and they came out to take him home. Nevertheless, Mary was with him at the end, and her grief must have been profound. Melvin too was broken-hearted. Sure, it was only a dog, but it had been a long-time companion. You could experience grief over the loss of a dog just as you could over the loss of a loved one or a friend. Lane knew that Melvin would be all right, for he had his wife and kids, but the absence of his companion dreaming dog dreams in the back of the bus would be felt. Eventually Melvin would be able to let it be.
    Lane drove up the narrow road towards the remains of Couston Castle and parked in a lay-by. He reflected on the last few days. The stone crashing through the window and the words on the note had rattled him. No doubt that the act had been done by someone being theatrical, but the words still wounded him. He had always thought of himself as at least trying to do the right thing. He was trying to do the right thing in relation to Inchcolm Abbey, and yet someone had threatened his life. Loss was always lying in wait around the corner. How would Katriona fare if she lost him? The family who had once lived here in the castle had known loss. They lost Gavin when he went into the monastery. Then at some point Gavin must have lost his father and mother. Had they made it into the burial grounds of the monastery when they died? Had the canon's mother and father made it into the monastery when they died? Had their names been inscribed on the Inchcolm *Obituary*? Did Gavin, at certain times during the week, pass by their graves and reflect on their absence? Loss was enduring. Lane shook himself and started up the car. He would need to stop this. He would need to stop writing a narrative about Gavin. Nothing like getting caught in the web of your own fiction. *Let it be*, Lane, *let it be*.

Chapter Twenty-One
Watcher

It was the middle of the afternoon by the time Lane got back home. The fluffy white clouds over Fife had joined forces to create a solid bank of grey. It was dull, and the air was heavy with impending rain. It was a relief to find the house quiet. Perhaps the demonstrators were done protesting, or if they weren't, perhaps the rain would keep them away. It hadn't been Lane's practice to pray for rain, but now . . . . He spent a while browsing through the yellow pages to look for a glazier to provide an estimate for replacing the window. The yellow pages seemed to be depleted these days. He looked online and found a number of glaziers whose telephone numbers he wrote down. The doorbell rang and Lane went through to open it. It was D.I. Hewitt.

"Mr. Lane, hello. You'll remember me?" Hewitt said.

"Of course," Lane said, "Come in, please."

Hewitt continued to stand on the doorstep. "Before I do, I take it that you just came to the door and opened it, not knowing who was there?"

"Yes, I did," Lane said.

"Remember," Hewitt said, "just the other day you received a death threat. I could have been the person who put that note through your window. Did you think about looking through your peephole first?"

"No, you're quite right," Lane said. "I've never been in the habit of using that."

"Perhaps," Hewitt said, "this would be a good time to start."

"You're right," Lane said. "Point taken. Come in please."

Lane led the way to the lounge and they sat down. Hewitt was wearing a wrinkled grey suit, white shirt and a yellow tie loosely knotted. He extracted a piece of paper from his jacket pocket, unfolded it and studied it as if trying to remember the incident.

"We've inspected the items from your bad experience the other night," he said. "There are no prints on the stone. The paper is the kind of paper you can buy nearly anywhere and there are no prints on it. The printing on the page is standard PC printer type, could have come from a thousand printers around here. There's really nothing there to give us a clue about the identity of the perpetrator. So . . . I'm sorry that we haven't made much progress."

"OK," Lane said, "It doesn't really surprise me. Did you send it to forensics to check for DNA?"

"To forensics?" D.I. Hewitt responded, "You mean like *seen on TV*?"

"Well, yes, I suppose so," Lane answered.

"Right, forensics," Hewitt said. "Let me see now," he said, looking intensely at Lane, "When you say *forensics* you're thinking very attractive girl in a pristine white lab coat, surrounded by the latest hi-tech equipment, right?'

"I suppose so," Lane said.

"I thought so," Hewitt said. "And she's got two phones on her desk, one to Interpol and one to the FBI, and the room has a glass wall for them to write down clues and so forth?"

'Yes, go on," Lane said, sensing a smile forming.

"And the girl says to me, 'Mr. Hewitt, I think I've got something here.' So I lean down to her as close as I can, so close I can smell her perfume. It's number 5 I think. Then she says, 'This rubber band that was around the stone. I think I know where it came from.'"

"And I lean in even closer to her lovely tanned neck and say, 'Right Senga', because she's from Glasgow and went to uni there. 'Where's that?' I ask."

"And she looks up, those deep blue eyes looking intently at me. She says, 'This rubber band is from W.H. Smith, the newsagent in Cardenden, right here in Fife.'"

"And I say, 'Well Ian Rankin must surely be our perpetrator then. That's his home town.'"

"And she says, 'Oh it can't be Ian Rankin.' And I say, 'Why not?' And she says 'Well, he knows about this sort of thing. He would never use a rubber band from his home town.'"

Lane couldn't help laughing.

"What I'm getting at, Mr. Lane," Hewitt went on, "is that Fife Constabulary might not match the television portrayal when it comes to forensics."

"I appreciate that," Lane said, "I was only pulling your leg a little. You know, it took me years to realise that *Senga* was really *Agnes* backward."

"Really?" Hewitt replied. "I guess that you haven't spent enough time in Glasgow."

"Probably not," Lane said. "But to be honest with you, I haven't thought a lot more about the note."

"I don't think you should dismiss it," Hewitt said, crossing one leg over the other and sitting back in the chair. "You did receive a death threat, and for all we know it could be serious."

"I hear what you say," Lane said, "but what do you want me to do, dwell on it all the time, stay inside the house, or what?"

"No, you can't behave like that," Hewitt said. "I appreciate that, but just exercise a little more care than usual, like checking who's outside the door before you open it, and like looking to see if anyone is following you."

"Fair enough," Lane replied, thinking that maybe he could get D.I. Hewitt and Naomi Fowler together. They could watch each other's back. "I'll try to do that."

"We'll continue to send up someone to keep an eye on you and the property," Hewitt said, "but you'll appreciate that it can't go on forever."

"Yes," Lane said, "I understand that. You've got a budget to operate to. Thanks." He showed Hewitt to the door and watched him drive off. At the moment, the *cul de sac* was quiet, so that was promising. Lane shut the door and tried looking through the peephole. He could see only an indistinct bunch of green leaves at the other end. He opened the door about a foot and assessed the location of the peephole in relation to the front porch. The peephole was situated about five and a half feet above the bottom of the door. The step on which any visitor stood to ring the doorbell was a foot below the bottom of the door. Heck, that would mean that a visitor would need to be at least six and a half feet tall before he could be seen. *Check on whoever is outside before you open the door*. Yeah, right.

It was hard to relax. Lane went through to the kitchen and looked into the freezer to find something for their dinner that night. He stood for a minute with the door open, trying to remember why he was there. Then he went through to the study to phone several glaziers to ask for estimates to replace the study window. The phone still had shards of broken glass trapped around the buttons. But his agenda comprised by these domestic tasks wasn't fulfilling its function very well. He was edgy and jumpy, wondering who it was out there that wanted to do away with him. He wished that he had never responded to the invitation, that he had never gone to Inchcolm, that he had never met Naomi and agreed to take this job.

He went to the front door to see if the peephole could be moved down to an ordinary person level. When he opened the door there were several people gathering with placards. He went out and marched down the path towards a woman who seemed to be organising the demonstrators.

"Excuse me," Lane said to her, "Who exactly are you?"

"Well," she said, "who are you?"

"My name is Lane," he said. "I happen to live here and I was wondering what you're up to?"

She surprised him by sticking out her hand. "Hello, Mr. Lane, my name is Betty Duthie. I'm with the Fife Wildlife Association, or FWA for short. I'm afraid that we've come to protest today. I hope that you'll understand."

"Betty," Lane said, "I appreciate that you at least are courteous, unlike the guy Falconer who was here last night, but why are you demonstrating, and why are you doing it here?"

"Mr. Lane," she said, placing a hand on his arm, "don't take it personally. We are greatly concerned about all wildlife, but particularly about the seals at Inchcolm. We're absolutely opposed to Alexander Morton commandeering Inchcolm for his own purposes. I don't know if you know it or not but Inchcolm is important for its pinniped population."

"I'm sorry," Lane said, "for its what?"

"Pinnipeds:" Betty Duthie said, "seals. Inchcolm has both common and grey seals."

"Oh yes," Lane replied. "I know about the seals. I counted forty-six of them the other day. I just didn't know the word *pinniped*."

"No, most people wouldn't," Ms Duthie replied. "It just means fins rather than feet. The point is that we need to protect them, and Mr. Morton's plans may well damage them or at least frighten them away."

"But my understanding is," Lane said, "that neither the common nor the grey seal are endangered."

"No, that's correct," she said. "But things can change more quickly than you realize with wildlife. For example, there could easily be an outbreak of disease or an oil spill or whatever. In any event, people who visit Inchcolm love to see the seals, and it would seem a great shame to frighten them away."

"Yes, I quite agree," Lane said. "Tell me, is there any other wildlife on Inchcolm apart from the birds?"

"No, not really," she said. "Nothing else except perhaps rats. Why?"

"Well," Lane said, "that surely means that the main concern, at least as far as wildlife is concerned, is the seal. Now, do you know that Alexander Morton has a plan for dealing with the seals?"

"No, I didn't," Ms. Duthie said. "Please tell me."

"OK," Lane responded, "but first of all, let me say that I am not working for Alexander Morton. You people seem to believe that, but it isn't true. I do research into the abbey in order to advise any interested party. So protesting here outside my house really has no point. I am not your enemy."

"I take your point," she said, "but you've been seen meeting with him, and the news stories in the paper and on TV link you to him very closely. We're not after you so much as we're after publicity."

"I know," Lane said, "and I'm unhappy about that, but when it comes to Inchcolm I am neutral. OK?"

"If you say so," Mrs. Duthie said, looking doubtful. "but how does the man propose to deal with the seals?"

"He tells me," Lane said, "that he is going to build and anchor soft platforms for them to lie on."

"Soft platforms?" she said.

"Soft platforms," Lane replied. "These things are to have a soft waterproof top and will be designed to float on the surface, whatever level the tide is at. They'll be much more comfortable that the buoy platforms the seals use now."

"That's a new one on me," she said. "I'll need to look into that. I suppose theoretically that it could enhance their living conditions. But there's still the issue of increased traffic in the estuary. He can't avoid that."

Lane was about to speak when a car pulled in to the *cul de sac*. He turned to see Steven Swinton and another man emerging. Swinton strolled over to Lane and held out his hand. "Hello again, Davis," he said. "I thought I would see what's happening with you. This is our photographer Alan Dawson. I see that you've got a demo on your hands again. I want to get some photos of that, and . . ." he said, looking at the house, "I see that you've had a little trouble with that front window." Dawson began shooting images of the demonstrators, at which point they stopped moving and held their placards higher.

Lane motioned to Swinton to accompany him up the path. "Look, Mr. Swinton," he said, "I'm happy enough to talk to you, but I don't want photos taken of my house. That would just help pinpoint where I live, and I've already had enough hassle. Please forego that."

"Fair enough," Swinton said, "no pictures of the house. But what happened here?"

"The other night," Lane answered, "there was a demonstration here, just like at the moment. Later on, after people had left, someone threw a stone through the window. It's as simple as that."

"Wow, pretty scary, eh?" Swinton asked.

"It gave us a fright," Lane answered, deciding he would say nothing about the note and death threat.

"What's your reaction to these demos, Davis?" Swinton asked, taking out his notebook and pen.

"I can understand that people are concerned about a number of aspects of Alexander Morton's plans," Lane said. "I am too, especially about the threat to wildlife and about the commercialisation of the island. But I am not on one side or the other. I'm only advising about the abbey, so there is no point in making me a target. And . . ." Swinton interrupted.

"Do you feel you're a target, Davis?" he asked.

"Yes, I do," Lane answered. "Otherwise these protestors wouldn't be here, outside my house. But the second point I was trying to make is that there are lots of other factors which you have to take into account. It would be good to see the abbey restored. The project would bring jobs where jobs are needed. People ought to think about these factors as well. It's not a single issue thing, not a black and white matter."

"Right, thanks for that comment, Davis," Swinton said. "We'll see if we can't get this into the paper tomorrow. By the way," he said, "glancing to his left, "I see that you have police protection here this evening." Two constables had parked down the road and were making their way towards the house.

"Yes," Lane answered. "I guess they feel we need it. Incidentally, could I suggest that you might want to interview Betty Duthie, who's here at the moment."

"Who is she?" Swinton asked.

"She's here for an organisation called Fife Wildlife Association. When you speak to her, ask her to comment on the fact that Morton plans to build soft platforms for the deals."

"I'm sorry," Swinton said, "soft platforms?"

"Yes," Lane answered, "soft platforms. Ask her for her opinion on the idea of providing more comfortable places for the seals to lie on."

"OK, I will," Swinton said, shaking his head. "You learn something new every day."

Later, at a largely silent dinner table, the Lanes were reflective and quiet. Katriona's plate had hardly been touched, her glass of wine left half full.

"How long is this going to go on, Davis?" she asked.

"I don't know," he said.

"We've got demonstrators outside, a boarded-up front window, policemen patrolling, and a death threat hanging over your head," Katriona said. "I get accusations at work, you're in the newspaper, and the neighbours are unhappy with us. It's not exactly ideal is it?"

"No, it's not," Lane answered. "I'm sorry that I ever got into all this, but it can't go on forever." And then, in an effort to lighten the mood a little, he continued, "I never for one moment though that a pinniped would turn out to be so important in this."

"I'm sorry, a what?" Katriona said.

"You know, a *pinniped*," Lane answered. "A mammal having fins rather than feet. Like seals."

"Davis," Katriona said, looking steadily at him, but she wasn't smiling.

Chapter Twenty-Two

Walkabout

It was another invitation to the island, and Lane couldn't refuse it. Alexander Morton rang to ask him to accompany him on a walk through the abbey and around the island. It would, Morton said, give him a chance to explain to Lane the nature of his development on the ground. It didn't seem like a bad idea, the only drawback being that to be seen with Morton was to once again elevate his profile with the demonstrators. Lane agreed to go the following day. Morton would, of course, arrange for his own private transport from Granton Harbour. If Lane went on the *Forthbelle* from North Queensferry it would lessen the chance of being noticed. Lane occupied himself with preparing a list of questions to ask. It would enable him to keep busy while glaziers came during the day to provide estimates for the repair of the front window.

There were whitecaps cresting in the blue-green water the following day as the *Forthbelle* set out. Banks of cloud, the edges rimmed with silver, crossed diagonally from southwest to northeast. At most there were a dozen passengers on board, rather subdued he thought, as the commentary began. By now Lane knew it well enough to mime it. There was lots of traffic on the road bridge, and a container vessel piled high was making its way slowly up the Forth, heading probably to Rosyth or Grangemouth.

The *Forthbelle* made its way down the estuary and finally pulled into the little harbour at Inchcolm to the screeching of gulls. Lane made his way up the path along with his fellow passengers. Alexander Morton and Lanson Brand were directly ahead, standing near the gift shop and toilets. Morton was wearing a blue jersey, open at the neck and an expensive suede jacket. He was writing something in a small spiral notebook. He turned as Lane approached.

"Davis," Morton said, hand extended, "good to see you. Thanks for coming today."

"Not a problem," Lane replied. "I always like coming here."

"I wanted to spend a while just walking around with you," Morton said. "I thought it would let me show you in more detail just exactly what we have in mind. Beyond that, there are some things I need to see anyway."

"That's fine with me," Lane said, "and there are questions I need to ask you as well."

Morton pointed to the gift shop and toilets. "Let's start right here. Look at this," he said, "All this is pretty ugly don't you think? If this building were taken away and we excavate into the hill behind, this can be made much more attractive. You saw the computer mock-up of the hotel. Don't you think that it would look much better than this?"

"I couldn't really argue with you on that score," Lane answered. "There is a question about scale though. If you're going to make a profit here then you have to have enough people staying. And if you have that many people as paying guests, you need a relatively large hotel with a lot of rooms. And if you put that large a building here, will it not overwhelm the abbey?"

"OK," Morton answered. "Yes, we do need a sufficient number of rooms, but the hotel will run right back into the hillside. It's not going to project up and out. You'll see the front of it but not much more."

"Fine, Lane said, "but when you do that surely the rooms at the back will be quite dark. My wife and I once strayed in a hotel where we were given a room which the desk clerk called a *city room*. We didn't think anything about that until we got to the room, when we realized that there was no window. There was only a large poster of a beach scene in Hawaii. We'd never had a hotel room without a window before. It was a strange feeling."

"Yes, I can understand that," Morton said. "But there are better ways of dealing with that problem. I've done it before. Have you ever been to *Caesar's Palace* in Vegas, or to the *Venetian*?"

"No, afraid not," Lane answered.

"Well, both these hotels have interior walkways and rooms with artificial skies and surroundings," Morton said. "The clouds move and the colours change and so on. They are very realistic. We'll do something like that in the very back rooms of this hotel. You'd be surprised how good it can be. In any event, our guests will spend very little time in the room. They'll be on the golf course or in the casino."

"Fair enough," Lane replied, "but I wouldn't like to think that your guests were spending that much time in the casino. I have problems with gambling."

"I appreciate that," Morton responded, "but you have to understand that the finance to support this whole development will come mainly from the gaming. There's not going to be that much margin on the hotel charges or the green fees, so unless we get it on the gaming, the whole thing is not feasible. Anyway, that's not really your problem."

"No, I disagree," Lane answered. "It is my problem because it's an ethical issue, and I'm supposed to be advising on ethical issues."

"Yes, OK," Morton answered, "I'm sorry and you're right." He put his hand on Lane's shoulder. "You know, that's what I like about you, Davis. You're a straightforward kind of guy. I like that. I can do business with people like that. We'll come back to that issue, but let's move on now."

Morton moved towards the abbey, with Lane in tow. Lanson Brand the minder followed a few yards behind. Morton led the way through the arched door and into the Chapter House, gesturing as if to open a curtain. "Isn't this a great room? I like the way they did the gothic arches over the abbot's and priors' seats, and the vaulted ceiling is just magnificent. This room will get the greatest attention from the restorers, along with the church of course. We're going to do this up exactly as it must have been, the masonry tidied up, the stonework and floor cleaned. Everything in here will be made pristine."

"Wasn't this where you were planning to have your poker room?" Lane asked. "I've got questions about that."

Morton held up his hand a smiled. "Change of plans about the poker room," he said. "Let me come to that later."

They moved on to the cloister walk, stepping through gothic patterns of sunlight formed by the arches. "The cloister will be completely rebuilt," Morton said. "The stonework here will be brilliant. The benches where the canons sat to talk will be built and set up here, and there'll be grass in the centre yard, probably better and greener than it ever was in the fifteenth century."

They turned to the right and went into the ruined church. Morton stood with his hands in his pockets, looking up at the sky. Lanson Brand remained outside the foundations, bored, prodding something with his shoe. "This is the hardest bit," Morton said. "There's just so much to rebuild here, and not a lot to go on. I've got architects working on this already. They say that we'll need to start at the transept on the south side and work from there. They'll do the transept and apse and then work back to the nave. But I want this to be absolutely right. It should be beautiful when it's finished, but I suspect that it may take longer than anything else."

Morton moved east to the space where the apse used to be. He pointed to the remains of the painted mural or fresco. "You know about this?" he asked Lane.

"Yes," Lane answered, "it depicts the funeral procession of John de Leycestre in the thirteenth century. Pity that the heads of the people aren't there. I suspect that someone is the distant past broke off the heads as a souvenir."

"My thinking too," Morton responded, "but I'm planning to re-head them."

Lane couldn't help laughing. "Re-head them?"

"Sure," Morton said. "If you can behead someone, you ought to be able to re-head them. We'll get some expert from Italy, some fresco guy to do that job for us."

Morton headed east out of the church ruins and then stopped. He turned towards Lane. "Incidentally," he said, "that site you found online, *St Jean des Vignes,* will be a tremendous help to us."

"Good, I'm glad to hear that," Lane said. "It's been very instructive."

They rounded the corner and moved on down towards the domestic wing of the monastery. "Even the *lavabo* will be restored just as it was," Morton said. "We'll include small modern restrooms within them, as unobtrusively as possible. If we're taking away the toilets over at the gift shop we need to have something somewhere. It's a shame in a way, but they'll be done as sensitively as possible."

Morton and Lane, followed by Lanson Brand, moved around towards the west side of the cellars and kitchen. Morton pointed up to the upper level. "The dormitory was up here, of course, and we plan to put in several beds like the ones the canons used. In the refectory down here we'll have several long dining tables with benches and a kind of lectern like the one they used for reading during meals. We're planning a café here, a place for visitors to get coffee and something to eat. The cellars underneath will be completely done, of course, with samples of the foodstuffs they might have kept in the various chambers. We hope to have three or four people on site acting as canons or lay brothers doing their various jobs. We could have one being a cellarer, one being a kitchener, one being a refectorer, maybe one acting as the worship leader, something like that. Each one can explain his job as visitors go round."

Morton put his hand on Lane's shoulder again. "Now," he said, "that brings me nicely to an important point."

"Which is?" Lane asked.

"Two things really," Morton said, "but they're connected. First, your friend Gavin . . ."

"Oh no, not Gavin again," Lane said. "I thought that we had dispensed with Gavin."

"No, we haven't," Morton said, smiling broadly. "He's great, absolutely essential. I want Gavin to act as the key interpreter of the abbey. We can follow Gavin through a whole cycle of life in the abbey. We see him getting up from his bed here in the dormitory, going to worship in the church, meeting with the others in the Chapter House, then going out in the boat to collect food at the farms on shore, then back here to worship and so on. You were right in thinking that the style of monastic life here had to be personalised, and Gavin is just the man to do it."

"I'm not sure," Lane said, actually feeling rather pleased. "Gavin just seems to cause problems."

"No, not really," Morton said. "That was just because James was foolish enough to pass your story over to some reporter. When this thing is restored, Gavin will lead people around here. There'll be *Follow Gavin* signs around the abbey, but we're also going to have an audio tour for people. They pick up their headphones when they get on shore and then walk though the abbey, and it will be Gavin who's doing the interpretation. So you've got to do even more with the man. In fact, I think that you should write a book about Gavin."

"A book about Gavin?" Lane said. "It would need to be a novel then because . . ."

"Because Gavin is fictional, I know," Morton finished the sentence for him. "Seriously, I think you should do it."

"Uhuh," Lane said.

"Now," Morton said, "here's the second point, and it's even more important than the first, but why don't we sit down somewhere." Lane thought that Morton looked out of breath. They moved to the low wall near the chapter house entrance and sat down on the stone.

"Here's the plan," Morton began. "We actually need someone here on site to explain how the abbey functioned. The audio tour will be fine, but when larger groups come for example, and when there are people who ask serious questions, then we need a live person here. I don't mean questions about the practical details so much as about the theological details. Why was the abbey important, for example? Why did people want to become members of this community? What shape did worship take? What did they talk about in the Chapter House? What did they believe about heaven and hell in a different age? All these things. Do you see what I'm driving at, Davis?"

"Sure," Lane answered. "It would be a great thing to be able to do that. It's an ideal set-up for a theological interpretation of the world. It's what I've been trying to do in the research."

Morton slapped Lane on the knee. "My point exactly," he said.

"I'm sorry?" Lane said.

"This is a job for you," Morton said. "In the United States, as you know, we would call this person a *docent*, a person who interprets important places or items. You know more about the abbey than anyone else by now, so you could come here two or three times a week and act as docent. Now, the salary wouldn't be that great, but it would be significant. I mean, you can't be earning that much as a freelance theologian can you?"

Lane was speechless for a moment. "No, well, not really, but . . . I'm floored. I had no idea that this is what you were talking about."

"Why not?" Morton responded. "It seems to make good sense to me. You're a theologian, you know about the abbey, and you live nearby. Why not take the opportunity to expand people's understanding in such a secular age."

"It's good of you to think of it," Lane answered, "but it's hard for me to think of myself in that kind of role."

"OK, I can imagine that," Morton said, standing up. "But I think that you should think long and hard about it. You'll come around to see it the way I do. The other thing that you could do is to perform weddings. I know that there are already weddings in the abbey as it is. When it's restored there will be a demand for many more. You could handle these. Now, I think that we should move on to other things."

Morton led Lane back down the path towards the east end of the island, followed dutifully by Lanson Brand. There seemed to be more people around the abbey now, some carrying what looked like picnic lunches. Morton stopped where the beach met the upward slope of the headland.

"The clubhouse will be set into the rise here," he said, pointing into the side of the slope, "almost all of it concealed within the hill. Light doesn't matter much for a display of clubs and clothes." He proceeded further up the hill, following an overgrown path. After a few yards the path stopped at a grey metal door set into the rock face. Morton produced a large key and with some difficulty turned it in the lock. Lanson Brand stepped forward to help Morton push the door open, its bottom scraping loudly against the concrete. Against a totally black backdrop Lane could see only a maze of cobwebs. As his eyes grew accustomed to the dark he could make out a tunnel formed by rust-coloured bricks.

Morton looked back at Lane and smiled. "My guess is that you haven't been in here, right?" he said.

"You're right," Lane answered, "although I have an idea of where you're taking me."

"Lanson, you first please," Morton called out. Brand went forward, extracting a torch from his pocket. "You lead the way, please," Morton said. Brand went slowly forward, brushing cobwebs out of the way and playing the torch's beam back and forth on the floor. They went a few more yards, when Morton again called to Brand. "Stop for a moment, Lanson, please." Morton took a step towards the wall and placed his hand on it, taking deep, measured breaths. Lane thought the man appeared edgy and nervous. When several minutes had elapsed he called for Brand to go ahead. After perhaps twenty-five yards they entered what seemed to be a much larger space. Brand shone his torch on the wall and found a light switch. He pushed the switch and the room was flooded with light. The large rectangular room was empty apart from cobwebs and the tracks and droppings of small animals. Morton stood with his hand against the wall and looked at Lane. "Do you know what this is?"

"I think so," Lane answered. "A tunnel was built during the First World War to link the men's quarters with the gun positions. We've come through that tunnel and ended up in the magazine, where they stored the ammunition."

"Absolutely right," Morton said, "you know your stuff. But not many people have ever seen this place. It took some hard negotiation for me to get in here."

"I can imagine," Lane said. "I didn't know where the entrance was or whether anyone could get in here."

"Not many people do," Morton said, "but I managed it. Anything can be done if you speak to the right people. Now, I have you to thank for bringing me here. Remember how you said that it wouldn't be right to have the poker room in the chapter house?" Lane nodded. "Well, that really set me back, because the poker room has to be unique in this set-up. A lot of the margin we need will come from the poker room, and it has to be different from any other room in the world. Now, Davis, this is it."

"This is the poker room?" Lane asked.

"This is it," Morton said. "A secret room set into a hill entered by a tunnel. Once we get this kitted out it will attract the best players from all over the world. This room will be as posh as you could imagine, thick carpet, tapestries on the walls, recessed side lighting and a heavy oak round table for the game. We'll need to extend the tunnel, cut it through the rock until it curves around into the casino. We'll put in art work, an artificial sky and a long bar. Now, Davis, you led me to a completely new design, so thank you." Morton put his hands together and gave a few claps in Lane's direction.

"Now," Morton said, "I think we should move along. The tunnel goes right out in the other direction to the northeast corner of the island, but that's a long way and I need out. Lanson, lead the way please."

Brand switched off the light and turned on his torch. The three men proceeded down the tunnel and through the door. Morton locked it and put the key in his pocket. "This needs to go back to the keeper," he said. They walked back towards the harbour where people were beginning to gather for the *Forthbelle*.

Morton took Lane's hand and shook it vigorously. "Davis, thanks for coming today. I trust that you're able to see how much we want to do at Inchcolm. I hope that you'll think about the things we talked about, really meaning the possibilities for you in the set-up. You're an important key to this development, and I hope that you'll tell this ridiculous umbrella group through Naomi just how great this can be. Safe trip back."

Lane joined the others on board. He found a seat out of the wind and sat down, determined to stay there for the entire voyage. There was a lot to think about, but his head was spinning at the moment. What exactly had happened on Inchcolm today? He'd been led around the island listening to Morton's plans. He had to admit that they were stunning, probably realistic enough, provided the man had the money. He had been informed that he was a key player and had even facilitated the gambling aspect, even though it was unintended. He'd been told that he ought to write a book about Gavin: a good joke that one! And, of all things, he had been offered a job, a job being a theologian of sorts. He started to laugh and then muffled it. If anyone else on the vessel saw him laughing on his own in the corner . . .

On the way home he stopped at the supermarket and bought the making for a lasagne and a bottle of Chianti. They would enjoy a good meal tonight and have some fun. He couldn't take the job of course, maybe not even recommend the project to Naomi, but they could laugh about it at least. He hoped that there wouldn't be a demo that night, and there didn't appear to be.

"So you had your little walkabout today?" Katriona asked.

"I did indeed," Lane answered.

"Well," she went on, "aren't you going to tell me about it?"

"Oh, I suppose so," Lane said, "pretty much the same old thing with a couple of new twists."

"And what were the new twists?" she asked, topping up their glasses with Chianti.

"Well, Morton thinks that Gavin is wonderful and wants to use him in producing an audio tour of the abbey."

"Really?" Katriona said. "Well, that's good isn't it? I knew that you couldn't keep a good man down."

"Moreover," Lane added, "he thinks that I should write a book about him. Of course, it would need to be a novel because Gavin is . . . . *a fiction*," Katriona joined in.

"Anything else?" Katriona asked.

"Well yes," Lane said, "there was one more thing."

"What was that?" Katriona asked.

"He offered me a job," Lane answered, trying to keep a straight face. Katriona spilled her wine.

"He offered you a job?" she asked, mopping up the pool of red with a paper towel. "What kind of job?"

"A job as a docent," Lane answered.

"And what does a docent do?" she asked.

"Well, a docent explains or interprets things. In this case the docent would explain how the monastery worked, what happened there, what their theology was and so forth."

"Well, that sounds pretty good," Katriona said. "It's right up your alley isn't it? And would you live on the island or what?"

"Well," Lane said, "No, I wouldn't live on the island, maybe just be present for three days a week or something like that."

"Oh, that's a pity," Katriona said.

"How's that?" Lane asked.

"Well," Katriona answered, "I was just thinking that if you lived on the island I could maybe find another man to keep me company."

"No, its all right," Lane said, "you've nothing to worry about. I have no intention of taking the job."

"Aw shucks," Katriona said.

Chapter Twenty-Three
Tales

When the mobile rang he knew it was Naomi. This time he was right.

"Hello, Davis?" she said.

"Hi Naomi, how are you?" Lane answered.

"Fine, thank you, but I'm sorry to say that I have a rather urgent request."

Lane held the phone away and sighed. He didn't really need this today. With the phone back in position, "Yes, Naomi. What can I do for you?"

"The umbrella wants a concise report from you, I'm afraid. Morton is putting pressure on everyone to come to a decision. They're looking to you for advice."

"Do you mean," Lane said, "that they want me to specify all the pros and all the cons and then tell them what to do?"

"Well," she answered, "obviously you can't tell them what to do, but something like that, yes."

"And when you say *urgent*, Naomi," Lane said, "do you mean like *now*, like today?"

"If it's possible, yes please," Naomi answered.

Lane found his diary and opened it. "I can probably do it, but it will need to be this afternoon. The glazier's coming to replace our window this morning."

"Oh, I see," she said. "I forgot about your window. Of course that's fine. This afternoon will do fine."

"Where do you want to meet," Lane asked, "the same place as last time?"

"No, perhaps not," Naomi said. "I think that it may not be safe there any more."

Lane held the phone away and sighed again. "OK, where do you suggest?"

"Well, you were Church of Scotland, right?"

"Yes, Naomi," Lane answered. "But I can't see what that has to do with it."

"The place I have in mind is just next to the great Scottish Reformer's house. You follow me?"

Lane tried to figure out what she was talking about. The great Scottish Reformer could only be John Knox. John Knox's house was on the High Street, down the Royal Mile. He knew that there was a café there called the *Storytelling Café*. "Do you mean," he asked, "the place where they tell tales?"

"Yes, exactly," Naomi said, pleasure obvious in her voice. "Let's meet there and I'll buy you a coffee."

Lane hung up, shaking his head. He would have to get his skates on now.

A summary had to be made now, a position taken. In a way, Lane thought, it was helpful having finally to tackle this. He had done his research, he had inspected the abbey and the island, he had seen the plans and talked them over with Morton, and he had walked through the plans on the island. It was probably time to work out *his view* on things, to come to a moral position. He set about trying to clarify the issues in his own mind.

On the positive side, the restoration of the abbey had to be the key element, If it were restored properly, as Morton had promised, it would not simply be beautiful but would afford great educational opportunities. Morton was right in believing that Inchcolm would attract great numbers of visitors, and they would come not just to play golf or the games in the casino, but to see the abbey. They would discover what a medieval monastery was all about. They would have to think about self-discipline and worship and the economical consumption of resources. They would have to think about life and death and heaven and hell. They would have to think theologically.

All this meant that money and work would be brought to the area. That was another key element. The money would not only enhance the lives of the people who were directly involved with Inchcolm, but would help to maintain other historic properties in Scotland. Finally, it had the potential of increasing the flow of tourists to every part of the country. Scotland's heavy industries of the past were all in the past. The country required developments like tourism.

On the negative side was the potential damage to wildlife. There would be an impact on the birds of Inchcolm. He couldn't see any way around that. Morton's suggestion of *Colony Definition* was weak, probably empty. He wasn't sure about damage to the seal population. If Morton did what he said he would do, the seals would probably be all right.

There was also the question of whether the restoration of the abbey was actually a good thing. People could, and actually did, say that they loved the ruins as they were. There was a danger that an insensitive restoration might commercialise the abbey. If there were too much investment in a café and a shop, if large numbers of extravagant weddings were held in the church, then commercialisation might take over. Lane couldn't bear the thought of photographers dominating and ruining ceremonies. There would need to be limits of some kind placed on the commercial aspects of the new abbey.

Then there was the casino. Gambling for Lane was a major negative factor. He hated the idea of money being wasted, and especially the idea of it being wasted by people who could least afford it. It was one thing for wealthy high rollers coming to Inchcolm from the rest of the word and losing money. It was another thing for people to lose money when they couldn't afford to so, especially in these hard times. And yet, Morton was clearly preparing to spend vast sums of money on the project. He would require a large profit from the casino to fund it, so the casino was essential.

There were other negative factors as well. The proximity of the island to Braefoot and Hound Point, the increased traffic in the Forth: these were factors to be considered. But these were really beyond his area of expertise. These issues would be to be dealt with by the other spokes in the umbrella. And it was hard to assess the political aspect of this development. The Scottish government could expect many people to be for and many others to be against it. That was up to them to judge. The issue was important enough to win or lose an election.

What, Lane asked himself, was the bottom line? What did he think, and what would he recommend? First, he needed to take himself out of the equation. Would he like a job as docent of the abbey, a steady income for a seldom-employed freelance theologian? No, it wasn't practical. He couldn't live on the island or travel there three days a week. Would he like to play golf with Callum McBain on the world's holiest golf course? Sure, but that was irrelevant. Would he fancy writing a book about Gavin? Unlikely, but that could be done whether the island were developed or not. This moral case didn't seem to be one which could be settled by the use of principles or laws. Any relevant principles contradicted one another. There wasn't a black and white about this issue. It was complex, with layers of moral issues. So it seemed to demand a *utilitarian ethic*, a matter of the greatest good for the greatest number of people plus other aspects of the creation. What, Lane asked himself, would constitute the greatest good for the greatest number? His answer was: *permit the development.* Having made up his mind, Lane spelled it all out, printed several copies, put them in a folder and got ready for his meeting with Naomi Fowler.

The new window had been installed by lunchtime. It was great having light in the room again. Lane ate a sandwich and headed for the train. There would be nowhere to park where he was going. The platform at Inverkeithing Station was nearly empty. A long-haired youth with a guitar slung over his shoulder sat on the bench next to a short blonde girl in tight jeans. Two older ladies chatted about the shops they were planning to visit. Lane studied the advertising over on the opposite platform. It suggested that the sure way to get a job was to enrol in a local college. Would there be much point in getting a college degree in these times? He doubted it. You would be better off being a plumber, a well-paid and technologically challenging job. The train arrived and he boarded.

From Waverly Station he walked up Cockburn Street, passing a gallery, a Mexican restaurant and a sports shop. It had all changed. Years ago he and Katriona had stayed at a hotel on this street, now long gone. All he could remember about it was that they had been awakened in the morning by kegs of beer being rolled down the slope, metal on cobblestones. Climbing up to the High Street, he turned left. *The Storytelling Café* was down the *Royal Mile* several hundred yards, just past John Knox's house. It wasn't clear that John Knox had ever lived there, but it made for a good story and was a method of attracting visitors. Lane went into the café. It seemed to feature bakery goods, coffee and tea as well as a storyteller. There was abundant space, so he found a table in the corner. Perhaps that would satisfy Naomi's anxiety about security.

She came through the door ten minutes later, wearing a grey suit and white blouse and carrying her umbrella. Lane stood up to greet her. "Thank you for coming on such short notice," she said.

"It's all right," Lane said. "In fact, it was quite useful having to crystallise things in a hurry."

"Will we just have the usual?" Naomi asked.

"Why not?" Lane said. She went to the counter to order. Eventually she returned with coffees and scones and set them out on the table.

"Did you get your new window in?" she asked.

"Yes, it's in place, and it's great having light in the room again," Lane said.

"And have you had any more death threats?" she asked.

"No, no more threats," Lane said, looking straight at her, "nor have I seen anyone following me."

That put her off a bit. "Oh . . . good," she said.

Lane reached for his briefcase and extracted a blue folder. "This is for you," he said. "There are two copies here. It's a summary of my thinking so far, but I reserve the right to change my mind if circumstances change." He handed the folders to her.

"Thank you very much," she said, opening one folder and removing a copy of the report.

"What I'd like to do now," Lane said, "is run through it verbally with you so that I can explain my conclusions."

"Yes, please," Naomi said.

Lane took her though it step by step. She listened carefully, asking the occasional question.

"And the bottom line is . . ." she asked at the end of his analysis.

"The bottom line is that I think the development should be approved, assuming of course that there are certain safeguards on everything that Morton promises. Of course, I'm only dealing with the island and the abbey. There are lots of other issues that are beyond my remit."

"Yes, of course," Naomi said. "But this is so helpful, and I'll present them with your report this afternoon, as soon as I get back to the office."

"Now, Naomi," Lane said, reaching across the table to touch her hand, "there are two things I need to ask you, if you don't mind."

"Go ahead," she said.

"First of all," Lane continued, "what is the state of play with your umbrella group? You've been very canny in what you've told me. You've said almost nothing about what your various institutions, companies and so forth really think."

"OK," she said, "I'll do my best. The Scottish Tourist Board is for it. They want it to go ahead and say so. My own agency would like the extra income from Morton but is afraid to say so, because it goes right against the main thrust of what we do. The government want it to go ahead, but are trembling at the idea of the political fallout. There are demonstrations at the Scottish Parliament every day now. The wildlife organisations are against it, as you already know. So are Forth Ports and the oil companies. As I said to you, Alexander Morton is putting pressure on us to make a decision. Every morning he's seeing someone or phoning them, wanting to know when a decision will be made. He can be quite intimidating you know."

"I suppose so," Lane said, "but to be fair I haven't seen that side of things yet."

"Well," Naomi said, "he's being nice to you because he wants you on his side. He's a shrewd operator. You do know that he's bulldozing or threatening several people in Fife, don't you?"

"No, I didn't," Lane answered. "Who are you talking about?"

"Oh, the farmer who owns the old quarry," Naomi said. "Morton wants the stone from that quarry. He offered to buy the whole farm, but the farmer doesn't want to sell. He likes living there, and says that the land means more to him than the money. Morton can't accept being refused. He's threatening to ask for a compulsory purchase order. He claims that the farm is a mess anyway, littered with rusting equipment. It's all very nasty."

"I see," Lane said. "I didn't know that."

"No, you probably wouldn't," Naomi said. "But I suspect that it will come out in the newspaper one of these days. What was the other thing you wanted to ask me?"

"It's more personal, Lane said. "I hope you don't mind.

"No, that's all right," she said. "On you go."

"You've been reading a lot of John Le Carre'," Lane said.

"Oh yes" she said, smiling. "He's my favourite author. I've read all his books at least twice."

"It's just that you've been so cautious about meeting me, looking over your shoulder all the time, changing meeting places, being guarded over the telephone. Has all that been really necessary? I mean, have you any actual evidence of anyone spying on us?"

Naomi hesitated then blushed. "I couldn't pinpoint hard evidence, but I'm sure that I've been watched."

"So you're not just imaging all this, conjuring it up as in fiction?" Lane asked? "And all this anxiety I've had over the last few weeks, all that was necessary?" Lane asked.

"Oh yes, I'm sure of it," Naomi answered.

"Fair enough," Lane said and smiled.

Later on that afternoon they watched the sun sinking behind the hills in the west, rose-edged clouds drifting in to fill the gap. Katriona stood looking out through the re-glazed window.

"Thank goodness this is done," she said. "Let's hope that it stays intact for a long time."

"I hope so too," Lane said, "but there are no guarantees."

Demonstrators were beginning to gather in the *cul de sac*, their signs beginning to look a little tattered. The bird people were there, as well as the seal people. There were no monks, but there were several people with signs demanding a *Yes to Inchcolm*. Lane turned to Katriona.

"I think we ought to go out tonight for a change."

"What do you mean," she asked, "go out for a walk, go out to a movie or what?"

"No, go out to dinner," Lane said.

"Us, just the two of us, go out to dinner?" she asked.

"Absolutely," Lane answered.

"What a good idea," she said." Where can we go?"

"How about *Room with a View* in Aberdour?" Lane said.

"Good idea," Katriona said, "but we'll never get in tonight. They'll be fully booked."

"No, we will get in," Lane said. "I made reservations earlier"

"Brilliant, what a guy," Katriona said. "So we can reverse the Cruiser gently through these people in the road, just like Moses parting the Red Sea?"

"Just like that," Lane said.

The restaurant was located at the corner of the harbour in Aberdour, in an imposing square grey stone building. The road to the house and several adjoining houses ran steeply downhill from the parking lot for the *Silversands Beach*. Lane proceeded cautiously down the hill and pulled into the small parking lot. Along the seafront, a garden with a few picnic tables ran along for a hundred yards. The remains of a timber pier projected above the water out into the Forth. In the days of old, passenger vessels had called in to pick up or discharge their passengers for the town. They were greeted at the door by Rachel, the girl who with her husband had started the restaurant. They followed her into the snug to wait, and she handed out menus.

"Mr. Lane," she said, looking intently at him, "Are you not the person who's working with Alexander Morton on his development on Inchcolm?"

"Well, yes," Lane replied, "except I'm not working with him as such. I'm just acting as a kind of adviser."

"I thought you were involved somehow," she said. "I recognised the name because it's been in the paper. We're not very happy with Mr. Morton, you know."

"Sorry?" Lane said. "You're against the development?"

"No, it's not that so much," she said. "It could increase our business in fact. It's that Mr. Morton wants to buy all these properties down here in order to put in a kind of terminal. He wants to run a ferryboat between here and the island for his hotel guests and golfers. It's just that we only started the restaurant three years ago, and we love what we're doing. The clientele is gradually building up. In any event, this house has been in the family for years and years. We don't want to move, but he keeps putting pressure on us. He says that he'll ask to get these properties by compulsory purchase. We're really angry and upset about this."

"I'm sorry," Lane said, "but I didn't know anything about this."

"When I saw your name on the reservation list," she said, "I thought that you were coming to badger us on Morton's behalf."

"No, honestly," Lane replied, "I knew nothing about this. Morton has never mentioned doing anything in Aberdour to me."

"Well," she said, "he's got plans for this place. He intends to force us all out, build a terminal for his ferry and a new road down to it."

When they were seated at the table, Katriona said, "That kind of puts the damper on things doesn't it? Did you really not know anything about this?"

"No," Lane replied, "I did not. Morton has never mentioned this."

"You know," Katriona said, her face hidden behind the menu, "I think he's taking a loan of you. He's really got you working for him."

"You're the second person to say something like that today," Lane replied.

Chapter Twenty-Four
Fog

A thick blanket of fog lay low over the Forth the next morning, burying Hound Point and the islands. The only things visible were the warning lights of the road bridge, just piercing the blanket with two bright flashing dots. The sun was a white incandescent bulb in the sky. The valley north of Inverkeithing was smothered in a white and heavy stillness. The doorbell seemed extra shrill. Lane opened to door to find D.I. Hewitt. He led the detective into the lounge.

"I see you've had your window repaired," Hewitt said.

"Yes," Lane replied, "I just hope that it stays that way."

"I think that you should be OK Now," Hewitt said. "That's why I've come really."

"You've found the culprit," Lane said.

"We have," Hewitt replied, "as much by accident as by design. There's been a rash of thefts of cycles lately, bicycles I mean. We suspected a lad who had a history of this, and when we picked him up he thought it was about the smashing of your window. He obviously felt guilty about it and just confessed. Roy Malloy is his name."

"Roy Malloy?" Lane asked, raising his eyebrows.

"That's it," Hewitt said. "It does have a certain ring to it, *Roy Malloy*. I think it's another one of these cases where the parents are trying to be cute with the names of their children. Anyway, it seems that Roy had been out with two of his mates, and they'd had a few beers. They came up the street here and saw the demo outside your house. So they just kind of joined in with the bird people, thinking this was great fun with the bird screeches and the seal groans and so on. One of the bird people explained about Inchcolm and why they were there. Anyway, when the demo ended the lads went home. But Roy was still a little high and thought he'd make a big splash. So he wrote the note, tied it onto a stone, came back here and heaved it through your window. He had no intention of doing anything to you. It was just a lark. Anyway, he's obviously felt guilty since then."

"I see," Lane said. "That's a relief in a way. I didn't take it too seriously, but it was always there in the background. Did he say anything about the bad grammar?"

"You mean the *Your* rather than the *You're*?" Hewitt asked.

"Yes," Lane replied.

Hewitt rolled his eyes towards the ceiling. "Come on, Mr. Lane," Hewitt said, "Roy's not that high on grammar. He's not exactly a bad lad, just heading in the wrong direction without any kind of moral compass. So many of the kids around here come from homes where there's alcohol abuse or drug abuse or one parent or unemployment. I mean, in lots of these homes no one works and no one has ever worked, and no one ever expects to work."

"Yes," Lane said, "I know. My wife's a social worker. I take it that Roy's home life is like that?"

"Absolutely," Hewitt replied.

"Can you take it easy on him?" Lane asked.

"We can try," Hewitt said, "but he has committed an offence, and it isn't the first one, so there's not a lot I can do."

"How about sending him around to talk to me?" Lane asked.

"Would you be willing to do that," Mr Lane, "point out to him how much anxiety and grief he's given you?"

"Of course," Lane said.

"I'll give it a try," Hewitt said, "but don't count on it. The culture around here is pretty impervious. Can I tell you a story, a true one Mr. Lane, assuming that you don't mind a bit of profanity?"

"Sure, go ahead," Lane said.

"Well," Hewitt began, "my wife's a teacher in the primary school, and she's got this teacher friend in the same school. So in her class there was a little girl, Susie. Susie was reasonably bright and all, but I guess that at home they didn't believe in baths or showers or anything. So Susie didn't smell very good, and the others kids were avoiding her, didn't want to sit next to her or play with her on the playground and so on. The teacher, my wife's friend, felt sorry for her and wrote this note for her to take home to her parents. She tried to be very diplomatic and all, you know, saying that maybe it might be a good idea, just a suggestion, that Susie could have a bath before coming to school. That would make her a lot happier and so forth. So the next day Susie comes back with a note from her dad and hands it to the teacher. The note says:

Dear Teacher:
 Susie comes to school to be telt, not to be smelt.
 She's not a fuckin' daffodil.

You can kind of see the problem. This father is certainly not daft. In fact, I'd say that he's a bloody good poet, but he's not acting responsibly for his kid. There's something embedded in the culture, something in their lives that makes it hard to fix things. All I know is that the law isn't going to do it for us."

"Yes, I know exactly what you mean," Lane said. "They seem to have everything stacked against them from the very beginning."

D.I Hewitt stood up to go and held out his hand. "So, at least you know how it happened now. I think you can relax now."

"Thanks for your help, detective inspector," Lane said and led him to the door.

"By the way," Hewitt said on the way out, "I hope that you used your peephole to spy me out."

"I only do the very tallest visitors," Lane replied.

"Sorry?" Hewitt said.

"Not to worry. It's just my little private joke," Lane replied.

Lane stood looking out the window, reflecting on what had happened lately. People talked about the fog of war but there was also a fog of peace, or at least non-war. Things were hidden and then suddenly emerged, objects became distorted, distances were altered. Naomi was paranoid and found conspiracies everywhere. Out of control kids did crazy things and damaged the fabric of society, Morton enthused over his plans to get you on his side but then performed questionable acts behind your back. It was difficult to penetrate the fog. He couldn't figure out the next step.

Later that evening Lane and Katriona sat having a coffee in the lounge. Lane had put a CD on, Copland's *Appalachian Spring*.

"Have you noticed?" Lane asked.

"Noticed what?" Katriona asked.

"Noticed the silence, noticed that we have no demonstrators this evening," Lane answered.

Katriona was quiet for a moment, listening. "You're right," she said. "What's going on?"

"I think," Lane said, "that the demos have moved on to the Scottish Parliament. They get much more publicity there than they do here. Last night it was only us and the neighbours who took any notice."

"Well, I won't complain about that," Katriona said. "What else is supposed to happen about Roy Malloy?"

"I don't know," Lane said. "I guess that it will go to court at some point. D.I. Hewitt didn't really say. I suggested that if the boy could come round I would have a chat with him."

"It'll never happen," Katriona said. "I can tell you that right now."

"You're sure, are you?" Lane asked.

"I'm sure," she said. "That's the way these families are. What I could do is to speak to the social worker in that area and make sure they get some support. I think I'll do that. However, at least there is no death threat hanging over your head. I'm glad about that. I quite like having you around."

"Really?" Lane said.

"Really," she said.

Chapter Twenty-Five
Activities

The next day Lane phoned Katriona at lunchtime. "Guess what?" he asked.

"I've no idea," Katriona said. "Tell me."

"We've been invited out for dinner tonight," Lane answered.

"Really?" Katriona said. "That's nice, but by whom?"

"By the Scobies," Lane answered. "Are we able to go?"

"Yes, I think so," Katriona said. "There's nothing else on. It'll be good to get out for a while."

Adam and Maggie Scobie had been members of Lane's church in Edinburgh for a number of years. Adam Scobie was an engineer employed by British Aerospace. When the company moved his office to Dalgety Bay the Scobies moved house. They weren't happy about it, but commuting between Edinburgh and Dalgety Bay via the Forth Road Bridge would have proved difficult. The move had proved beneficial in spite of their reservations. Adam had taken up sailing and was now deeply involved in the sailing club. The two couples had seen each other only a few times since the move, but Adam Scobie had phoned Lane that morning to invite them over for a meal. The Scobies had heard of the demonstrations and thought that it would help the Lanes to get away for an evening. Their house, right on the bay near Homeward Point, enjoyed a 160 degree view of the Forth. Adam Scobie had suggested that if the weather was good they might like to walk the Coastal Path to the house and then he would drive them back home at the end of the evening, making it possible for Lane to enjoy a dram. Lane was grateful for the suggestion, for more than one reason.

At 6:30 PM the Lanes closed the front door, stepped out into a quiet evening, and walked down the path into a *cul de sac* devoid of demonstrators. Lane was sorry in a way, for he harboured an image of the two of them ambling slowly past gulls and seals and waving goodbye. But it wasn't to be. They turned the corner and headed northeast on the coastal path. The old pier, disjointed and rusting, lifted its head above the grey waters of the Forth. On the left, Prestonhill Quarry, enclosed by a rusty chain link fence, maintained a dark silence. Lane suddenly upped his pace.

"Hey, wait for me," Katriona said, as she hurried to catch up. "What's up? Why the Olympic sprint?"

"I don't like this part of the path," Lane said. "It's something to do with the dark water lapping the stone in the quarry. You could drown someone here and no one would know for years."

"Davis," Katriona said, "Roy Malloy has confessed. Your life isn't being threatened any longer."

Lane slowed down and put his arm around her. "Yes, you're right. Sorry."

The path took them along the fringe of Prestonhill Woods and then beside the curving beach adjacent to St David's Harbour. Below them on the sandy beach a tall blonde girl threw a ball for an energetic black lab. They reached the gate to the next section and Katriona stopped and looked at Lane.

"What is it?" Lane asked.

"Do you realize," she said, "that we're out together in our own neighbourhood, just the two of us, taking an innocent walk? When did we last do that?"

"That's true," Lane answered. "It was a good idea, but I wish that I had thought of it."

They followed the coastal path as it wound around the flats at St David's, then past the harbour and up the hill. Hound Point had its quota of tankers moored alongside. A long, low freighter with a white bridge headed out towards the North Sea. From the top of the hill they could see Dalgety's bay and small beach. Adam and Maggie Scobie's front window looked directly out over the estuary. They were waiting on the porch when the Lanes reached the house.

"You escaped from the gulls and seals," Adam Scobie said as they shook hands and were ushered them into the lounge.

"Unfortunately, they weren't out there this evening," Lane said. "It would have been satisfying if they had, I mean just walking past them casually as if they weren't there. However, they have a legitimate reason to protest, so I'm not complaining."

"Fair enough," Adam Scobie said. "I may be doing the same sort of thing soon enough."

"Why is that?" Lane asked.

"Oh, he's talking about the beach," Maggie came in. "The radioactive issue has raised its head again. All of us who live along the bay are getting rather frustrated."

"I'm sorry," Lane said. "I didn't realize that this was still an issue. I guess I've been too preoccupied with Inchcolm."

"So, what's happening?" Katriona asked.

"Before I answer that," Maggie said, "let Adam get some drinks."

Later, when they were supplied with drinks, Maggie returned to the question. "It's just the same issue, except larger in scale," she said.

"You know how during the war, they dismantled aircraft here at Donibristle," Adam said. Lane nodded. "Radium was used in the dials, but they didn't seem to appreciate that radium was dangerous."

"So," Maggie went on, "they removed all these dials and so forth, burned them, and then buried them along the foreshore. They obviously thought that they had disposed of the stuff safely."

"And now?" Lane interjected.

"And now," Adam continued, "they're finding radioactive pieces of material out on the seabed. Obviously, you would have to consume some of it to put yourself in danger, but it is pretty alarming. Anyone with kids who want to come down here and play in the sand is angry. The Ministry of Defence keep coming and investigating and talking about it, but they've done nothing."

"I can see that it's a worry for you," Lane said. "I'm sorry that the problem was under my radar. Sorry, no pun intended. I've been so caught up with Alexander Morton and Inchcolm that I haven't paid much attention to anything else. Surely the MOD just *have* to deal with it."

"One hopes so," Adam said. "Our member of parliament has taken it on board, so we continue to put pressure on the government. As always, they're reluctant to spend money. Anyway, tell us about Inchcolm and the famous Mr. Morton."

"Sorry to interrupt," Maggie said, "but I think that the dinner may about be ready. Give me a few minutes and then move through to the table. We can carve up Mr. Morton there if you feel like it."

They discussed the plans for Inchcolm over dinner. Adam was opposed, feeling that the development plans were unrealistic and that the increased traffic on the Forth might interfere with the events of the sailing club. Maggie was for the development, enthusiastic about having another golf course for her to play.

"So this is really a divided household," Lane suggested. "One of you is for and one is against. You've cancelled out each other's vote."

"Well, that was on the cards," Adam said, "but it doesn't really matter. We invited you tonight because we're concerned about what you're going through. It can't be nice, having people shouting outside your house every night. And I heard that someone had smashed your front window."

"Yes, that's true," Lane said.

"And, I also heard that someone had sent you a death threat," Adam went on.

"Also true," Lane answered, "but that's been resolved. It was no more than a mindless prank."

"I'm glad to hear that," Adam said. "Now, however, I want to know what *you* think though, about the development."

"I'm supposed to be neutral, Adam," Lane answered. "I just provide some research so that others can make a decision."

"But surely you can't be in favour of it," Adam said.

Lane studied him for a moment. "Adam, do I detect the voice of the sailing club in that question?" he asked, smiling.

"Well, not exactly," Adam answered. "That's my opinion you're hearing, but it is true that the club put pressure on me to speak to you when I said that I knew you. I wasn't keen since you're a good friend, but it was hard to say no to them."

"It's OK Adam," Lane said. "I can understand, but what is it that they object to?"

"The sailing here is complicated enough already," Adam said, putting down his fork and using his hands to propel imaginary vessels. "We've got the tankers coming in and out of Braefoot to cope with, as well as tugs, freighters, the *Maid of the Forth*, and so forth. Every time we want to run an event we've got to check with a dozen other people to set it up. If

Morton does his development there'll be even more traffic and we might as well give up."

"Yes. I think that's a valid argument," Lane said, and I admit it's one I hadn't thought of. "I'll state your case the next time I talk to my contact. How's the sailing going anyway?"

"Not that well, to be honest," Adam said.

"Why not?" Lane asked. "Do you need a faster boat?"

"No, it's not that simple," Adam responded. "Speed is important, but it's not the whole thing. I'm not that good yet at reading the conditions on the water. You've got to have a good sense of when to tack, when to come about and so forth. I haven't got it yet. Plus the sailing here is tricky. The wind can come up suddenly and throw you off course in a minute."

"Right, I see," Lane said, "but you can't blame Alexander Morton for that."

It was eleven o'clock before Adam Scobie drove the Lanes home. They are all agreed that it had been a fine evening and they would do it again, but next time at Inverkeithing.

"Well, did you enjoy that?" Katriona asked once they were in the house.

"I did," Lane answered. "It was good to see them and talk, although we didn't exactly get away from Inchcolm."

"No," Katriona said, "but we didn't talk about that *all* evening. We covered lots of other ground as well. I enjoyed just having a more or less normal evening, kind of like other people do."

"Yes, I know what you mean," Lane said, "but you're sort of implying that I'm not normal aren't you?"

"I couldn't possibly comment," Katriona answered.

Chapter Twenty-Six
Walkabout II

When his mobile rang fairly early the next morning, he couldn't interpret the ring. He didn't expect Naomi to ring him after the hard time he's given her. It was Sophie.

"Davis," she said, "I'd really like to talk to you on your own." This gave him a little kind of buzz in the spine, and he stood up straighter.

"Sure, Sophie," he said.

"It would be great if it was today," she said. "I'm sorry that it's short notice, but it's kind of important."

"That's OK, Sophie," he said. "Let's make it today. Where do you want to meet?"

"Can you suggest some place in Edinburgh that would sort of safe. I mean, somewhere where there won't be reporters and demonstrators and so on?" Lane looked out the window while he racked his brain. It was bright and dry.

"Have you been to the Royal Botanic Gardens, Sophie?" he asked.

"The Royal Botanic Gardens?" she said. "No, I haven't been there."

"OK," Lane said, "we'll go there. We can talk as we walk around. I'll show you the gardens and we'll have a coffee. Is that OK?"

"Sounds fine to me," Sophie said. "Where do we meet?"

"We'll meet at the east gate. Just ask someone at the hotel reception where the botanic gardens are. They'll tell you how to get there."

Lane drove into Edinburgh, giving himself plenty of time for slowdowns on the bridge, detours, roadblocks and whatever. He found a place to park on Inverleith Terrace, dug into his pocket for the small change he'd extracted from the coin jar, and bought a ticket to stick on the windscreen. He had to wait about ten minutes before Sophie appeared, coming through the gate accompanied by Lanson Brand. He strode over to them and greeted Sophie and her minder. Sophie turned and spoke to Brand.

"Lanson, I'll be all right here, honest. You don't need to come with me. Davis, we'll be safe enough won't we?" She had a pleading look in her eye.

"I don't think so," Brand said. "Mr. Morton said I had to keep my eye on you."

"Look, Lanson," Lane said, "this is a safe place. It's a royal garden and they have security guards. You can see for yourself that there are no demonstrators and no suspicious characters. The worst thing that can happen here is that we might be attacked by a squirrel."

Brand frowned at Lane and then looked at Sophie with a query in his eye. "Are you sure?"

Sophie put her hand on his arm. "Lanson, I'm sure. Don't worry. Go somewhere and have a coffee and try to relax. We'll meet you back here in a couple of hours."

"OK," Brand said, "I'll do what you want, but I'm not happy." Then looking steadily at Lane and pointing his index finger at his chest, "You better take care of her mister."

They left the entrance and walked up the south path towards the rock garden area.

"Do they really have security guards?" Sophie asked.

"Well, not exactly," Lane answered. "I was stretching it a little. They do have keepers who keep their eye on things, but mainly they give rows to the children who are running or being noisy."

"I see," Sophie said.

"What did you want to talk to me about, Sophie?" Lane asked. She walked on a few steps before answering.

"Could we go on for a bit before I tell you about it?" she asked. "It's kind of difficult, and if we talk about other things for a while it would help. Is that OK?"

"Of course," Lane answered. "There's no rush. I'll tell you a little about the gardens."

The cloud covering was thin, hardening the sky into blue and white marble. The sun was beginning to penetrate the cloud cover, casting the shadows of trees and shrubs onto the grass. Lane gestured to the rock gardens.

"This is just about my favourite place," Lane said. "It's something about how they've shaped the alpine areas coming down the hill, so that it looks like a stream or river which then widens out to create little islands of colour and texture. You see what I mean?"

"Yes," Sophie said, "gorgeous. Some of the coloration is like what I've tried to produce in the hotel's soft furnishing. I like the way it kind of beckons you to climb up into it."

"Do you want to go up?" Lane asked.

"Sure, why not?" she said.

Lane led the way up the narrow path, crunching the gravel under foot. Sophie took his arm to negotiate a boulder and it produced the same little buzz he's gotten through the phone. The reached the top of the hill, dominated by an ancient cedar twisted by the wind. From here the pattern of alpine islands were even more discernable.

"Beautiful," Sophie said.

"Yes," Lane answered. You can see why I like it." They stood watching for a moment. "Now let's move over this way," Lane said. Fifty yards along the path they reached the grove of sequoia.

"Wow," Sophie said.

"Aren't they great? Lane asked. "These are my favourite trees. They're massive, even though they're really only youngsters. We were in *Yosemite National Park* several years ago, and the ones there were four or five times this size. One had an opening wide enough for a road cut through it."

"What are the little plaques on these trees?" Sophie asked, moving closer to one.

"They indicate that someone has adopted the tree. I guess it means that they've contributed money to the gardens for its upkeep. As a reward they get to have their name on the tree."

"What a good idea," Sophie said.

"Yes, I thought so too," Lane answered. "In fact, I wanted to do it myself, but then I found that all the trees had been adopted. I wondered if you could foster them."

Sophie laughed, and Lane realized it was the first time that morning he'd seen a smile. They continued on the path as it wound its way down onto the lower level of the gardens. The route curved to the left and then up the hill through the rhododendron section, where a middle-aged couple sat reading on a bench. Lane stopped and gestured up the path.

"Now, Sophie, this is an important place in the garden and I want to tell you about it as we go."

"OK," she said, looking a little anxious.

"No. It's nothing to worry about," Lane said, "just a kind of vantage point that I think is special." They moved on up the hill and Lane pointed to the left.

"Over here," he said, "Edinburgh suddenly comes into view across the gully. We've been walking along and you could be anywhere out in the country. You can't see any streets or buildings and you can't see or hear any traffic. You could be miles away from anything. But then suddenly as you climb a little higher the top of a city emerges, and you can see the castle, the buildings on the Mound, and St Giles Cathedral, and it's all just there, so close."

"Yes, I see what you mean," Sophie said, shading her eyes with her hand.

"But that's only part of it," Lane went on. "If you look to the right . . ." Sophie turned to the right. "You'll see this lawn sloping up to the grey building. It used to be an art gallery. Now, in front of you is an empty space, and that's a pity because there used to be a piece of sculpture here. They moved it and it's now over at the *Gallery of Modern Art*. Anyway, it used to stand right there. It's a sculpture of Christ, called the *Risen Christ*, by Jacob Epstein. OK, so far?"

"Yes, OK," Sophie said. "What about it?"

"Well," Lane said, "Try to imagine it. You're walking along up this hill, pretty much sheltered by the rhododendrons. Then you turn the corner, see the city, and suddenly there is the *Risen Christ* in front of you. I'm talking about the way it used to be. Anyway, there he is, quite tall and gaunt, standing erect and holding out his hand towards you. He is greeting you, surprising you. But he is also pointing to that hand and showing you his wound, the hole formed where they nailed him to the cross. It is, rather it was, quite an experience."

Sophie was quiet, concentrating, trying to see what Lane was describing.

"Now the reason that was so important to me," Lane said, "was that it seemed faithful to the New Testament, to the way things actually happened."

"I don't follow you," Sophie said.

"Well, the resurrection of Jesus was a complete surprise to the disciples. For them he was dead, everything they had done together was lost. They were depressed. And then suddenly, surprisingly, he was alive and it changed everything."

Sophie was shaking her head. "I'm listening," she said, "but this is hard for me. I don't know how to take the resurrection. I can't really believe it, sorry."

"No, that's all right," Lane said. "I don't believe it either, at least not a bodily resurrection. This is what I'm coming to."

"Yes, OK," Sophie said. "Go on."

"The crucifixion and the resurrection," Lane went on, "are not so much two different events, but only one event seen in different ways. It's like two sides of a coin. Better yet, it's like two sides of a hand. Let's take this hand that the risen Christ is holding up. It has a front and a back like all our hands. But his hand has a wound in it, a hole which connects the two sides, so they are different but have continuity."

"I'm not sure I see what you're getting at," Sophie said.

"I realise that," Lane said. "It is difficult, but let me try to explain. The one side of things is the crucifixion. Jesus is dead. His faith in God and his love for others is gone, dead, down the drain. But the other side of the hand is that the disciples suddenly realise that the quality of his faith and love was stronger than what the establishment did to him. He didn't allow the fear of death to divert or stop him. He was stronger than death. He broke its back. The disciples suddenly saw that, and in that sense he was for them alive. It doesn't matter if the physical body is still in Palestine or not. Our way of seeing things is crucial. When people talk about the Holy Spirit they really mean that there is a spirit of comprehension which gives us a new way of seeing the world. We construe the world in a different way. Sorry, I'm going on a bit, but do you follow me at all?"

"I'm not sure," Sophie said. "It seems rather complicated."

"Yes, I know," Lane said, "but lots of important issues are complicated. The idea that faith is just something simple is wrong. It helps if you just keep in your mind that the resurrection is a profound way of seeing the crucifixion. Jesus' faith and way of love was stronger than death. That's the thing to focus on. In any event, I think we should go on up the hill and get a cup of coffee."

"Good idea," Sophie said, "but I'm buying because you were great to find the time to meet me today."

"No, Lane said, "I'm buying today. No arguments."

There were a dozen young mums with pushchairs and children at the outside tables and spread about the lawn. Eventually Lane found a table. Sophie sat down while he went in to join the queue for coffee. Lane suddenly realized why this was for so many people a good place to come. There was plenty of space for children to roam, lots of things to see, and best of all it was free.

Lane brought the coffee and shortbread and sat down.

"Coming back to what you were saying," Sophie said, "this means that I don't have to believe in a physical resurrection?"

"That's what it means," Lane said, "although there are lots of Christians who would disagree with me. For them the physical reality is very important."

"It's just that it's always been a kind of barrier for me," Sophie said. "I just don't think that dead bodies can rise up."

"No, I appreciate that," Lane said. "I feel the same way. Moreover, do you see what problems it poses if Jesus' body was raised physically?"

"What do you mean?" Sophie asked.

"Well, what happens next? When he is no longer with his disciples, where does he go? The New Testament answer was that he ascended up to heaven, the body I mean. Is that easy to believe?"

"That's even harder," Sophie said. "It's the visual thing, the body going up and up like a rocket."

"That's right," Lane said. "That's exactly the problem. Now, that takes us to the bigger problem, or have you had enough?"

"No, this is interesting" Sophie said. "It's good to talk to someone who knows about these things. We're Episcopal, or at least we're supposed to be. We don't really go to church very often, mainly to weddings and christenings and things like that. I think that daddy is more interested than mom, but he's always too busy, and she's always at one of our houses around the world furnishing it or upgrading it or something. So I've never really had much of a chance to talk about this stuff."

"Well," Lane said. "You're no different from most people. But I want to come back to this body ascending into the heavens because that provides us with the key to unlock other doors."

"OK," Sophie said, raising her coffee cup and smiling once again. "Go on. I'm ready."

"Good," Lane said. "The people who wrote down what's in the Bible, the Old and New Testaments, were a primitive people. I don't mean primitive in a bad sense. I just mean that they didn't have the benefit of science or any tools to investigate the world. So they saw the world as a three-storied world: a flat earth, the heavens above, and a hell below. The earth had seas around its edges and monsters swimming in the water, and it was dangerous to go too far out. The heavens had a kind of rigid firmament with God above it and holes within it to allow the rain and snow to come through. You could see the stars through the holes, and the sun and moon moved across the sky. So God was up there, in the heavens, usually pictured as an old man with a beard. If you look at our old Bibles, these were the kinds of images on the pages. So, going back to what we were saying about the resurrection, you can see that with that kind of view of the world, the risen Jesus *had to ascend*. There was no other way of dealing with a physical body. Now Sophie, is that how you view the world?"

"No," Sophie said, "of course not. The earth is round, it goes round the sun, the moon goes round the earth, and space is infinite."

"Exactly," Lane said. "We can't live with a three-storied universe. We have science and it's able to describe the world pretty well. We learn more about the earth and the universe every day. But the language that was used in relation to that primitive view of the world still exists. That language and that way of thinking is still in our heads, even in the heads of people who are not religious. So that means that we often hold to a kind of adolescent faith. We think of God as being above us, *up there*. So even today, if you talk to someone about God, he or she will think *up*. I'll bet you would as well. If I mention *God*, you'll think *up*. And that means that we're forced to talk about God *coming down* when he acts in the world. Lots of our prayers and hymns contain language like that. In a typical prayer, for example, we ask God to *pour down* his love upon us, and in a hymn we sing *point me to the skies*. We have to get beyond that kind of language and that way of thinking. Theologians talk about *transcendence*, which is a word that refers to how God goes beyond us or is different from us. Now, if he's up in space, then he goes beyond us in the medium of air or space itself, so we are bound to feel disconnected. And since we've been up in space and even on the moon, we know that the old man with the beard is not up there. And that knowledge is fatal, absolutely fatal, because our intelligence says *No, God can't be up there*. So the odd thing is that it's our own faith-language that tends to undermine our faith. Our intelligence, which after all is a gift of God, stokes up our religious doubt. Are you following me, Sophie?"

"I think so," she said. "You don't want me to think of God as being up in space."

"That's right," Lane said. "Demolish that three-storied universe because it's not credible any more. I mean, does the God who gave us intelligence expect us to have an outmoded view of the universe? Surely not. If we employ our intelligence properly we can come to a better grasp of faith. It makes a lot more sense to think of God as being *down*. There was one theologian who spoke of God as being the *Ground of Being*. In other words, God is under us, that source from which we spring and upon which we stand. What do we mean by transcendence then? Does he really go beyond us or is he only a product of our imagination? He is not a product of our imagination because millions of people from the beginning of time until today experience his reality. You can't just write them off. We are connected to him, but he goes beyond us in *depth* as the ground of our being. The New Testament spoke of Jesus as the *Son of God*. That means that his relationship with God was unique. Jesus is like us in that he is human. He is different from us in that he is *more* human. He penetrates more deeply into the being of God. People make the mistake of thinking of Jesus as different because he is more pious or more *holy* in some way. That's not right. He goes beyond us in humanity, not divinity. He's more human than us, and in that deepest humanity he is the face of God."

"I'm sorry," Sophie said, "but you really have lost me now. I thought that Jesus was supposed to be both human and divine."

"Yes, that's right," Lane said. "But his divinity lies in his humanity."

"Say that again," Sophie said.

"His divinity lies in his humanity," Lane replied. "He is different from us not because he's more pious or holy than us but because he's more human than us. He does love perfectly, he does forgive perfectly, he is able to sacrifice himself for others. So he points us downward to our true being. You see what I mean?"

"He's divine because he's more human. Is that what you mean?"

"Yes," Lane said. "That's the nub of it. It's a hard thing to grasp because it reverses what we normally think. But yes, that's it."

"OK," Sophie said, "but I'll need to think about that."

"Sophie, I don't want to go on any more," Lane said, "but there is one other thing that's important. Do you mind?"

"No, this is interesting," Sophie said. "On you go."

"A lot of the scientists don't like religion because they can't separate the outmoded view of the universe from the substance of faith, so they want to dismiss the whole thing. What that means is that they also dismiss all these people through the ages who've had experiences of God and relate these experiences in the Bible and elsewhere. The scientists are really saying to them: 'Your experience is so much rubbish.' The scientists want us to enjoy nature and express wonder at its beauty and at the genetic code and so forth. Now, it's good to enjoy nature and express our wonder at the marvellous world we live in. That's exactly what we've been doing this morning. But you can't really talk to nature or to the genetic code. You can't have a continuing dialogue with it. If I had started talking to those redwoods back there you would have run a mile. But you can have a dialogue with the God whose face we see in Jesus. Everyday I'm talking to him, and that's what keeps me sane and preserves my identity. He judges me, tells me what I've done and haven't done, what is good and what isn't so good. OK, I've done it again, sorry. I'll shut up now."

Sophie touched his arm. "No, I've really appreciated hearing all that, and I promise you that I'll think about it. I've never really had the chance to do that."

"Right," Lane said. "Now what did you want to talk to me about?"

Sophie sat up straighter and took a deep breath. "It's about my dad," she said. "I'm worried about him. He is so determined to do this development. He's like a bulldog when he gets his teeth into an idea. He can't take *no* for an answer, especially when lots of people are saying that it can't be done. He is just so competitive, and that leads him into becoming a bully. He tries to bulldoze people into his way of thinking. He doesn't mean to be nasty to people, but he can't see when he's hurting them. Have you seen that?"

"Yes, I have to admit that I have," Lane said. "It surprised me in fact, because I like your dad."

"He's always had to struggle to do his developments," Sophie said, "and he's almost always been successful. Losing isn't the name of the game for him. But this one, well, I don't know. I'm not sure."

"What do you mean?" Lane asked.

"He's not really getting anywhere. The people he talks to are just stonewalling. They won't make any decisions about things. So he gets more and more determined, and James is even worse. He just eggs daddy on even more. When the two of them get going . . ." She shook her head.

"So you're concerned that he's being frustrated by the various agencies and the demonstrations and by the government's inaction?" Lane asked.

"Oh," Sophie answered, "he's not bothered by the demonstrators. He's had all that before. What I'm worried about is his health. Just before we came over the doctor told him that he was hypertensive. There's a risk of a stroke or a heart attack, and you can see the symptoms sometimes. But he just shrugs it off. He won't give up on this development, and I'm afraid that the more he goes into battle the more risk there is to his health. Mom doesn't realise it's so bad and James doesn't seem bothered."

"I see," Lane said. "I'm sorry to hear that. When he and I were walking around the island the other day I thought that once or twice he looked kind of fragile."

"What I wish," Sophie said, "is that something would convince him to call it off himself. That would be the only way."

"Yes," Lane said, "I see what you mean. If it were his decision he could live with it, save face as it were. I suppose it could happen, Sophie. Don't despair." Lane looked at his watch. "Now, however, I see that our time is up, and if I don't get you back to dear old Lanson he'll blow a gasket."

"What a thought," she said and gave a little smile.

That evening, Lane told Katriona the story of their walk in the garden.

"What was Sophie wearing today?" she asked.

"Oh gosh," Lane replied, "I don't remember."

"You mean," Katriona said, "that you walked around with her all morning but were so taken up with your chat to her that you didn't notice her appearance?"

"You know," Lane said, "you hit the nail on the head. But I thought that you might feel some sympathy for the girl."

"I know," Katriona said. "I'm sorry. I do feel for her in that situation. I was just teasing you a little. The battle is getting worse and increasing the stress on everyone. Seriously, can you see any end to this? What are you going to do? You're probably the only one who understands."

"I do have an idea rolling around in my head," Lane said, "but I'll keep it under my hat for a while."

"Fair enough," Katriona said, "but I sense that you have a problem with your metaphors. If it's rolling around in your head you hardly need a hat."

Chapter Twenty-Seven

Table Games

Lane wasn't expecting to hear from Robert McCord again, but there it was—a call on his mobile first thing in the morning.

"I've been thinking about you," McCord said. "How are you doing?"

"Oh, I'm fine I suppose," Lane replied. "My life has been threatened by a teenager, we've had demonstrators on the driveway, I have no idea what I'm doing, but apart from that I'm fine."

"It's good to hear you being so positive," McCord said. "I sense that you might be ready for something a little different."

"What did you have in mind?" Lane asked.

"Let's go for lunch in the country," McCord said. "How does that sound to you?"

"It sounds great," Lane said. "What's the plan?"

"I'll pick you up from the station at Inverkeithing in an hour. OK?"

Lane switched his mobile off and dropped his shoulders. It would be good to do something different.

Lane got to the station fifty minutes later and stood by the bus stop. The sign across the way was still advertising courses at the local college. A half-dozen taxis waited in the taxi rank, the drivers shuttling back and forth to complain to one another about either the meanness of their customers or the lack of them. A black Daimler pulled up beside him precisely on the hour. The driver emerged and held the door for Lane.

"Mr. Lane," the driver said, "nice to see you." Lane did a double take: the man looked familiar, but he couldn't put a name to him.

"Hello, how are you?" Lane managed to say. He got into the back and shook Robert McCord's hand. The driver got in and slid the glass panel dividing the front of the car from the back shut.

"I think I must know your driver somehow," Lane said. "He knows me at any rate."

"You probably do know him," McCord said, "He works for funeral directors and usually drives for them at funerals. Frank is his name."

"Of course," Lane said. "Frank. He used to pick me up at the manse and take me to the crematorium all the time. I haven't seen him in years. How is he driving for you?"

McCord stretched out his legs and turned slightly towards him. "Our own car and driver are out today on another mission. We have a standing contract with these people for livery. This little jaunt today is regarded as low risk, so Frank is driving us."

"I'm sure," Lane said, searching his memory, "that it was Frank who was so keen on his vegetable garden. I remember once when we were headed to Warriston Crematorium. Frank was telling me about his garden. He told me that he had planted carrots in this row and then potatoes in the next and sprouts in the next, and so on. Well, we arrived at the crematorium and I had to get out. I mean, after all, I was taking the service! So Frank stopped talking and I got out and went in and conducted the funeral. I spent a little time with the family afterwards, you know how it is. Then I came back to the car and got in, and Frank just continued the story where he had left off: 'And in the next row I planted beans.'"

McCord was laughing. "Tell me about it," he said. "I get this every time he drives for me. That's why I have to keep asking him to keep the window shut. He's got a collection of his vegetables in the glove compartment, I kid you not. He brings them out when he thinks he can entertain a passenger. So the other day he brings out two carrots and a peapod. He holds the carrots and the pea in his left hand and drives with his right. All the time he's turning around to talk to me. He puts the carrots up on the dashboard with two fingers, moves the peapod towards them with his thumb and index finger, and then says, 'This one carrot says to the other one, *There are times when you just gotta take a pea.*' He puts these vegetables away and brings out an onion and a beet. He has the onion and the beet nodding to each other and then says, '*I'm an onion, how are you?* The other one says, *Oh, I'm OK, just a little beet.*' And then, as if that weren't enough, he brings out a runner bean. You know, one of those *Fine Runner* beans? So he's running it along the top of the dashboard, back and forth, back and forth. And then he says, 'This is a fine bean, a runner bean. He's in training for the 2012 Olympics.'"

Lane placed his hand over his mouth and tried to stop laughing. "You sure know how to pick'em," he said.

The car had left Inverkeithing and was now going north on the M90, slowing down to comply with a reduced speed limit in a construction zone. The road was full of white vans and large lorries.

"Where are we going?" Lane asked.

"Well, I kind of figured you could use a break," McCord said. "I've been keeping track of your altercations with gulls and seals and monks and Alexander Morton, so I thought that some TLC would be in order. We're going a few miles up north to a place I know, the *Grouse and Claret*. I have a feeling that today at lunchtime it might be quiet. I have a few more insights to pass on to you."

"Fantastic," Lane said.

Lane could see the waters of Loch Leven to his right, the sky beyond it was bright with scattered clouds. To the west the sky was growing darker. The Daimler turned off on the slip road as they approached Kinross and then left onto a single-track road for about a mile. The *Grouse and Claret* lived all by itself under a grove of trees with a small lake to the back. The receptionist took them into the restaurant and seated them at a large window overlooking the lake. A few ducks came out from the water and shook themselves. A couple sat at a table in the corner studying the menu.

"I have a suggestion," McCord said.

"OK," Lane replied, "you have my attention."

"Well, we have some serious stuff to talk about today. Neither of us is driving, so I suggest we might indulge in a bottle of wine. What do you say?"

"It sounds good to me," Lane said. "You choose."

"When they had ordered, Lane said, "So what is this serious stuff we have to talk about?"

"It's about your plan," McCord said. "It's about your exit strategy for your role in the Morton affair."

Lane studied McCord. "What makes you think I need an exit strategy?" he asked.

"It seems to me that they dropped you into the middle of this," McCord said. "I think that you're supposed to be the fall guy. Everybody is kind of hiding behind you and letting you take the blows of bad publicity.

Morton's getting it too, of course, but he's got to be used to it. You're not used to it and an easier target."

"Do you think that was the original idea?" Lane asked.

"Probably," McCord said. "But that doesn't particularly matter now. The question is: how do you extract yourself?"

"Tell me how you see the state of play from outside of the situation," Lane said.

"Not too complicated," McCord said. "They all go on talking to Morton, trying to sound like they're being very reasonable, but then pointing out the obstacles. Every time Morton hears about another obstacle he gets more and more determined. The actual plan of the development, the details, are now superfluous in a way. Morton will by now be angry and have gone into war mode. In his mind he'll be fighting against *enemies* who only want to thwart his wishes, and that will result in a lot of collateral damage. It doesn't really matter now who is for it and who is against it or the strength of their arguments. The government will ride the fence until something breaks. It won't happen."

"What do you mean: it won't happen?" Lane asked. "You mean the whole development? How do you know?"

"OK," McCord said, "let me show you. The thing is through, you have to do this objectively. You have to think strategically. You can't simply say, 'The idea of restoring the abbey is good', or 'This development will destroy the wildlife.' You have to consider the island as a whole in the context of geopolitics." McCord reached over for the sugar bowl and then grabbed the salt and pepper shakers. The waitress arrived with their starters.

"I'm sorry," she said, "I couldn't have set the table properly."

"No, No," McCord said. "That's just me moving things around. My apologies. It's all right."

They waited while the starters were placed on the table.

"We might as well begin," McCord said.

When the plates had been removed McCord began again. "Let's say that this sugar bowl is Inchcolm," he said, placing it in the centre of the table. "Now the salt is Braefoot, and notice how close it is to the island. Then the pepper down here is Hound Point, and over from it in the form of your wine glass is the tank farm at South Queensferry. We'll put the bottle here for the rail bridge and the candle there for the road bridge. We'll put my glass up here for the naval shipyard at Rosyth, and in the middle we'll snake my knife down for the pipeline supplying North Sea oil. And, I almost forgot, we'll take your spoon for the refinery at Grangemouth. Now that everything's in place, what does it look like?"

"It looks like a mess," Lane said, laughing.

"No, you need to be serious now," McCord said, shaking his head. "Look at this. Look at it strategically. What have you got? You've got a loading station for combustible gas, you've got a loading station for crude oil supplied by a major pipeline, you've got a refinery and tanks filled with oil, you've got the two major transport links to the north, and you've got a dockyard where Britain's new aircraft carrier is going to be assembled. And right here in the middle on Inchcolm you're going to send all kinds of vessels, thousands of tourists and probably helicopters flying in and out. Now what does that look like?"

Lane was struggling to find the right word. "Precarious maybe, or risky?" he said.

"Precarious or risky?" McCord said. "I think we should do stronger. What about disastrous or explosive? The island would be a bomb sitting in the midst of all these strategic assets. Do you not see that? It's a staging post for some terrorist to hijack a boat and run it into Hound Point, rupture the line and drop thousands of tonnes of oil into the firth. Or he could hijack a tanker filled with natural gas and explode it under the bridge. I mean, there are so many possibilities for terrorist activity that it doesn't bear thinking about."

"I see what you mean," Lane said.

"It's obvious when you look at it like this," McCord said, pointing to the cluttered table. "Now, what wouldn't be obvious to you is that this sort of thing is probably being planned already." McCord lowered his voice. "We know that right now El Qaeda have guys in training, learning how to hijack ships. We have tabs on a number who have enrolled in nautical colleges. We know that several have infiltrated the pirates in Somalia. I mean, if you want to learn how to take a vessel just go on a boat trip with these guys. They're good."

"So," Lane said, "you're saying that because the island, if developed, would pose such a risk, somebody would veto the whole thing?"

"Sure," McCord said. "This estuary, the Firth of Forth, has to be one of the most strategically important regions in the UK. Think about it, Davis. What you would have at Inchcolm is a UK site and an American enterprise rolled up into one. Moreover, because of the gambling, you would have a prime example of western greed. What a great target! You can't imagine a better one. The two governments can't let this project happen. They won't at this stage say that because it wouldn't be politically wise. But they can't let it happen. If the Scottish government didn't kick it into the long grass then the UK government would."

The waitress arrived with the main course. "Oh dear," she said, holding their plates and looking at the table.

"It's all right my dear, "McCord said. "We're only playing our table game again. Just leave it with us."

As they walked to the parking lot and the Daimler after lunch, McCord said to Lane, "Is there anything else you want to ask me or talk about on the way back to Inverkeithing?"

"No, I don't think so," Lane answered. "You've done enough for one day. You're put this thing in a wholly new perspective."

"Fair enough," McCord said, with a wink. "In that case I'll tell Frank to leave the panel open on the way back."

Lane told Katriona about his meeting with McCord that evening.

"So it wouldn't be permitted to go ahead regardless?" she asked. "All this discussion and the demonstrations and all your work are basically pointless? Is that what Robert is saying?"

"Yes, I think it is," Lane answered. "I suspect he has access to information that we don't have. They must talk to MI5 and MI6 on a regular basis. I suppose that they're always analysing the risk level in various developments."

"Does that not rather change your role in the business?" Katriona asked.

"Yes, of course it does," Lane said. "On one level it makes me redundant. But on another level I might still have a role to play."

"So you still have ideas rolling around in your head?" she asked.

"Oh of course," Lane said.

"That's comforting," she said.

Chapter Twenty-Eight
Requiem

It had been another largely sleepless night. Lane finally got up at four in the morning and sat at the window. The Forth was empty of traffic. The lights of Edinburgh could be seen across the water, and in the east the sky was gradually turning pink. He'd lain in bed most of the night tried to think through the issue. Now he was still at it, but with a more methodical approach. McCord believed that the development would never be allowed to go ahead. Lane had to accept that this was probably true. On the other hand, the various parties were allowing discussions to continue, and this could go on for years. The longer it went on the more vitriolic it would become. And poor Sophie, in the middle, would grow more and more concerned about her father. What should he do? What could he do?

Lane listed the possibilities on a sheet of paper. There weren't that many. He went through all the notes he made over the weeks. He made breakfast, and the two of them ate in a kind of sympathetic silence. When Katriona was ready to leave she came over to Lane and put her arms around him.

"Don't allow yourself to become too anxious about this," she said. "It looks like it's beyond your control. They've gotten good value from you, so there's no point in letting yourself to be exploited any longer."

"I realise that," Lane said, "but I still feel there must be something I can do to ease the pain."

"Ease the pain for whom?" Katriona asked.

"I'm not sure," Lane answered, "maybe for everybody."

Over a second cup of coffee, Lane went over his list of possibilities and his notes and looked more closely at the idea rolling around in his head. By ten o'clock he had made a decision. He phoned the Caledonian Hotel and asked to speak to Morton.

Morton came on the phone sounding cheerful, "Davis, good to hear from you. What can I do for you?"

"Good morning Mort," Lane said, trying to find exactly the right words, "I think it would be a good idea for us to get together on the island. I've discovered something that could be important for you to know."

"Well, I'm going out there today," Morton said. "I have a meeting with Callum and Fadi. Can you get out there this morning?"

"I'm sure I can," Lane answered. "I'll see you when I get there."

He went on the *Forthbelle*. The sky was blue, the sun was a golden sphere, and there were only a few white clouds drifting aimlessly. As the Belle pushed out into the current under the rail bridge, Lane was surprised to find that he was a little emotional. It was, after all, possible that this might be the last time he would set foot on Inchcolm, at least in an official capacity. He thought back to that first time, when he'd come in response to the mysterious invitation. He had studied every passenger to find the one who had issued the invitation, and it had turned out to be the one least likely. He had become intrigued by the ruined abbey, being drawn into its hidden life, and spurred on to create Gavin the canon. He had been under siege by the demonstrators and his life had been threatened. He had even been offered a job. They were nearing the island. The seals were resting on the buoy, and the birds flying in and out. He had enjoyed his work with the abbey, but now it looked as if it was coming to an end.

Lane saw Morton standing on the south beach, along with two men. He recognised one of them as Callum McBain. Alexander Morton turned his way and called to him.

"Davis, down here," he shouted. Lane climbed over the rocks and walked across the sand.

"Davis," Morton said, grabbing his hand and pulling him into the group, "I think you know Callum here, and this is Fadi. We're just arguing on how far out the peninsula ought to go. Would you say a five iron or a seven iron?"

"Oh well, what a question," Lane said. "What's this hole to be called again?"

"This tee is looking more or less south," Morton said, "so this is St Cuthbert."

"Right, let me think," Lane said, stroking an imaginary goatee. "St. Cuthbert, on the basis of what I know, I would say that St Cuthbert is definitely a seven iron."

"There you go," Morton said, turning towards McBain and looking triumphant. "A seven iron shot, Callum." The two men looked blank.

"OK," Morton said, "I'll leave you two to work this out. Davis here has something important to talk about." He put his hand on Lane's shoulder and they climbed back over the rocks and onto the grass. "Now, what's this all about?"

"Let's walk around the abbey and I'll tell you," Lane said. They went through the chapter house, out into the cloister and stopped.

Do you remember the details about the early history of the abbey?" Lane asked. "I'm talking about the material that was in the paper I wrote."

"I remember a lot of it," Morton said, "but refresh my memory. I've had too many other things to think about."

"Of course," Lane said, "I realise that. You remember that Alan de Mortimer gave half of his lands to the canons so that the abbey could be built?"

"Yes, I've got that," Morton said.

"The arrangement was," Lane went on, "that in return for this gift, Alan would be buried in the abbey."

"Yes, I know that," Morton said. "But it didn't happen, did it?"

"No," Lane said. "It didn't happen because when they were taking Alan out to the abbey in his coffin, they stopped and dumped the coffin overboard."

"Yes," Morton said, "why was that again?"

"We don't know," Lane said. "No one knows. It was a strange thing to do since he had done so much for them."

"Right," Morton said. "There must have been some reason that we can't fathom. Sorry, no pun intended." Morton grinned broadly. "What next?"

"And then," Lane went on, "later on, Alan's son William had another skirmish with the canons. The abbot and the canons had the right to nominate the priest to be in charge of St Fillans Church. But William put his own man in charge and that infuriated the canons. So, if you remember, on the night that the new man was to be inducted the canons went ashore and barred the door to the church. For this they got beaten up."

"Yes, I do remember this vaguely," Morton said. "But I don't really see yet what this has to do with what I'm proposing to do now. All this was back four or five hundred years."

"I'm coming to that," Lane said, "but let's walk around a little farther. There's an important place here." They turned to the right and went into the ruins of the church. Lane led Morton to a point near to the south transept of the church.

"This, I think, is quite an important place," Lane said, pointing to the wall.

"Why is that?" Morton asked, frowning.

"It was here, in the wall," Lane said, "that the remains of a person were found."

"OK," Morton said, "correct me if I'm wrong, but surely remains were found in many places around the abbey. You said yourself that people were desperate to be buried here. It was a little encouragement towards heaven. Alan de Mortimer expected to be buried here, and so did everyone else. So what's special about this place?"

Lane took his time in answering the question. "What's special about this place, Mort, is that this person had been buried standing up."

Morton looked at Lane. "Buried standing up?" he asked. "You mean he was vertical in the wall?"

"That's what I mean," Lane said. "He was put into the wall standing up."

"Well, OK," Morton said. "But lots of people must have been buried like that."

"No, not really," Lane said. "There were very few. Now, can you think of any reason why he might have been buried standing up?"

Morton scratched his head. "The only thing I can think of is that maybe he was a warrior, so if he were standing up he would be ready to come out fighting." Morton assumed a pose like a boxer.

"Well, that's a reasonable guess," Lane said. "But think for a minute about what this place is. It's a monastery, an abbey in the Augustinian tradition. One of the rules was to avoid quarrels, because anger might grow into hatred and anyone who hates his brother is a murderer. That's what Augustine said. This place is to be a place of peace in the world. Is it likely they would have honoured a warrior by putting him here?"

"No, I suppose not," Morton said.

"Now," Lane went on, "think of all the cathedrals you've ever been into. I take it that you've been into some of the great cathedrals in Britain or in Europe?"

"Of course," Morton said, his body language saying *frustration*, "We've been to dozens, especially in England and in France. They're brilliant, beautiful. That's why I want to restore this church. You know that already."

"Yes, I do know that, and I share that vision with you," Lane said. "But I want you to think about all the tombs you've seen in the cathedrals. What is true of all of them?"

"Well, let me think," Morton said. "I suppose that they're mostly all constructed of marble or granite or something similar."

"OK," Lane said, "but think more basically than that. How are they positioned?"

"Positioned?" Morton asked. "You mean facing east or some other direction?"

"No," Lane said. "I mean, are they lying down?"

"Well, yes, of course," Morton said. "They're all lying down, all horizontal."

"Why is that?" Lane asked.

Morton looked at Lane and laughed. "They're all dead."

"Absolutely," Lane said. "They're all dead and they're all at . . ." He was rolling his hand, prompting Morton to supply the word.

"Well, they're all at *rest*, "Morton said.

"That's it," Lane said, "that's the key word I was looking for. I'm sorry, I didn't mean to put you to the test but I had to get to these key words—*at rest*. You see, in the Christian faith the idea of being at rest after death is quite important. In the Roman Catholic Church the mass which is said at death is called the *Requiem Mass*. It begins with the sentence *Requiem aeternam dona eis*, or *Grant them eternal rest, O Lord*. The prayer goes like this:

> *Eternal rest grant unto them O Lord,*
> *And let perpetual light shine upon them.*
> *May the souls of the faithful departed, through the mercy of God,*
> *Rest in peace. Amen.*

"Now," Lane said, "I have to ask you this. Would the person who was buried here standing up, would he have enjoyed eternal rest?"

Morton studied Lane's face for a moment and studied the wall. Then looking back at Lane, he replied, "No, I suppose not."

"Exactly," Lane said, "because he's not lying down. You can't rest standing up. This chap had no rest, no rest for an eternity, because he was standing up."

"OK," Morton said, "I get the point. But I still don't understand what that has to do with me."

"That," Lane said, "is precisely what I'm about to tell you."

Chapter Twenty-Nine
Cartulary

Lane hung around the house all the next morning. It wasn't because it was raining, which it was, but because he expected a phone call. By one o'clock in the afternoon three calls had come. He went out to take the Cruiser out of the garage. The gutters on the house were overflowing with rainwater and it was running down the driveway onto the road. He saw not another soul on the street. Lane drove to the supermarket in Dalgety Bay. He required a better supply of groceries for what was going to be a different kind of day. He felt altogether different, more buoyant, like a cork that had been pressed under the water for a long time and then allowed to bob up into air.

By the time Katriona got home he was ready. He handed her a glass of bubbly.

"What's this, champagne?" she asked.

"No, not really," Lane answered. "It's only sparkling wine, but it's a good one."

"Why, are we celebrating something?" she asked. "Let's see, it's not my birthday and it's not your birthday, and it's not our anniversary."

"We're not exactly celebrating," Lane said, "just marking an important event."

"Would you like to tell me about it?" Katriona said.

"No," Lane said, "I'd like you to find out on your own. Let's watch the six o'clock news."

They sat in the lounge and he switched on the TV. It was the second item in the format. The commentator said:

Alexander Morton, the American property tycoon, has given up on his effort to create a casino and golfing complex on Inchcolm in the Firth of Forth. Mr. Morton said that he had become frustrated by the failure of several agencies and institutions to commit to the development. 'Scotland is very important to me because my origins are here,' he said. 'I wanted to build something here that would be world class and bring in millions of pounds for the Scottish economy, as well as hundreds of jobs. But it's not going to be because people can't make up their minds. I can't wait here forever because I have too many other irons in the fire. It's a sad day for Scotland.' Spokesmen for Historic Scotland, the Scottish government and several other agencies declined to comment, but representatives from bird and wildlife groups welcomed Mr. Morton's withdrawal from the development. Mr. Morris Falconer, representing the Save our Birds Society, said that the birds of Inchcolm had won a major victory.

The camera moved from the newsreader to Edinburgh Airport, where Morton, Sophie, James, and Lanson Brand were seen going into the terminal. Morton turned and waved to the cameras.

"Wow," Katriona said, turning to Lane. "That is news. Talk about a significant event. Did you know this was happening?"

"I didn't know for sure until a little earlier today," Lane said. "I thought it would happen after what I did yesterday."

"What did you do yesterday?" Katriona asked.

"Well," Lane said, "let's have another glass of bubbly and I'll tell you." He refilled their glasses.

"I phoned Morton and asked to see him on the island," Lane began. "He seemed in a good mood in spite of all the hassle with everyone. So we walked around the abbey to the transept of the ruined church. Had I told you about Morton's superstitious nature?"

"I don't think so," Katriona said. "At least I can't remember it."

"OK," Lane went on. "Early on, when I asked Robert McCord if he had any information about Morton, he said that the man was very superstitious. Wouldn't sit with his back to a door or window, wouldn't walk under ladders, that sort of thing. Then later, when we were on the island, I noticed him on a couple of occasions seeming sort of unsure or hesitant. For example, he wasn't happy in that tunnel, even though he wanted to use it for his poker room. Anyway, I didn't think a lot about it until the other day. You know that Sophie told me she was worried about his health and wished that he had a way out. And you know that McCord said this project wouldn't happen regardless. That seemed to be the clincher. I knew I had to do something. Are you with me so far?"

"Yes," Katriona said. "Carry on."

"Well," Lane said, "I took him around to where these remains were found, the person who had been buried standing up. I asked him what he made of this, and he suggested it might be a warrior. I said no, that couldn't be, and I asked him what would it mean if you were buried standing up rather than lying down. And eventually I got him to see that the person would never be at rest, and that that was particularly significant in a monastery. I Mean, *eternal rest* is the whole point of being buried there.

"Yes, I can see that," Katriona said, "but what does that have to do with Alexander Morton?"

"Well," Lane went on, "I reminded Morton of how the canons had treated Alan and William de Mortimer. There really was a major flow of bad blood there, as if from an theological artery. These canons and the abbot were basically peaceable people as far as we know, and yet there was some kind of war going on with the de Mortimers. So I reminded him of that, and then I said that I thought the person whose remains had been found in the wall had been one of the de Mortimer family. And I said that I thought the abbot and canons had placed a curse on the family, so that any of that family who became involved with the abbey would never have eternal rest.

"You told him that?" Katriona said, her eyes opening wide.

"I did, and I saw the man shudder. I mean, you read about people shuddering, but I'd never actually seen it before: his whole body, starting with his shoulders and all the way down. Then he became pale. I was actually quite worried about him."

"I should think so, the poor man," Katriona said. "But what you told him wasn't true was it?"

"You mean about no eternal rest for someone being buried standing up and about a curse on the family? Lane asked.

"Yes, that wasn't true."

"Well," Lane said, "I don't know that it wasn't true. I think that they were deliberately denying eternal rest to this man. After all, it was a Christian community and they believed fervently in eternal rest. I think that my thesis is quite logical. I can't think of another explanation, can you? I mean, the guy's feet weren't even touching the ground. How can you rest like that? Now, as for the bit about a curse on the de Mortimer family, it is the case that I don't have any hard evidence for that. But the theory does fit the facts we have doesn't it?"

"Maybe," Katriona averred. "I'm not sure."

"I'm beginning to think," Lane said, "that the line between truth and fiction is finer than I thought. We have certain experiences, see certain things, and we need to form stories to explain them, and the stories can become compelling. I guess they are compelling because they help us to deal with reality. And the stories can live on even when others discount them and claim that they are only fiction. Look at that story about Gavin, for example. I kept saying that the Gavin narrative was a fiction, but no one would listen. People kept Gavin alive because he enabled us to shine a light into a dark area of history. I hate to say it but to some extent I agree with Pilate when he asked 'What is truth?' He was being cynical, but the truth is pretty slippery isn't it? We all see things in slightly different ways. It just seems to me that there are lots of stories that you can think of where the question about truth or fiction is not the key question. Somehow it's also about a story being *accurate* or *useful,* about portraying life in the world under God as it really is.

"Would you include the biblical stories, like some of the Old Testament stories?" Katriona asked.

"Well, yes," Lane answered, "but these accounts have the weight of canonical authority, because they convey something about the nature of God. It's just that most of these stories were never meant to be taken literally. They contain humour and insight and express profound truth. If you try to take them literally you destroy them. Take the Genesis account of creation. The idea is that there is a close relationship between God and man. God and Adam have a habit of walking around the garden and conversing in the cool of the evening. They give names to all the creatures together. Temptation comes very subtly: the serpent says, 'Did God really say that you couldn't eat from any tree in the garden?' The man blames the woman and the woman blames the serpent. This is a story offering a profound description of life: this is just the way that God relates to man, man relates to man, and man relates to the world. This is the way things are. But take the story literally and you've ruined it. The fundamentalists destroy it by insisting that it is the actual account of creation and by doing so they allow scientism to dismiss it as absurd. So a wonderful story falls between a rock and a hard place, destroyed by fundamentalists on the one hand and discarded by scientism on the other. Stories are about more than facts. They're about the interpretation and shaping of life itself. That story I told to Morton appears to be fiction, but it could be true. We'll never know. The point is that it may have saved his life and spared all of us from a battle that could have gone on for years."

"And how do you feel about things, Davis?" Katriona asked. "Are you happy or unhappy that the battle of Inchcolm Abbey is over?"

Lane studied his glass for a while. "The battle is over, but no one had a victory. Morton saved face to a degree, but on the whole most everyone lost. The birds and seals won, I suppose, but they're about the only ones. The abbey is still in ruins, and no other historic properties will benefit. The various institutions and agencies lost credibility, as did the government. I feel sorry for Mr. McBain because he had put his heart into the course. No one will get any jobs of any kind. On balance I suppose I'm unhappy," he said. "I would have liked to see the abbey restored. I can visualise young people going around it, listening to the audio commentary and learning for the first time about medieval faith. I would have enjoyed writing a script and using Gavin as the key figure. And I would have liked to see a number of people get good lasting jobs around the place. I guess that's how I feel."

"So," Katriona said. "that's the end of it then?"

"Well, not quite," Lane answered. He got up, went over to the stereo and put on Mozart's *Requiem*. He came back holding several sheets of paper. "I got three phone calls today. Naomi came first. She told me about Morton's decision and thanked me for all my help, adding that there would be a cheque in the post. She was a little cool, I thought, after all the secret conversations we'd had. Then Sophie called and thanked me. She sounded relieved and said that she was grateful for what I'd done. She was a lot warmer than Naomi."

"I'm sure she would be," Katriona said, smiling sweetly, "Sophie just likes you."

"Then Morton himself phoned," Lane said. "He told me he had decided to pull the plug, but he said that he had really enjoyed meeting me, had learned a lot from me and was sorry that the project couldn't go ahead."

"Was that it?" Katriona asked.

"No," Lane said. "There was something else. He said he wanted to do something for Inchcolm Abbey, leave something in recognition of what he had tried to do there."

"I see," Katriona said. "And what's that going to be?"

"He's going to re-head the fresco, you know, the one that sits in the nave of the church at the moment."

"You're joking," Katriona said. "Re-head it?"

"Yes," lane said. "I'm sure I told you about the before. He's going to bring in his Italian artist and put new heads on all the figures. He says that Historic Scotland has given him permission." Lane handed her a piece of paper. "This is the fresco as it is now. It portrays the funeral process of John Leycestre. And this," he said, producing another sheet of paper, "is an artist's reconstruction of how it must have looked when it was complete."

Katriona studied the paper. "There are seven people in the funeral procession."

"Yes, that's right," Lane said.

"One of them is a bishop or something," she said, "He has a mitre and a shepherd's crook."

"I think that's probably the abbot," Lane said.

"So what heads is the artist going to use? I mean, whose heads will be put on? Sorry, I don't know how to phrase the question."

"Well," Lane said, "What do you think?"

Katriona thought for a while. "I think that Alexander Morton will want to be on there and possibly James."

"You're right," Lane said, "James and Alexander will be there, and which body will Mr. Morton head up?"

"Oh, no doubt about it," Katriona said, "He'll be the abbot."

"No, you're wrong," Lane said.

"Well, who then?" Katriona asked. Lane studied his glass, saying nothing.

Katriona looked steadily at him. "It's not you is it? Are you going to be the abbot?" she asked.

"Yep, yours truly," Lane replied. "Morton said he really appreciated my help. I'm going to be the new abbot."

"That's wonderful," she said. "According to this drawing, though, you'll need a shepherd's crook."

'We've got one," Lane said. "Don't you remember our old neighbour, the one who made walking sticks with antler crooks?"

"Oh yes," Katriona said. "I had forgotten that. What about the haircut though? This drawing of the procession shows them all having . . ." She hesitated, looking for the word.

"Do you mean tonsures?" Lane asked.

'I guess," Katriona said, "If that's the word. Can Melvin give you one of those?"

"I suppose that he could," Lane answered. "He's always asking me if I want some off the top. It might throw him if I said I wanted it all off the top, leaving just a neat round bald patch."

"So if you're going to be the abbot," Katriona asked, thoughtfully, "can I be your wife then?"

"No, sorry," Lane said. "Abbots don't have wives."

"Well, in that case," she asked, "can I be your mistress?"

"Absolutely," Lane answered. "I'd like that."

"Would that be permitted, having a mistress?" she asked.

"No," he said, "but it wouldn't be unusual. In fact, you would immediately put me in St Augustine's shoes."

"How is that?" Katriona asked.

"I would be praying, 'Lord, make me chaste, but not yet,'" Lane answered.

"So I can come and sleep with you in the dormitory?" she asked.

"Not in the dormitory," Lane said. "Everyone else is sleeping there. No, I'll be in the abbot's camera."

"That sounds exotic," Katriona said. "Can I sneak up the back stairs to the camera?"

"Of course," Lane said.

"That's even more exotic," she said. "This just gets better and better. How would I get to Inchcolm?"

"You'd have to get someone to row you across Mortimer's Deep," Lane answered.

"Who would I get?" Katriona asked.

"Who do you think?" Lane answered.

She thought for a minute. "Oh, I know, Gavin. He would do it."

"That's right," Lane said. "Good old Gavin."

"So," she said, "in the abbot's camera we would make mad passionate love?"

"That's right," Lane said. "And then I would get up in the middle of the night for Matins, and you would have to leave."

"Oh," she said, "in the middle of the night?"

"That's right," Lane said.

"And how would I get back across to the mainland?" Katriona asked.

"I don't know," Lane said. "Gavin couldn't take you because he's at worship as well."

"I see," Katriona said. "In that case, I guess I'll pass."

Lane started to say something and then stopped.

"Davis, what's wrong?" Katriona asked. 'You're looking all anxious."

"I just thought of something," Lane answered. "Time and chance . . ."

"Davis, you're mumbling," Katriona said.

"Time and chance . . . ," Lane said, rolling his hand forward and entreating Katriona.

"Time and chance happen to all men," she said. "So what . . . ?"

"I may have done Alexander Morton a very serious injustice," Lane said. "It came to me just now. I hadn't thought of it before. I'm stupid."

"How have you done him an injustice?" Katriona asked. "What are you talking about?"

"When I was trying to figure out why the canons dumped Alan de Mortimer overboard, I assumed that they had some kind of grudge against him. It seemed so out of character. It just didn't seem right that they would do that to the man who had given them the land for the abbey. I've never been able to reconcile what they did with how I see them," Lane said.

"Yes, I understand that," Katriona said, "but I'm still not with you."

"Well," Lane said, "you remember the Havkong incident? The night that the Havkong was being loaded with gas at Braefoot? A squall came up suddenly and she slipped her mooring and drifted out into the estuary?"

"Vaguely," Katriona said, "but I'm getting an inkling of where you're going."

"Suppose," Lane said, "and try to visualise it at the same time. The canons are carrying Alan de Mortimer's coffin out of the gate to the castle. It's very heavy, being lined with lead. Some of the peasants from the castle have come to help because the canons are not used to heavy labour, at least most of them. So they struggle down the hill alongside the Dour until they come to the harbour. The boat is there, waiting. With difficulty they load the coffin onto the vessel. There isn't much room left for the canons themselves, but they squeeze in around it and take up their oars. They push off and head for the island, west by southwest. They get out into the channel and suddenly . . ." Lane looked at Katriona.

"Suddenly a squall comes up," she said.

"Exactly," Lane said. "A sudden squall like the one that hit the Havkong, like the one that hit King Alexander I as he was crossing the Forth from Edinburgh, like the one that hit St Paul off Crete, and like the one that hit Jonah on the way to Tarshish."

"I'm with you," Katriona said.

"So the wind is battering the boat," Lane continued, "driving them east, farther and farther out into the estuary. The boat's not for turning and begins to take in water. They become increasingly alarmed, looking around at each other, wondering what to do. They row harder, trying to turn the vessel around, but with no luck. They stop rowing and look at each other and at the coffin, and without speaking make a decision," Lane went on.

"There's only one thing to do," Katriona said.

"Exactly," Lane answered. "It doesn't make sense to risk all their lives for one man who's already departed. So they stand up, lift the coffin up high enough and dump it over board. Then they sit down and say a silent prayer."

"So it was the greatest good for the greatest number," Katriona said. "a utilitarian ethic?"

"I guess so," Lane answered.

"And without the coffin, "Katriona went on, "the boat is more manageable. They get it turned round and head back to the island."

"That's right," Lane said. "The abbot has been waiting for them down at the little harbour, worried because of the weather. He's relieved when he sees the vessel approaching but then flabbergasted when they pull in and there is no coffin. He can't believe that de Mortimer went overboard, but they explain how dangerous the situation was and he begins to understand. They all proceed to the church and have a spontaneous service, praying for forgiveness for their failure. What do you think?"

"I think you could be right," Katriona said.

"I think so too," Lane answered. "And now I feel very bad that I've done Alexander Morton such an injustice. I should have thought of this before, especially when Adam Scobie mentioned the sudden changes of wind in the bay."

"OK," Katriona said. "So it is unlikely that the canons placed some kind of curse on the de Mortimers, but it's still true that the family did suffer a string of unfortunate events. And it's also the case that because Alexander Morton is superstitious and believes in bad luck he was always going to be anxious about his fate. You did give him a way out and may have saved his life."

"I suppose so," Lane answered.

"Anyway, Katriona went on, "we believe in forgiveness don't we?"

"Yes," Lane said sighing, "we believe in forgiveness."

Later, when they were eating dinner, Katriona said, "This is so nice, your best lasagne and some good Chianti. Thanks for making dinner."

"That's OK," Lane said. "We needed to mark a special occasion."

"How do you like the green beans in tomato sauce and oregano?" he asked.

"Delicious," Katriona said. "This evening has been just great. It's nice to have you back again, relaxed and happy."

A few minutes later, Lane was holding a green bean and running it back and forth across his plate.

"Davis," Katriona asked, "what on earth are you doing?"

Holding up the bean, he replied, "This is a runner bean, a Fine runner bean."

"I think I can see that," Katriona said. "But what are you doing with it?"

"It's a Fine bean, a runner bean practicing for the 2012 Olympics."

"Davis," Katriona said, "Stop it, now."

"OK," Lane said and sighed, putting the bean into his mouth and chewing, "but that's the end of a Fine career."

THE END

Lightning Source UK Ltd.
Milton Keynes UK
UKOW051721290212

188134UK00001B/174/P